WHEN
THE
PAST
IS
ALL
DECEPTION

WHEN THE PAST IS ALL DECEPTION

R. MICHAEL CASSIDY

a novel

atmosphere press

© 2024 R. Michael Cassidy

Published by Atmosphere Press

Cover design by Matthew Fielder

No part of this book may be reproduced without permission from the author except in brief quotations and in reviews. This is a work of fiction, and any resemblance to real places, persons, or events is entirely coincidental.

Atmospherepress.com

The Four Quartets

The tolling bell
Measures time not our time, rung by the unhurried
Ground swell, a time
Older than the time of chronometers, older
Than time counted by anxious worried women
lying awake, calculating the future,
Trying to unweave, unwind, unravel
And piece together the past and the future,
Between midnight and dawn, when the past is all deception,
The future futureless, before the morning watch
When time stops and time is never ending;
And the ground swell, that is and was from the beginning, Clangs
The Bell.

        T.S. Eliot
        1943

1

Mark Price's grandmother used to believe that idle hands were the devil's workshop. "Boredom brings mischief just as sure as sugar on the counter brings ants," she would say, sometimes to no one in particular. Now in his 49th year, Mark was extremely bored, both in his job and his personal life. He should have seen trouble brewing. He should have listened to his grandmother.

Staring out the wide picture window of the faculty library, Mark watched as dozens of law students ambled lazily across the quadrangle in the afternoon sunshine, stopping in small groups occasionally to chat before they headed off to their classes. The well-manicured lawns and the leaves slowly turning from green to amber glistened in the late September light. Scanning these images, Price daydreamed about his own days in college and law school decades earlier. Back then he had wanted to freeze time, to find some way to stay a student forever. Spotting his own reflection in the picture window, Mark noticed the spreading crow's feet at the corner of his eyes and realized how naïve he had been.

Now in his late forties and well past the half-way mark of his career, Professor Price didn't know if he could stomach university life one day longer, let alone one more decade. Striving mightily to stay awake, Mark listened wearily as a senseless debate rambled on at their monthly faculty meeting.

One of his younger colleagues, recently tenured and rambunctious, thought that the law school cafeteria should serve only free-range chicken. "These animals are kept in cramped, filthy conditions for the duration of their lives and reach slaughterhouses too sick to stand. Our inaction, passivity and economic support fuel the industry."

"Let's file a petition with the Executive Vice President," a recently hired junior professor added in unctuous support. Mark doubted that either professor had ever met the Executive Vice President, or knew her name for that matter. A third colleague suggested that the subject of free-range chicken might be a matter better left to the University Faculty Senate. Sensing an escape hatch that would allow them to be both principled and expedient, the Dean asked for a motion to refer the matter there. By show of hands, a majority of the faculty concurred.

Packing up his laptop when the meeting was over, Mark felt demoralized in a way that he was not normally accustomed to feeling so early in a semester. He did not fit in very well with his faculty colleagues at the Louis D. Brandeis School of Law. Mark had practiced law longer than most of them did before becoming professors, and at heart he considered himself more of a lawyer than an academic. He also thought that much of his colleagues' scholarship was completely unmoored to the realities of day-to-day law practice. This estrangement only intensified as the years passed; today's pointless faculty meeting served as but one example.

Having achieved tenure and middle-age, Price couldn't care less what anybody else at "LDB" thought of him. As a full professor, Mark no longer needed anybody's approval or support. He had a handful of friends with whom he occasionally enjoyed a cup of coffee in the cafeteria or a beer after work. But he was disconnected from most of the others. Although he didn't usually dwell on it, today it unnerved him just slightly to feel like such an outsider among his peers.

Mark climbed several flights of stairs to his office, taking two stairs at a time. A former high school and college athlete, Mark had worked hard to stay in shape during the past three decades, notwithstanding the gray beginning to creep into his dark brown hair. He tried to watch what he ate, and he worked out regularly to keep extra pounds off his 6'3" frame. Even still, climbing the stairs, like suffering through faculty meetings, did not come as easily to Mark as it once did.

Mark reached the fifth floor without breaking a sweat, ready to get an hour's worth of work done in quiet before he had to leave for the day. As he rounded the hallway corridor to his office door, he almost stopped in his tracks as he saw a student sitting on the floor outside his doorway. "Shit," he thought to himself. "Brandon Gould. I promised him I would review his exam." Mark had completely forgotten.

Mark feigned tardiness and invited Brandon into his office. Reviewing exams and papers with disgruntled students was probably the least favorite part of his job. Brandon had been a student in Mark's Criminal Procedure class the previous semester, and had emailed Mark when grades came out over the summer asking Mark if he would be willing to sit down with him and show him what he did wrong. Mark had agreed on a date with the student, but then had completely put it out of his mind.

Sometimes students were sincere in wanting to learn how to do better. Sometimes they were secretly hoping that the faculty member would change their grade. Mark suspected that Brandon Gould fell into the latter category. Twenty years of academic life had taught Professor Price how to spot a grade grubber. Brandon had been excessively eager during class, raising his hand much more frequently than other students, and loving to hear the sound of his own voice. Mark suspected that Brandon was a poser, overly impressed with his own abilities.

Mark fished Brandon's exam out of a stack piled up in the

corner of his office and handed it to his pupil. Scanning the top of the front page, Mark said, "I see you received a B-, Brandon. Sorry if you were disappointed." Mark knew from experience that the students most likely to come by his office were the students who received the B's, not the students who received the C's or D's. The former group believed they were "A" students, and their egos were deflated by what they thought were aberrant grades. The second group were hanging on by a slim margin and just hoped to graduate.

With years of experience under his belt, Mark had developed a protective measure to deal with students like Brandon. "Why don't you look at an 'A' paper while I go over the notes I wrote in the margins of your essays to remind myself what I thought of your answers." Usually in looking at the best paper in the class, the contrast between a stellar performance and a mediocre one took the wind out of even the most disappointed student's sails.

Mark quietly looked over his notes in the margins of Brandon's exam. When he was finished he tried to explain to Brandon in a constructive manner what he could have done better. Yet Brandon's reaction completely blindsided him:

> "I don't think you graded the exam fairly, and I don't think you conducted the class fairly. As the semester went on, you stopped calling on me. I think you disagreed with my progressive views on criminal justice issues and with my criticisms of the police. You also played favorites in class. As a vocal member of the LGBTQ+ community, I was clearly not one of your favorites."

The accusation left Mark momentarily speechless. But today he was in no mood to take any crap from a twenty-three-year-old, wet-behind-the-ears law student.

"I don't care what your political views are, Brandon. I also don't care if you are a member of the LGBTQ+ community or what your sexual preferences are. All I care about is training you to be an excellent lawyer. Under our grading policy, a 'B-' is defined as 'a competent grade demonstrating an average command of the assigned material.' That is what your essays exhibit. They are pretty good—but they are not excellent. Moreover, under law school policy, I could not change a grade even if I wanted to without a full vote of the faculty. So there is nothing I can do about it. If you have any further complaints about this, you should go see the Dean."

Mark's office phone rang, saving the pair from further awkwardness. Glancing at the caller's number, Mark saw that it was his wife.

"I'm sorry Brandon, but I have to take this call," he said, gesturing toward the office door.

Mark picked up the receiver just as Brandon closed the door behind him.

"What's up, honey?"

Susan Price was sweet but short on the other end of the phone. Mark could tell from her tone that she was busy at work and had no time for small talk.

"Katie missed the bus back from her field hockey game at Milton Academy. She needs a ride home. Can you go get her?"

Mark was confused. Katie was a junior in high school and normally drove to away games with friends who had their drivers' licenses.

"Didn't she go in a friend's car?"

"I thought so too, Mark, but they left without her for some reason and now she needs a ride. She didn't explain it. I'm running into a meeting with a client and I do not have time to get her. Can you please go?"

Mark agreed and hung up the phone. Milton Academy was in the complete opposite direction from their home in Cambridge. At the beginning of rush hour, this trip would add at least two hours to a very long day. But Mark quickly packed his briefcase and headed to the campus parking garage.

After eighteen years of marriage, Mark had learned to recognize in Susan's voice when things were negotiable and when they were not. They had met as young, idealistic prosecutors working side by side in a district attorney's office. Mark had left the office early to begin an academic career. Susan had stayed for over two decades, trying the most serious felony cases and eventually serving as the First Assistant District Attorney. She then left the office for a big law firm representing corporations in white collar criminal defense matters. Susan now worked longer hours than Mark, and earned much more money than he did. It was an unspoken understanding between the two of them that when compromises had to be made, the burden fell on him.

Listening to "The Sports Hub" on 98.5 helped Mark mitigate the stress of traffic on the way to Milton. But that ridiculous faculty meeting and a tense student encounter left him in a sour mood. Mark had not had an opportunity to prepare for class tomorrow morning, or to finish the edits on a law review article that a co-author was patiently awaiting.

As Mark pulled into the Milton Academy parking lot, he spotted Katie sitting on a bench in the main circle. Katie's sandy blonde hair was tied back in a ponytail, which protruded from the back of her BB&N baseball cap. Like her mother,

Katie was both beautiful and athletic. Even in her field hockey skirt and jumper, she looked iridescent. Katie's blue eyes shone in the fading sunshine, and the remnants of a summer tan caressed her toned legs. As usual, Mark's heart swelled with love and pride at the sight of his daughter.

That momentary peace was shattered when a text message flashed across Mark's dashboard display just as he popped the car's trunk. It was from Julia Hoffman, Mark's teaching assistant.

"Why are you ghosting me?"

Shit! Mark minimized the text quickly as Katie finished storing her field hockey gear and jumped into the front seat.

"Hi sweetie. Did BB&N win?"

"Ya, we won 4-2."

"Did you score?"

"Coach sat me out—I didn't play."

That was a huge surprise. Katie had been playing varsity field hockey since sophomore year, and she was the best striker on the team. Mark couldn't imagine why the coach would completely bench her during her junior year.

"Does this have something to do with why you missed the team bus?" Mark asked.

"I don't want to talk about it."

"Well, I just took an hour of my day to pick you up, so I feel like you owe me an explanation."

"I didn't miss the bus. That bitch Shannon Harrington left without me. I was supposed to go home with her."

"Why would Shannon do that?"

"I don't want to talk about it."

"Well, why didn't you just get on the team bus?"

"God, Dad, the coaches didn't *know* I was coming on the team bus. They thought I was driving home with Shannon. Would you please just leave me alone?"

With that, Katie inserted earbuds and turned on her music, signaling the conversation was over.

It was going to be a long drive home. Mark scrolled restaurant contacts on his cellphone searching for takeout options for dinner. He also stewed privately over how he was going to respond to Julia Hoffman.

2

Susan Price's phone alarm sounded on their bedside table at 4:45 am on Tuesday. She had laid out her gym clothes in the walk-in closet the night before. She squeezed her lithe frame through the crack in the closet door and changed her clothes quietly so as not to wake Mark. Once down in the kitchen, she sat at the granite island and poured herself a cup of black coffee, scanning her news feed and text messages as she stared out the window. These fifteen minutes of solitude in the morning—when the house was peaceful and nobody had yet made any demands on her time—were perhaps the happiest of her day.

Susan placed a high value on structure and routine. She was considered a "top performer" at her law firm precisely because she squeezed a lot of activity into a single day. Susan started almost every weekday with spin class at 5:30 am at Barre & Soul, a small boutique gym near their Brattle Street home in Harvard Square. She returned to the house, showered and changed, and left for the office no later than 7:30 am. The convenience of having parking in the basement of her building and a smoothie stand in the lobby allowed Susan to be at her desk most days by 8:15 am, at least when she was not traveling for out-of-town clients. The flexibility of Mark's schedule gave him time to get the kids off to school, a luxury that Susan had begun to take for granted.

The 5:30 am spin class on Tuesday morning was led by Corey, one of Susan's favorite instructors. Corey was in his young twenties and incredibly fit; strong biceps, pecs and thigh muscles were accentuated by black spandex bicycle shorts and a neon colored Under Armour jersey. Corey had the sort of chiseled face and impeccable bone structure that one rarely saw on figures other than models and department store mannequins. He wore his shoulder-length blond hair tied up in a man bun. Susan considered him just the sort of innocent 'eye candy' worth starting her day with, no strings attached.

While his workouts were intense, Corey used hand weights only in the first section of the spin class, allowing Susan to use the second half of her workout to glance briefly at the notes section of her iPhone, where she maintained a "to do" list for each day. This type of multitasking allowed Susan to hit the ground running when she got to the office.

When the class ended Susan grabbed her water bottle and towel and headed quickly for the door. As she passed the front desk she felt a presence behind her and turned to face a familiar face. Tony Garcia, a homicide detective and former colleague from the District Attorney's Office, was coming out of the same class.

"Hey Susan. Great workout, huh?"

"Tony, what a surprise. I didn't know you belonged to this gym!"

"Just joined a week ago. I was two rows behind you on another bike."

"I didn't take you for the spin class type. Not running and lifting anymore?"

"Too many years of pounding. My doctor says I have to be careful of a disc at L4-L5. Plus, this place is half way to the office—I live in Watertown now."

"You'll love it. Sorry I have to run, Tony. You look great. Please give my best to Barbara."

Susan quickly made her way down JFK Street to the intersection of Brattle and the short walk home. Harvard Square was just starting to come alive with people hustling to work, merchants opening up their stores, and students trudging back to their houses after a long night studying or partying. You could tell who were students and who were Cambridge residents by whether they looked purposeful or languid in their morning pace. Susan dodged expertly between MBTA buses exiting the underground station and commuters leaving Flour Bakery carrying their morning coffees.

Later, on the commute down Storrow Drive, Susan was too preoccupied to notice the idyllic image of rowers sculling on the Charles River. Instead, she let her thoughts drift to Tony Garcia. They had worked closely together in the DA's office for over twenty years—having met when she was straight out of law school and he was fresh "off the road" in his first detective role with the State Police. Over the years they had staffed many cases together, from rapes and burglaries to bank jobs and homicides. While they had not kept up their friendship since she left the office, back then they had forged a close bond in trying circumstances—distraught victims, turncoat witnesses, evidence suppressed by judges, and ruthless defense attorneys. There was even a brief period during her courtship with Mark—after two or three years of dating, but before they had become engaged—when Susan and Tony had a fling. Susan and Mark had taken a break to sort things out—at Mark's suggestion. The break had only lasted five or six months—but during that time, one night while they were working late, Tony made his move. What followed was an intense affair that they kept secret from their co-workers. It was fueled mostly by romantic interest on Tony's part and revenge on hers, with sexual desire being their common denominator. Susan had let Tony down gently when Mark came crawling back on his knees a few months later. Intense memories of those passionate nights with Tony came rushing back to Susan now as she drove into the city.

Parking her car, Susan entered the building steeled for battle and ready to tackle the day. At the 14th floor of Wright & Graham, she stopped by her secretary's station for a perfunctory 'good morning' and to collect her messages. Susan's primary task on Tuesday was to prepare for a conference call with the general counsel of Luminex, a major pharmaceutical client based in Atlanta. One of their insulin products had been linked to a small number of deaths across the country in patients who had received doses allegedly tainted with a fungus. Although the client very much hoped that the investigation would not lead to any criminal charges, Susan was assigned the case due to her familiarity with manslaughter prosecutions. This was a big test of Susan's ability to satisfy a major corporate client on a high profile matter.

As Susan was thumbing through her messages, she noticed a phone call from Bridget Moore. Moore and Price served on numerous civic and bar association committees together, and their children were classmates at the toney Buckingham, Browne & Nichols school in Cambridge. They were also college classmates at Dartmouth and longtime, albeit not especially close, personal friends. Although Bridget Moore could be calling for a dozen reasons, Susan was excited about one in particular. Moore served as Legal Counsel to the State's Governor, Richard Jeffries. Susan had recently applied for an opening on the state Supreme Court occasioned by the mandatory retirement of one of its seven justices. She had interviewed last month with the Judicial Nominating Commission and submitted forms for the background check; the next step was to hear who had made it onto the "short list" to be interviewed by the Governor.

Susan resisted the temptation to return Moore's call right

away—she had billable work to focus on and needed to concentrate on the immediate needs of paying clients. Fortunately the day passed quickly with Luminex phone calls and meetings with colleagues. At 4:30 pm, Susan returned Moore's call, taking the liberty of dialing her personal cell phone. Moore answered on the second ring.

> "Susan, so glad it's you. The Governor wanted to make sure I contacted you before the day was out."
>
> "Hi Bridget. Do you have news? Is it good?"
>
> "It's good. You made it down to a list of three that the Governor is going to interview."
>
> "Bridget, thank you! I'm thrilled. Now I have to figure out how to tell my firm."
>
> "Well, you'd better figure that out soon; a story will probably appear in the Globe tomorrow morning," Moore responded.
>
> "I thought there weren't going to be any public announcements until a finalist was selected?"
>
> "That was our plan, but it looks like there was a leak. I got a call with a request for comment a few minutes ago from a Globe reporter, and they have the names."
>
> "Who else is on the list?" Susan asked.
>
> "Carter Ellis and Annette Casper-Jones. Your interview with the Governor will be next week. His scheduler will call you tomorrow with a time. Plan on an hour. I'm so happy for you Susan! Now, I've got to jump. Talk to you later."

With that, Moore's line went dead.

Susan wasn't buying the "leak" story for a moment. The Governor's office had intentionally disclosed the names of the three finalists as a trial balloon to assess public reaction before they made a final decision. That way, if there was any negative information that had not yet surfaced in due diligence, the Governor could pivot in another direction.

Today's development put Susan in a very awkward position with her firm. She had only given the names of two colleagues as references during the application process, and those friends had been sworn to secrecy. Now, she needed to find the Chairman of the firm's Executive Committee to fill him in before she left for the day.

Stewart Katz was just finishing up a phone call when Susan did a quick soft-knock on the frame of the open doorway and strode into his office. Katz gestured for Susan to sit down, but she remained standing, not wanting to get comfortable because she did not want to stay long. Standing up in front of Katz's expansive desk also put Susan in a slightly more advantageous posture, standing with feet shoulder-width apart, as if braced for a hit. She stared just over Katz's right shoulder out the floor-to-ceiling windows of his corner office, noticing dusk begin to descend over Boston Harbor.

"Susan, how is the Luminex investigation going?"

"I think we're containing it nicely, so far. But that's not why I stopped in to see you, Stewart. I just received word that I'm one of three finalists for the open position on the Supreme Judicial Court. I'm going to be interviewed by the Governor next week."

"Wow. I'm surprised, Susan. I didn't know you had applied."

"Well, I didn't let many people know at the firm. I thought it might be a long shot, and I didn't want to alarm anyone. But it's always been a dream of mine."

"If you get selected, the Luminex people are going to be worried about transitioning the case to another lawyer. I went out on a limb grooming you for that case."

"I thought you'd be excited for me," Susan replied defensively. "It's good marketing for the firm to have one of its partners being considered for a prestigious appointment."

"That may be. I'm just hoping this doesn't jeopardize our relationship with the client, that's all. How much time do I have before the matter becomes public?"

"Tomorrow morning."

Susan had not expected a warm and fuzzy reaction from Stewart Katz. But the stream of four-letter invectives that then streamed out of his mouth would have made a truck driver blush. Katz was concerned first and foremost with protecting the firm's bottom line, and that meant keeping big corporate clients happy. He chastised Susan like an errant teenager for not letting him know earlier about her judicial application.

As she left the Managing Partner's office, Susan silently churned about how the charm that Katz so generously bestowed upon the firm's clients was not shared with his colleagues, particularly those whom he perceived as junior to him. No wonder the associates and younger partners had a nickname for him—"TF"—for "two-faced." Nobody in the firm trusted him, but everybody feared him.

On the drive home, Susan rehearsed her conversation with Mark. On one level she knew that her husband would be happy for her; Mark had always been tremendously supportive of her career. But she also knew that he felt a little trapped at his job, unhappy with the year-after-year routine of teaching, and frustrated by leadership at the law school that he perceived as ineffectual. Because they had started their careers together and were of the same age and level of experience, Mark couldn't help but be a bit envious of Susan's opportunities. And, of course, he would feel nervous about Susan taking a tremendous salary cut just as the kids were approaching college. It was one thing for Mark to pick up the slack on parenting and household responsibilities when Susan was bringing home a hefty paycheck. Whether he would be willing to shoulder that responsibility with good humor when she was compensated as a public servant was entirely another issue. Plus, Susan's time commitments in her new role were not going to be reduced dramatically to make up for that salary loss.

Susan's hope for a quiet opportunity to chat with Mark was shattered as soon as she opened the mudroom door. Mark and the kids had started dinner without her, as she had expected. Susan could see the signs of pasta bolognese on the stove and countertops, one of Mark's signature dishes. The pungent smell of garlic and roasted tomatoes filled the space. But any semblance of family harmony was broken as soon as Susan heard the scene playing out at the kitchen table. Mark was demonstratively waving his fork, his face reddened with frustration. Katie was crying. And Archie, their fourteen-year-old, was silently staring down at his cell phone under the rim of the table.

"Maybe that *is* the best I can do," Katie choked through tears.

"Go see the teacher and ask for extra help."

"Mr. Cooper is ridiculous. He's the hardest teacher at the school. I knew I should never have taken his class. It's way too hard for me."

"That's just one paper grade," Mark explained. "It's not your final grade. The teacher is probably trying to motivate you."

"I'm never going to get into Williams if I can't get better than a C in AP History."

"It's just your first paper," Mark explained. "Don't judge a whole class by one grade."

"Why won't you let me take Adderall? Everyone else at BB&N is on Adderall!"

Mark glanced up at his wife as she put her briefcase down, implicitly pleading for help. Susan had no idea where to jump in. Sensing an easy mark, she said:

"Archie, put your phone away. You know it's not allowed at the dinner table."

That mollified absolutely nobody. But it bought Susan some time to gather her thoughts, pour herself a glass of wine, and get settled at the table.

"Why are you so upset about one history paper?" she asked Katie.

"Because everyone will think I'm stupid. You don't understand, Mom. I'm never going to get into a top college if the honors teachers think I'm a 'C' student."

"Your Dad's right. It's just your first paper. And what's this about Adderall? You don't have ADHD."

"Tons of kids at school take it, and they don't have ADHD either. Or, their parents pay some quack to say they do. I could buy it under the table like other kids do. I'm just asking you to get it the honest way."

"Meds are not the answer," Mark interjected. "If your schedule is so tight that you need drugs to help you focus, that means you need to give something up. Cut back on yearbook or student council, or one of your other activities."

"May I be excused?" Archie asked, stifling a yawn but not a roll of his eyes. He had barely uttered a word since he sat down at the table, classic for a second child. Katie tended to suck up all the oxygen in the room.

"You may both be excused," Susan said. "Please go to your rooms and finish your homework. Dad and I will do the dishes."

The couple lingered at the table, enjoying a brief moment of silence before delving into the sensitive topic of Katie's outburst.

"There's obviously something else going on with her," Mark said.

"What makes you think that?"

"She's fighting with her friends. Shannon ditched her for a ride home from the Milton game last night, and for some reason the field hockey coach didn't play her yesterday."

"Why is this the first I'm hearing about that?" Susan asked. She regretted the accusatory tone as soon as the words left her mouth.

"You got home from work at ten o'clock last night and I was in bed."

"I'm sorry. I'm just frustrated. Why would Shannon ditch her? Why didn't the coach play her?"

"She wouldn't talk to me on the way home. She was clearly upset about both."

"I'll see if I can get to the bottom of it," Susan said. "And tomorrow morning, when she is being more rational, can you please see if you can encourage her to go see Mr. Cooper about the History paper? Katie always listens to you about school stuff."

When the kitchen was clean and they were in bed for the night, Susan finally told Mark her news about the possible judicial appointment. It seemed premature to celebrate, because she still had to get through an interview with the Governor and, if selected, approval by the Governor's Council. But Mark was proud of her nonetheless, and delighted to hear that it was going to be written up in the morning edition of the Boston Globe. "Fuck the firm," Mark said. "They should be thrilled for you. Trust me, if you get the final nod, Wright & Graham will find every possible way to kiss your ass and milk the publicity."

Mark was a little less sanguine once he heard who Susan was up against. Carter Ellis was one of the most senior judges on the state's intermediate appeals court. He was a distinguished jurist and had much more civil litigation experience than Susan. Annette Casper-Jones was a trial judge in one of the busiest urban courts in the heart of the city, and had been a prominent criminal defense attorney before being appointed to the bench. As an African American woman, Annette would add much-needed diversity to the state's highest court. Mark knew that Susan's big firm experience, civic engagement and fundraising for the Governor were three of her major credentials. But he was not sure that they would be enough against those two impressive candidates.

3

Even the brightest afternoons in early October can evoke feelings of winsomeness for seasoned New Englanders. The sun hanging slightly lower in the sky as it began its afternoon descent signaled to those paying attention that there was a long winter ahead, full of shorter days and colder nights.

Tony Garcia was sitting outside on the second floor balcony of his small, two-bedroom Watertown apartment, wearing a Northeastern Huskies sweatshirt and quietly sipping a Michelob Ultra as he basked in the unseasonably warm 62 degree temperature. Tony was built like a middle weight boxer—six feet tall, square jaw, broad shoulders, massive pecs, and a narrow waist. His olive skin and jet black hair made him look like a Mexican Adonis, which, not coincidentally, was exactly what his female classmates used to call him behind his back at the police academy.

Tony's seven-year-old daughter Anna sat across from him at the patio table, eating dried fruit snacks and playing Animal Crossing on her Nintendo Switch. Usually, Tony didn't let her play video games after school, but today Anna was disappointed that a play date with her best friend Bianca had suddenly fallen through.

Watching Anna play in the waning sunlight, Tony marveled at her beauty and her innocence. A lump rose in his throat as he considered just how quickly their cozy family life had been shattered. His soon-to-be ex-wife Barbara had their house in Arlington, and Tony was living in a shitty rented apartment in Watertown with second-hand furniture scrounged last minute from his parents' attic in upstate New York. He saw Anna every other weekend and two nights during the week.

Tony's wife Barbara announced one evening last spring, when Anna was on a sleepover at Bianca's house, that she had "fallen in love with someone else." She was sorry, but she "realized she did not love Tony anymore" and perhaps "had known this subconsciously for quite some time." Barbara "never wanted to hurt him," but this was "just part of discovering who she was." It turned out that the "someone else" was an English teacher/aspiring poet at the same high school where Barbara taught history.

Tony had been tempted to seek primary custody of Anna and the house, because Barbara had been the moving party behind the split. But he knew that this would entail a costly legal fight, and he was not willing to put Anna through that battle. He also knew that his hours at work were highly unpredictable; being called out to a murder scene at 2:00 am would be untenable when you were raising a seven-year-old by yourself. So, Tony had quietly moved out of the house and agreed to have the couple's separation agreement mediated. But he increasingly felt bitter at receiving the short end of the stick in the breakup. And Barbara looked more joyful every time he saw her—radiating freedom, energy and relief. Tony wondered whether he would ever feel that kind of exuberance again.

"Let's go to the park," Tony called out to Anna as he jumped up from his seat. "It's way too nice out to stay inside."

Tony grabbed a soccer ball and helped Anna find and lace her sneakers. They drove to Casey Park, which was only five minutes from Tony's apartment. Anna would have preferred to go to the playground near her elementary school in Arlington, which was in their old neighborhood. That was where her friends from school would be on a beautiful sunny afternoon. But Tony wanted to avoid the awkward conversations with the mothers from Anna's grade. Some were friends of Barbara who would report back everything Tony said. Some were gossips who were looking for information about the breakup, particularly the more titillating aspects of Barbara's affair. Others were interested in Tony's newfound sexual freedom, sometimes subtly or overtly hitting on him. He found all these interactions extremely uncomfortable.

When Tony first moved out of the house six months ago, he believed every weekend or afternoon alone with Anna had to be carefully orchestrated with museum trips, amusement parks or sleepovers. He felt exhausted and inadequate trying to make plans on such a grand scale. As he eased into a more comfortable routine, Tony began to realize that some of the most enjoyable and loving moments were the spontaneous ones.

At the park, Tony and Anna had fun kicking the soccer ball and playing tag on the jungle gym. After that, a Cavalier King Charles Spaniel occupied Anna's undivided attention for close to forty-five minutes. The soft breeze glancing their skins cooled them down from the unusually warm October sun as they played "keep away" between a soccer ball and an adorable puppy.

Dinner back at the apartment consisted of Anna's favorites—chicken fingers and Annie's Mac & Cheese. Cooking was not Tony's strong suit, and he always opted for what was quick and sure to satisfy. He also whipped up a salad for the two of them, just in case Barbara asked Anna what Tony served for dinner. Anna didn't touch hers, but Tony didn't care. He had not reached the point in his co-parenting routine where he was enforcing Anna's fruit and vegetable intake. He was just getting by, day to day.

Drop off on a school night was at 8:00 pm, per their separation agreement. Tony made sure he drove Anna back to Barbara's place in Arlington at the agreed-upon hour. He stayed in the car and waved to Barbara as Anna ran up to the doorway. Tony was too tired and too frustrated with his ex-wife to walk Anna up the steps, feign pleasantries and review the events of the afternoon.

As he drove home, Tony thought about the work that lay ahead of him for the rest of the evening. Tony was the lead detective and therefore main witness in a murder case that would be presented to the grand jury in Superior Court at 10:00 am the next morning. He had to spend the rest of the evening reviewing all of the police reports, photographs taken at the crime scene, forensic analysis and the medical examiner's report from the autopsy. Tomorrow's case was a complicated matter involving blood splatter evidence and DNA extracted from multiple locations. There were no eyewitnesses to the crime, only friends and neighbors who told police about an argument between the victim and the suspect in the weeks before the death. Tony would have to be sharp tomorrow to convince the grand jury that there was probable cause to link the suspect to the murder.

Lying in bed that evening with papers from the case spread all around him and the Red Sox-Orioles game playing on the television, Tony remembered just why he loved law enforcement. He felt like he was protecting the public by investigating serious crime, and it was rewarding to see the faces of victims and their families when perpetrators were brought to justice. As the most senior detective at the District Attorney's office, Tony now received the most difficult and high profile case assignments. He also got to train and mentor younger officers, a task he relished.

Tony had just been passed over for promotion to Captain and head of the detective's unit, in favor of a colleague named

Emily Cronin, two years his junior. Tony understood the politics behind this appointment—the Department was facing calls to promote more women to positions of authority, and his friend and female colleague who received the promotion was highly competent and a good public face for the unit. Not incidentally, her father was a well-liked career officer in the State Police before his retirement. Tony hadn't exactly bristled at Emily's appointment, but he was disappointed nonetheless.

When Tony was informed about Emily's promotion, it was suggested to him that in order to be promoted from Lieutenant to Captain he should probably leave the District Attorney's Office and return to "the road," assigned to a barracks leading uniformed officers patrolling the state's highways. Because he loved detective work so much, Tony was reluctant to return to uniform, even if it meant a promotion and more money. That Faustian bargain, combined with his impending divorce, had put Tony in a funk as he approached his forty-seventh birthday.

Re-reading the medical examiner's report in preparation for tomorrow's testimony, Tony noted that the victim had metacarpal fractures on the fourth and fifth digits of his right hand. These were defensive injuries, likely caused by the victim raising his hand to protect himself from being stabbed, or trying to grab the knife away from his assailant. Tony was reminded of a domestic homicide earlier in his career where Susan Price was the prosecutor; she had prepared him deftly for a cross-examination on this same injury, where the defense attorney was trying to raise the possibility that the victim had broken her hand by beating her own children. Tony was prepared to counter that cross-examination only due to Susan's impeccable preparation and foresight.

Bumping into Susan at the gym earlier that morning had reminded Tony of what great partners they had been—both in and out of the courtroom. He had dated a lot of women over the years, but Susan may have been his one true soulmate. Tony barely contained his attraction to her at the office the whole time they worked together. At the time Susan had been dating one of their more reserved colleagues, Mark Price. When the two of them broke up, Tony seized the opportunity and asked Susan out for dinner. Tony believed that the intense physical and emotional attachment that he and Susan forged thereafter was the real thing. When she suddenly told him it was over, he was publicly stoic but privately inconsolable. Tony met Barbara within six months after Susan dumped him. Looking back, he now realized that his marriage to Barbara was likely a rebound relationship.

Remembering those nights together with Susan almost eighteen years ago, Tony was aroused. His hand moved under the bed sheet and he closed his eyes, allowing himself the physical release of reliving experiences with the most passionate woman he had ever known.

4

Criminal Law class on Wednesday morning was not going well for Mark. They were covering the topic of accomplice liability, and how little one had to do to assist in a joint crime to be considered responsible for the whole venture. First year students usually reacted strongly to the harshness of this doctrine, and engaged in a fierce debate about where the concept came from and whether it should be modified. Today, their minds seemed to be elsewhere. Several times Mark saw some of them smiling at their computers distractedly, as if sharing a private joke among themselves.

When he returned to his office and dumped his books, Mark picked up a voice message from the Dean's secretary. "Mark, this is Judy. Sydney would like to see you this afternoon if you could stop down. She has an opening in her schedule between 1 and 2."

Mark was somewhat taken aback by the call; when the Dean needed him for something, she usually called or emailed him herself. They were on friendly terms since Sydney arrived from a West Coast law school four years ago—an outside scholar brought in to 'shake things up.' Dean Sydney Taylor and Professor Mark Price did not share a lot in common—her field was labor and antitrust law, his was criminal procedure; she was far left on the political spectrum, he was just to the right of center. But as a somewhat new Dean, Sydney had needed Mark's alliance to chair important committees and marshal votes in faculty meetings. So she had been cordial to him—at least when it served her purposes.

Mark grabbed a sandwich and a cup of coffee at the cafeteria before heading down to Sydney's office. The Dean's suite off of the main rotunda was decked out in mahogany and leather, befitting the law firm partners and top donors who numbered among the school's prominent alumni. It stood in stark contrast to the cookie cutter, cinder block faculty offices on the floors above. Mark did a head pump to Judy in the outer office to see if Sydney was still free, and was given the visual okay to enter. As soon as he did, he could tell by the Dean's face that it was not going to be a pleasant conversation.

"Do you know a student by the name of Brandon Gould?" Sydney asked.

"Yes, he's a third-year student. He was in my Criminal Procedure class last spring."

"Well, he penned a very unflattering essay about you last night on the law student blog, 'Impressions.' Brandon writes, and I quote, that you told him you 'do not care about' the LGBTQ+ community here at the law school."

Mark suddenly understood the smirks on his students' faces in Criminal Law class just one hour ago. He had not remembered—if he had ever known—that Brandon Gould was a writer for "Impressions." At Mark's rank and tenure, he hardly ever felt the need to read the student blog. But it was clearly important to the Dean because she now had it up on her monitor—which she turned to face him.

Mark quickly scanned the on-line essay.

"Absolutely not. I did not tell Gould that I did not care about the LGBTQ+ community," Mark protested.

Even as he uttered those words, Mark felt increasingly indignant that he was having to justify his teaching methods to the Dean.

"What did you tell him?" Sydney asked.

"He came to my office to review his exam from last semester. Gould got an average grade—a 'B-.' When I explained what he did wrong on the exam and why it was not an 'A' grade, he accused me of viewpoint discrimination and alleged that I had stopped calling on him in class because of his political positions."

"How did the subject of sexual orientation come up?" the Dean asked.

"He brought it up. He said I stopped calling on him because he was a vocal critic of law enforcement and a member of the LGBTQ+ community. I told him I didn't care about his political views or sexual preferences, all I cared about was teaching him the material and making him a competent lawyer. And that's true."

Mark saw Sydney wince. Her body language suggested that both her political allegiance and sympathies might lie with the student.

"In retrospect, Mark, can you see how that language might have been unfortunate?" the Dean asked.

"It was a very brief conversation, Sydney. I don't have a transcript of it, and neither do you. But I stand by the gist of what I was trying to convey. A student's political persuasion and personal life are not important to me."

"Mark, you know you can't divorce law from political discourse. Pretending that you can becomes an apology for the status quo, whatever your field."

"Sydney, I feel like you are trying to micro-manage my teaching. You weren't there. Brandon Gould loved the sound of his own voice and raised his hand to speak several times every period. At some point you have to cut those students off for the good of the whole class."

They seemed to have reached an impasse. Mark was not at all clear what the Dean wanted from him. He let a couple of seconds pass in awkward silence and took a bite of his sandwich.

"Mark, the student 'Impressions Blog' allows guest contributors to post if they are invited by the editorial board. Would you consider posting a reply essay explaining what you meant in your conversation with Brandon—that is, that you care deeply about the LGBTQ+ community at this law school, but you do not take the sexual preferences of individual students into account in conducting the class or grading the exams."

"Sydney, I'm not going to blog about a private meeting I had with a student talking about his grade. That would violate federal privacy laws, and you know it."

The Dean did not like having educational privacy law thrown in her face. So she tried another tack.

"Mark, we are coming up on Admissions season at LDB, and this essay on our website is a little embarrassing to the school. I should also tell you that Brandon Gould is the great grandson of Jason Gould. Do you recognize the Gould name?"

Mark thought for a second and remembered that one of the biggest law firms in Boston was founded by a "Gould," who had also been a member of the State Supreme Court and an alumnus of Louis D. Brandeis. Shit.

"What do you want me to do, Sydney? We can't let grade-grubbing students use social media to bully faculty members. And just because his last name is Gould does not justify violating federal privacy law."

"How about this," Sydney interjected. "Would you agree to meet with him again? Soften your tone? You could explain what you really meant to convey in slightly different language. Perhaps if you did that, Brandon might voluntarily take this post down."

Mark thought about that for a moment. It seemed like a compromise that would be both private and face-saving. Most importantly, he would not need to reconsider the student's grade.

"Sure, Sydney. I'm happy to do that."

Mark began to rise from his chair, thinking they were done. But Sydney held up her hand to signal there was something more.

"Mark, the student in his essay also notes that you are one of a very few faculty members at this law school who has not put your preferred pronouns on your faculty webpage or the signature line of your email account. Gould uses this as evidence that you are not supportive of LGBTQ+ issues at the law school."

Mark was flabbergasted. While many of his younger colleagues had joined the "he/him/his," "she/her/hers," or "they/them/

theirs" bandwagon, Mark had not felt the least bit inclined to do so. He considered the practice virtue signaling, which he abhorred.

> "Sydney, there is no requirement at the University that faculty include their preferred pronouns in their correspondence with students."
>
> "I know there is no *requirement* in the faculty handbook, Mark. At least not yet. But I am asking you as a colleague to consider how the absence of your preferred pronouns might make students feel, from their perspective. I include my preferred pronouns."
>
> "I don't think anyone is confused about my preferred pronouns, Sydney. And if they are, I am willing to undertake the risk that they will use the wrong one in referring to me."
>
> "That confidence alone suggests a cisgendered perspective, Mark. It could turn off some members of your audience. As it did Mr. Gould. I am just asking you to think about it. Please."

Mark sensed that any further debate about this issue would just entrench their respective viewpoints. So he politely told Sydney that she had "given him a lot to think about," and bowed out of the office.

After getting back to his desk and returning a couple of emails, Mark left school early, confident that he was not in the proper frame of mind to undertake any serious research or writing. Indeed the Dean had given him a lot to think about during their meeting that day—but not in the ways she had intended. On the drive home, Mark thought about how students had become soft and entitled since he attended law school twenty-five years earlier; he thought about how faculties at top programs had increasingly become bastions of liberal elitism, intolerant of political perspectives that were conservative or even moderate; and, he thought about how white male privilege had likely reached a reckoning point in society.

Mark could deal with each of these realities individually. When he thought about them collectively, however, they made him feel very anxious about the next fifteen years of his career.

5

Mark arrived home at around 4:30 pm and parked his car on the street, leaving ample room for Susan in the driveway. He grabbed the mail and walked through the side door, dumping his briefcase in the mudroom as he meandered through the house. Katie would be at field hockey practice. Archie should be home by now, but there were no telltale signs of food on the kitchen counter.

When a sound of cymbals came crashing from the garage, Mark remembered that Archie had his band members over for rehearsal. Archie was the band's drummer and its unofficial leader; one of his friends from elementary school played the keyboards, and another served as lead vocalist and bass guitar player. Susan and Mark had encouraged Archie to keep this garage band together because it provided Archie a link to his childhood friends during the year he headed off to private school. One of the prices they paid for this continuity was Archie's freedom to have adolescent boys over the house two afternoons per week, unsupervised.

Mark entered the garage through the mudroom door, not even considering whether to knock. There was a scurry of shuffling as Archie's friend Max hid something under his jacket, and Archie kicked his backpack. The unmistakable smell of weed permeated the small space. Mark fanned the air in front of his face and coughed. The idiots hadn't even had the good sense to open one of the small transom windows at the side of the garage. Mark didn't know if he should consider that oversight a sign of innocence or disrespect.

"Hi Mr. Price!" Max belted out defensively.

"Time to head home boys," Mark ordered. "Rehearsal is over. Be sure to take whatever stuff you brought here with you."

The intended irony of that last statement likely escaped the teenagers. Max and Charlie eyed Archie warily as they grabbed their backpacks and headed for the door. They looked relieved to be escaping without admonishment.

Mark knew better than to scold Archie in front of his friends. That would only make it less likely that his son would be able to process anything Mark said to him.

"When did you start smoking pot, Archie?"

"I don't 'smoke pot,' Dad."

"I know what pot smells like, Archie. Don't insult my intelligence."

"You make it sound like it's some sort of regular thing. It's no big deal. I barely inhaled."

"You're in 9th grade, for God's sake. Where did you get it?" Mark asked.

"I didn't get it. One of my friends bought it off of some kid at Rindge and Latin."

"Max or Charlie?"

Archie's hesitation signaled that he was either crafting a lie or weighing the risk of ratting out one of his friends.

"I don't know Dad. I was in the bathroom when one of them pulled it out. It was less than an ounce. It's not even illegal in Massachusetts."

"Don't quote the law to me. It's against the rules of this house. Having kids over is a privilege—which you just blew. And you are way too young to be smoking weed."

The Prices had been close friends with Max and Charlie's parents since the kids were toddlers. Now they would have to decide whether to tell the boys' parents. Mark knew that he was too tired and irritable to confront that issue without Susan's support. So he decided to make Archie stew about the potential consequences.

"Go to your room and start your homework. Mom and I will talk to you about this after dinner."

What had started as a rather straightforward day was now turning into a disaster. Mark was still replaying in his mind the meeting with the Dean and how he was going to react to the negative web post written by Brandon Gould. Mark had no choice but to tell Susan about that controversy, because any whiff of hostility to LGBTQ+ issues could affect Susan's chances of being appointed by the Governor. Now he needed to talk with Susan about Archie smoking pot. It was going to be a tense evening.

As he began to prepare dinner at the kitchen island, Mark was preoccupied with worries over Archie. Mark felt guilty about encouraging Archie to attend BB&N, which was a bastion of privilege where many students exuded significantly more confidence than his son.

Archie's transition to BB&N this year had been unusually rough. Mark and Susan thought it would be easier for the family if Archie was at the same school as Katie, and naively believed that Katie would pave the way socially for her younger brother. Neither assumption had turned out to be accurate. Archie did not particularly excel at sports and was not considered popular with the jock crowd. He was way too self-conscious to throw himself into his studies and brand himself an intellectual. So Archie had not yet figured out where he fit in, and this was painfully apparent in his comportment. Physically, Archie had not quite grown into his own body after the onset of puberty—he was still a little pudgy around the middle, and hadn't yet sprouted in height or developed any significant muscle mass. Add reddish brown hair and burgeoning acne to the mix, and Archie was the epitome of an awkward fourteen-year-old boy.

Why had they been so thoughtless to give him a name like "Archibald," anyway? In retrospect, this seemed like a pompous and selfish act. Archibald Cox had been Susan's favorite professor at Boston University School of Law. She had even served as Cox's teaching assistant in his Constitutional Law class. Mark had admired Cox's integrity as Special Prosecutor in the Watergate break-in during the seventies, and the reputation and stature he brought to Mark's alma mater, Harvard Law School, before he was forced to retire. Naming their only son after a scion in the national legal community seemed like an appropriate way to honor a man they both admired. Now, it seemed like an act of vanity that had saddled their son with one more basis for ridicule.

Mark was sautéing chicken when he heard the mud room door open. Susan dropped off her briefcase with a sigh and came up from behind to give him a peck on the cheek.

"Thanks for starting dinner. You seem to have gotten home early."

"Bad afternoon at school, so I packed up and left. I surprised Archie and his bandmates, though. They were smoking pot in the garage."

Susan's furrowed brow alerted Mark that she was going to take this seriously. His wife had always been the primary disciplinarian in the family. Her own history of abstemiousness with respect to controlled substances made her less tolerant than most.

"Where did they get pot? He's not even fifteen for God's sake."

"I didn't want to cross-examine him in front of his friends. I told him to go upstairs and do his homework, and we would talk to him about it after dinner," Mark said.

"Great. Now he has time to concoct a story with his friends. We'll never get the truth out of them."

The tone of disapproval in Susan's voice annoyed Mark. If Susan came home at a more regular hour she would shoulder her own fair share of parenting issues.

"What time do you expect Katie home?" Mark asked.

"She's having a team dinner with field hockey. Be home later."

"I thought she had a falling out with her teammates. Did you get to the bottom of what happened Monday at the Milton game?"

"I haven't had a chance to talk to her about it," Susan responded. "I spent the last two days putting out fires on the Luminex case and fielding office gossip about my judicial application. Stewart Katz has a very big mouth."

If they were being graded on their parenting skills this week, Mark felt sure that they would receive a C+, at best. Susan did not seem to be carrying her fair share of the load. In the interests of marital harmony, though, he kept that observation to himself.

"So, what's our game plan with Archie?" Mark asked.

"This needs to be a big punishment. We have to take drug use seriously. I hate to think of Archie having a supplier out there."

"Why don't we cancel the band rehearsals for a month? No more having friends here after school?" Mark suggested.

"That's just going to deprive him of social interaction, which he needs right now. I hate to see him so miserable at BB&N."

Over dinner that evening, they discussed the dangers of drug use and how Archie had violated their trust by allowing marijuana in the house. They had decided to take Archie's cell phone away for a week. When Archie learned of his punishment, he exploded. That was the equivalent of the death penalty for a fourteen-year-old. "You all treat Katie as a complete angel in this family. She has you completely snowed. If you knew half of what she gets away with, she would be grounded for a year!"

Archie left the dinner table red faced and near tears, but not before powering down his cell phone so that his parents could not snoop on the device. "This family sucks," he blurted under his breath as he climbed the stairs.

In their bedroom, when the dinner dishes were done, and the downstairs lights turned off, Susan brought up the subject that Mark had foreseen was inevitable.

"Do you think that we should call Max and Charlie's parents?"

"I don't know," Mark said. "We don't actually know who brought the weed into the house. It seems like that would be opening a can of worms."

"Well, I would want to know if I were in their shoes," Susan replied.

"Then you should call them. But if it were up to me, I would let it go."

Mark was dog tired, and already thought that they had spent sufficient time on this subject. He was also discouraged that they were falling into their familiar pattern of using bedtime to rehash family controversies. Once the locus of intimacy, the Price's bedroom in their middle years had become like the site of a nightly board meeting.

"Don't you think it would be weird if I called them? You were the one who walked in on them and saw what happened. I would just be repeating what you told me."

"But I don't think we need to call them. You disagree. So if you think we should make the call, you should make the call."

Mark rolled over and turned out his bedside light. As he dozed off, Mark remembered that Susan had never asked him why he had had a bad day at work. In her younger days, when she was not quite so self-absorbed, at least she would have inquired.

6

The District Attorney's office in Middlesex County was tucked inside a drab office park in Woburn, about one mile from the Superior Courthouse. The DAs had been pushed out of the main courthouse due to the need for more courtrooms. The prosecutors were forced to lease space in a nearby office building that could just as easily have housed a bank or an insurance company. From the outside, the offices looked sterile and common. Victims and witnesses coming to the office to meet with prosecutors often drove right by the building.

Tony Garcia loved being in court and out in the field interviewing witnesses. Days when he was stuck in that drab office doing paperwork seemed to drag on endlessly. A pit of cubicles in the windowless interior of the building served as the hub where State Police officers did their work. Despite his seniority, Tony did not have his own office but was assigned a 6' by 8' cubicle like all the other detectives. Only the Captain assigned to the CPAC unit had her own office. Having been passed over for that promotion, Tony continued to be treated like everyone else.

Garcia was reviewing the forensic and toxicology reports on an arson case and trying to piece together the suspected timeline of a tenant's death inside an apartment building. The victim had suffered blunt force trauma to the head, but the cause of death was asphyxiation from the fire. Tony was trying to figure out whether the apartment was torched as an attempt to cover up a murder, or whether the victim fell and accidentally lit the fire by knocking over a candle possibly used for shooting up heroin.

Tony was trying to make sense of the Medical Examiner's report just as his cell phone rang. The number was from State Police headquarters in Framingham. Calls from "the brass" always made Tony nervous. He liked it when his superiors stayed out of his way and just let him be a police officer.

"Tony Garcia."

"Tony, please hold for Major Kelly."

Marty Kelly was the head of the criminal investigations bureau of the State Police, second in command under the Colonel. All of the Crime Prevention and Control (CPAC) units in the various District Attorney's Offices reported through Kelly. Tony rolled his eyes and took a long breath, preparing himself for what he suspected was coming next.

"Tony, Marty Kelly here. Glad I could reach you. How's everything in Middlesex?"

"Really busy, Major. But everything's good."

"Great to hear. Listen, Tony, I want to talk to you about a transfer. I'm ready to promote you to Captain if you will take a road assignment for a while and lead one of our highway barracks. Put your time back in uniform and I can pretty much guarantee that you will head the next CPAC unit that comes open. There should be some retirements coming up in the next twelve to eighteen months."

"I'm flattered, Major. But I think I would be wasted on the road. All paperwork and personnel issues. I'm a detective. It's in my blood. That's what gets me up in the morning."

"I get that Tony. But we all need to pay our dues. It's part of the job you signed up for. You don't want to be a Lieutenant forever. Think about the salary bump. Think down the road to your next assignment. It's temporary."

In fact, Tony had thought a lot about this issue since Emily Cronin was promoted over him to serve as head of the CPAC unit in Middlesex. She likely felt threatened having him still in the office, notwithstanding their friendship. Tony also knew that if he turned down this promotion, there might not be another one offered to him.

"Where 'on the road' would you put me?" Tony asked.

"C-1 Barracks. Athol."

Crap, Tony thought. The far side of Worcester County. It would take him over an hour to get to work every morning, on a good day. Getting an apartment out there would upset the applecart in his custody arrangements with Barbara.

"Major, I'm grateful that you're thinking about me. But I need some time to think about this. I am going through a divorce right now and I have to consider managing time with my daughter."

"Yea, I heard about that, Tony. I'm sorry. But you can make it work. Plenty of guys do."

Tony knew a lot of police officers who tried to "make transfers work" with their child custody arrangements, but few were truly successful.

"Major, can I have a couple of weeks to think about it, and maybe talk to some people who have worked in Athol?"

"Okay, Tony. But don't keep me waiting. These opportunities don't come up every day."

When Marty Kelly signed off, Tony was left wondering how much of this conversation was real and how much of it was just smoke being blown up his ass. Would it only be one year? Would he be given the next CPAC assignment that came up, or would the Department have 'other priorities' then too? And, perhaps, most importantly, did Emily Cronin want him out of her unit in Middlesex?

Tony's mind was racing, and he was unable to focus. After about thirty more minutes of work, he felt the presence of another officer bending over the wall of his cubicle. Tony looked up to see Ray Jones, a fairly new detective fresh off the road.

"Lieutenant. A few of us are going to J.J. Foley's for a beer after work. Want to join us?"

Tony had a real fondness for Jones, having taken him under his wing for the past year. While Tony wasn't in a great mood to socialize, he also had little appetite for spending another evening alone in his Watertown apartment, eating takeout and flipping through ESPN. With the affable Jones leaning over his desk, Tony was forced to make a quick decision. Maybe a night out bonding with other officers was just what he needed to evaluate the decision Kelly just forced upon him.

"Sure. I'll wrap this up and meet you there. But I can only stay for one beer."

J.J. Foley's was a true cops bar on the border of Chinatown and the South End. On any given week night, you were sure to find a mix of troopers, Boston cops and DEA agents milling about its long oaken bar or sitting in small booths and high tops around the bar's perimeter. Foley's had not yet lost its character by being infiltrated by young professionals moving into the neighborhood. Its dark, paneled interior gave patrons a sense of privacy from the outside world.

Tony drove his undercover vehicle and parked not too far from Foley's entrance on East Berkeley Street. Even though it was before 6:00 pm, he didn't bother to feed the meter. If a meter reader ran the plate—unlikely around Foley's—they would see that it was a state vehicle.

J.J. Foley's was just starting to get packed on 'Thirsty Thursday.' Tony quickly found the table of his younger colleagues at the back of the bar. Their conversation was lively and typical of cop banter—cases going to trial, rumors about pending retirements or divorces, and sports.

Tony felt at ease among cops in a way he seldom did with friends who were not in law enforcement. After a couple of rounds, the younger detectives' lips started to loosen. Tony's protegee Ray Jones was the first to ask him pointedly:

> "Lieutenant, is it true that you are being promoted and sent back to the road?"

Tony admired Jones' courage in asking. He also understood how quickly rumors could travel among cops.

> "It's been offered, Ray. But I'm not sure I'm going to take it."

> "Why wouldn't you take the promotion and the extra money? It would probably just be for a couple of years, right?"

Tony had to walk a fine line between wanting to mentor the younger guys and wanting to keep his actual feelings about his superiors on the State Police close to his vest. So he chose his words carefully.

"I love being a detective. It's like putting the pieces of a puzzle together. I'd miss that challenge if I went back to the road. One thing about detective work is that there's always going to be a 'next big case.' The thrill of that gets in your blood."

Tony excused himself to go to the men's room, taking his beer with him. As he scanned the bar on the way back, he saw a table of young women in the front corner who worked in the courthouse. One of them, a probation officer by the name of Patti King, caught his eye and waved.

Tony decided to drop by and say hello. Patti had been assigned to many of Tony's defendants over the past few years. Patti exuded warmth and charm without sacrificing a serious devotion to her job. Attractive and extremely well dressed, Patti also liked to stay in shape—a quality that Tony appreciated.

One beer turned into four or five for Tony Garcia that evening. His conversation with Patti and her friends felt breezy and light, just like the old days. Tony hadn't blown off any steam in a while. A night out at J.J. Foley's was just what the doctor ordered.

A little before 10:00 pm, Patti and her friends paid their bill and packed up to leave. Tony walked out of Foley's with them as they continued their conversation on the sidewalk. Tony found Patti's smile and her laugh completely disarming. She told him that she lived four or five blocks away in the South End. Tony knew that a city walk on a warm October evening would do him some good before he drove back to Watertown. So he left his car on the street and offered to walk Patti home.

Garcia never made it home to Watertown that night. As

Patti King and Tony stood under the streetlamps illuminating the pretty brick row houses of Appleton Street, Patti invited Tony up to her apartment for a glass of wine. Once inside, the attraction between the two of them intensified. Tony drew Patti into his arms and kissed her at the kitchen counter. Her perfume smelled of lilac, and she greeted his preliminary kiss with ardor, gently wrapping her hands behind his head. Soon they were pulling at each other's clothes. Patti let her skirt drop to the floor as Tony unfastened her bra, freeing large, supple breasts warm to the touch. Tony lifted Patti in his arms, and she straddled his hips with her bare, powerful legs.

Tony carried Patti King into the bedroom, where they fell onto the bed. Patti was adept at unbuckling Tony's pants and helping him slide his trousers onto the floor. She nibbled at his thighs and scrotum before discovering his erect penis with her tongue and taking him into her mouth, masterfully stroking his genitals with her lips and soft hands until he had to fight back the urge to climax. Tony pulled lightly on Patti's arms until she moved up on his body and straddled him on his back, working one hand on top of his bare, muscular torso as she used the other to guide him gently inside of her.

As they rocked each other to powerful orgasms, the warmth of Patti's thighs, her taut, athletic abdomen, and the luminous brown hair that cascaded across her shoulders reminded Tony of an earlier time and an earlier girlfriend. Susan Price.

7

Professor Price hadn't slept well, and it showed in his Criminal Law class on Friday morning. The large Dunkin Donuts iced coffee that he habitually brought with him to class barely improved his energy level. Mark had lots of things on his mind, both at home and at work.

After fielding some questions from a handful of eager students once class had ended, Mark made his way back upstairs to his office. Mark was anticipating a meeting with Brandon Gould in fifteen minutes. He had followed the Dean's suggestion and sent Gould an email inviting him to a meeting to discuss the LGBTQ+ blog post. Gould had tersely agreed.

Mark spent the remaining few minutes before his meeting with Gould tidying up his desk and returning a few emails. The clock ticked past eleven o'clock, and Gould still hadn't shown up. Eleven ten. Eleven fifteen. "That little bastard is standing me up," Price thought. "He's enjoying the limelight of the recent blog post and making me squirm." While Mark's thoughts normally didn't tend toward paranoia, he had become suspicious of the motives of this particular student.

When it was clear that Gould was not coming, Mark closed his office door and decided to use the unanticipated free time to call Susan. They still had not had an opportunity to talk about the blog post and Mark's conversation with the Dean. Mark felt like he owed Susan a "heads up" on this topic, given the public scrutiny she was about to go through with the Governor's office.

Susan picked up on the first ring.

"Hi Hon, what's up?"

"Just got out of class. How's your day going?"

"Trying to carve out a few minutes to get ready for my interview with the Governor this afternoon," Susan explained.

"Oh, I didn't know it was today. Did you tell me that?"

Mark regretted that question as soon as it came out of his mouth. He had just entered a familiar minefield over marital communications—or lack thereof.

"Yes. I told you on Tuesday."

"I'm sorry. We have not exactly had a lot of time to sort things out this week."

"What's up?" Susan pressed, obviously eager to get off the phone.

"Well, it sort of relates to your judgeship. There's a situation here at the law school that has now become public. I wanted you to know about it in case you get any questions."

Mark then briefly explained to Susan his exam review with Brandon Gould, the website post accusing him of anti-LGBTQ+ bias, and his meeting with the Dean.

"Shit, Mark, this couldn't come at a worse time for me."

"I know. I'm sorry. But this student is totally off base."

"Can't you get him to take the blog post down?" Susan asked. "I have it up on my screen now. It makes you look like a prick. If anyone from the Governor's office searches your background, they're going to see this."

"I tried setting up a meeting with the student this morning, but he blew me off. I don't know what else I can do."

"Well, you could at least get your preferred pronouns up on your signature line. That would be a healthy start."

"Susan, I can't allow myself to be bullied by a student. And even if I took that step now, it might not make the blog post go away. It's going to be perceived as insincere."

Mark felt like he was spinning his wheels with Susan the same way he had with the Dean. He understood Susan's predicament, but he wished she could be more sympathetic to his.

"Mark, I gotta go. Please try to handle this. We'll discuss it after dinner tonight. And we have to talk about Katie. I think I know what's going on with her field hockey friends. I saw some really fucked-up texts on her phone yesterday."

"Okay," Mark replied, fearful of what further controversies awaited him that evening. "Good luck with the Governor. You're going to be awesome."

After Susan clicked off, Mark tried to concentrate on the overdue manuscript that lay before him. As he slogged through it during the afternoon, his thoughts kept drifting back to the possibility of Susan's career change and the likely impact it would have on their family, their income, and their social lives. Mark tried to feel happy for Susan. She was a great lawyer, she had worked hard, and she deserved the shot. Susan's ambition and boundless energy were two qualities that had attracted Mark to Susan from the beginning of their relationship. Still, Mark could not help but feel troubled that his wife's career was now in ascendancy in a way that his was not.

8

The walk from Susan's office in Boston's seaport district to the State House normally would have been delightful, but for Susan's rising level of anxiety over the impending interview. Susan barely noticed the seagulls soaring above Rowes Wharf against a bright October sky, or the majestic foliage of the Boston Common. As she climbed the steps of Beacon Hill past the statues of Daniel Webster and Horace Mann, Susan rehearsed the points she wanted to make to the Governor, much like she would prepare for an important argument in court.

Susan entered the State House through its side door on Bowdoin Street. A friendly security guard recognized her from previous visits and quickly waved her through the scanning equipment. Susan was in familiar territory and about to have a conversation with someone she knew fairly well; although not personal friends, the Governor's and Susan's paths had crossed on numerous occasions throughout their careers. She recognized that this might be the most important "pitch" that she had ever made, and felt a nervous energy appropriate for the occasion. That morning she had chosen a navy blue Halston suit that fit her size four figure perfectly and accentuated her trim but feminine physique. An expensive silk blouse revealed just the right amount of neckline to be both subtle and dignified. For good luck, Susan complemented her outfit with a matching jade earring and necklace set that Mark had given her for a tenth anniversary present. An attractive and well-dressed woman in her late forties, Susan felt comfortable knowing that she still exuded the type of grace and power that turned heads when she entered a room.

Susan found her way to the reception area of the Governor's suite and was invited to sit in its well-appointed foyer. The eyes of six former Massachusetts Governors, including John Hancock and Samuel Adams, stared down at Susan from their expansive portraits hanging on the walls. It was hard not to feel intimidated by the sheer weight of history reflected in that room.

Soon, Bridget Moore, the Governor's Chief Legal Counsel, joined Susan in the waiting room. Moore informed Susan that she would be sitting in on the meeting and taking notes, although it was likely that the Governor would be doing most of the questioning. For the next few minutes, Bridget Moore kindly put Susan at ease by engaging in small talk about their families and school.

Minutes later, an assistant came out to escort Susan and Bridget into the Governor's inner office. Governor Richard Jeffries offered a cordial handshake and gestured toward comfortable leather chairs across from his desk. Jeffries was a tall, broad-shouldered black man close in age to Susan herself. Family photographs lined the credenza behind Jeffries, leading Susan's gaze out the floor-to-ceiling windows toward a sweeping vista of the Boston Common and the Back Bay.

Jeffries started the conversation by congratulating Susan for making it past the Judicial Nominating Commission and progressing this far in the appointments process. He also commented enthusiastically on her impressive career. What followed was a casual, almost breezy conversation about the law, the justice system in Massachusetts, and the role of the courts. They covered a wide range of topics, including the state constitution, policing, abortion rights, mandatory sentencing and educational inequity. Susan felt at ease as she put forward her views on these subjects, almost like she was having a conversation over a glass of wine with a friend.

When the conversation was over, Bridget Moore escorted Susan to the exterior door of the Governor's suite to say goodbye. Bridget was circumspect and professional, avoiding any direct feedback about how Susan had done. But Susan could tell from Moore's facial expressions and body language that it had gone well. Bridget also dropped one piece of inside baseball that surprised Susan: "You may hear as early as next week. The Governor has already interviewed the other two finalists."

Susan felt triumphant as she walked down the Boston Common toward her car. For the first time that day she heard the birds singing, the street musicians playing their keyboards, and the scatters of laughter from small groups of tourists crisscrossing the city. It was another gorgeous October afternoon, and Susan basked in the beauty of the Boston skyline as the autumn sun began its descent. Susan thought she had nailed the interview. The college athlete and competitor in her had come out, and she had left nothing on the field.

Susan's euphoria dissipated somewhat on the drive home as she contemplated some of the family controversies that loomed ahead. Susan knew she owed Mark some uninterrupted time to discuss what was going on at the law school. She also had some disturbing news about Katie that she had been putting off sharing with him. Increasingly for Susan, the small joys of family life felt outweighed by its complexities. This left her feeling wistful about her days as a single woman, able to focus solely on her personal and professional ambitions.

After dinner Susan suggested that she and Mark pour themselves a glass of wine and retreat into the den. Mark wanted to hear all about Susan's interview with the Governor, which she gladly shared with him, detail by detail. She then sought an opportunity to steer the conversation toward Mark's work.

"Mark, you know what comes next on this judge thing. If the Governor picks me, there will be increasing public scrutiny and an interview before the Governor's Council. Every aspect of my life will be fair game at that point. Have you gotten that student to take down the blog post about you?"

"I set up a meeting with him today, but he stood me up."

"Have you reached out to him again?"

"I tried. I sent him an email asking him if there was any confusion about the time, but he hasn't responded."

"What are you going to do now?" Susan asked.

"What can I do? I can't force students to take down blog posts about me."

"Well, you could add your preferred pronouns to your website and email signature. I think you're being just a little bit stubborn on that issue. It may mean a lot to students who are non-binary or questioning."

"They might still keep the blog post up, unless I issued some form of apology for what I allegedly said about Gould in private, which I cannot do because he has misrepresented the conversation."

"Maybe if you took that first step about the pronouns, the Dean could convince the student to remove the blog post," Susan replied.

"Blog posts don't simply 'go away,' Susan. That is not how the internet works. Even if it was taken down, a record of it still exists somewhere that some Governor's Council member could find."

"I'm just asking you to try, for my sake."

"I am trying. But I am not willing to engage in political posturing about something I don't believe in to avoid being criticized for something I didn't do. That is not how tenure and academic freedom work. The Dean should respect that. Instead, she appears to be siding with the student."

"Could you at least meet with Sydney again and tell her the efforts you have made? Maybe she can think of a way to intervene."

Mark agreed, although groveling before a Dean stuck in his craw. Middle-aged, right of center white males were no longer in power at universities like his. Sydney seemed to be taking advantage of that political moment to put him in his place.

Just when Mark thought he might finally relax for the evening, Susan brought up another difficult subject. She was whispering now to avoid being overheard.

"We need to talk about Katie. I think I figured out what is going on with her. It probably has nothing to do with field hockey."

"What is it?" Mark asked.

"She left her cell phone on the kitchen island Wednesday morning when she ran upstairs to find some books. I scanned her messages, and there was some sexually suggestive stuff on there."

"You looked at her phone? How did you unlock it?"

"Please. . . I've seen her swipe her code a thousand times. It's her field hockey number twice, backwards."

"That's a huge invasion of privacy, Susan. She's going to be furious with you."

"She's barely seventeen, Mark. We pay for the phone. We have a right to know what she's using it for."

"What was on the phone?"

"Texts from someone she listed in her contacts as 'Stickhandler.' Wanting to hook up with her and suggesting stuff they could do together. Pretty graphic. What bothers me most is that Stickhandler is reacting to a photo that Katie must have either deleted from her message history or sent to him on Snapchat. He says her 'tits and ass look smokin.'"

"What can we do? At least Katie had the good sense to send the photo on Snapchat so it couldn't be passed along to other kids."

"Mark, you're really not getting it. You're assuming 'Stickhandler' is some horny highschooler on the BB&N lacrosse team. We have no idea who he is. It could be some disgusting fifty-year-old pedophile trying to kidnap her. We have to do something."

"Did you try a reverse look up on the phone?"

"Yes, it doesn't come up. Blocked."

"Okay, what do you think we should do?" Mark asked.

"I think you should confront her and demand to know who Stickhandler is. We have to explain to Katie the dangers of sending sexually explicit photographs. If she doesn't tell us what's going on, we confiscate the phone."

Susan was at a clear advantage in this argument because she had had a few days to process the problem. Mark was annoyed that she was now trying to shift the responsibility to him.

"Why me? You are the one who discovered the texts. You need to own that."

"Katie will just blow up and redirect the focus from her behavior to mine. Besides, you have always been better able to reason with her. She's going through a real oppositional phase with me right now."

Mark let the irony of that sink in for a few moments. One of the reasons Katie had become oppositional with Susan during her teenage years was that Susan did not respect personal boundaries.

"I'm not going to do it, Susan. Sex stuff with a daughter really has to be a mother's job. Besides, you found the texts. Since I didn't see them, she could just deny it."

Susan was exasperated. As a successful litigator, she hated to lose an argument.

"How about I hire a private investigator to find out who Stickhandler is?" Susan asked.

"We just can't throw money at a problem and hope it will go away. We need to have a conversation with Katie about having respect for her body and protecting her personal safety."

"What do you mean 'we?'" Susan asked, pouncing upon Mark's verbal misstep. "You just said it was my job."

"Well, I'm willing to do it *with you* if you want to do it *together*," Mark emphasized. "I'm just not willing to do it alone."

Susan stood up from the couch hurriedly and collected her wine glass. She muttered, "Fine, I'll handle it, just like I handle everything else around here," as she backed out the door.

The unfairness of that last barb left Mark seething.

9

Saturdays were Archie's only real days to be lazy. He could sleep in, play video games to his heart's content, stay in raggedy sweatpants, and eat what he wished, when he wished. Homework could wait until Sunday. For a fourteen-year-old boy, Saturdays during the school year seemed like the last remaining vestige of childhood.

On this third Saturday in October, Archie slept late and then rode his bike over to his bandmate Max's house to jam in the basement. Max's mom did not work outside the house; a stout woman of Italian heritage, she loved to cook and dote on her family, especially her youngest son, Max. Mrs. Palitano was very good about making sure they always had lots of food in the house on the weekends; homemade meatballs, fresh bread, lasagna, biscotti and Italian cold cuts of every variety were stocked in the kitchen.

Archie loved Mrs. Palitano precisely because she was so different from his own mom. She was unapologetically devoted to her family, and always put them ahead of herself. Saturdays were boy time, and Mrs. Palitano knew better than to interrupt their activities in the basement. When she wanted to check on them or offer them something fresh out of the oven, she shouted down from the top of the stairs.

On that particular Saturday, the childhood friends turned their attention to the most pressing of their problems. They had gotten permission from their parents to attend a concert at the Orpheum Theater in Boston the following weekend. Their favorite rapper, Machine Gun Kelly, was headlining the venue. The boys' night out promised to be epic.

Weed was the drug of choice for Archie and his gang. But they had been debating for weeks about experimenting with ecstasy. The Orpheum concert seemed like the perfect opportunity. They decided to make this night memorable by trying to score some Molly.

Their problem: since Archie's cell phone had been confiscated, the boys had lost their ability to reach out to their drug connection, "Mullet." Mullet was famous among Cambridge teenagers mostly for his hairstyle and his bountiful stash. They had first met him about one year earlier while hanging out on their skateboards at Harvard's Holyoke Plaza. For the past twelve months, they had reached out to Mullet only for weed, and only using Archie's cellphone.

"Why don't you just text him on my phone?" Charlie asked.

"He's not going to answer a text from a line he doesn't know. He's way too careful," Archie responded.

"Why don't we just go to Holyoke Plaza and look for him there?" Max interjected.

"He never brings anything but weed to Holyoke Plaza. He's too afraid of the cops in the Square. He won't have any Molly on him," Archie explained.

Eventually the boys arrived at a solution. Archie would text Mullet using Charlie's phone, but explain to him in the text that it was Archie reaching out and that his phone had been taken away by his parents for a week. Archie would then ask Mullet to call him back on Charlie's line. If he did, Mullet would hear Archie's voice and know it was someone he was used to dealing with.

It worked. Mullet called back within twenty minutes, and Archie picked up. After a brief conversation about the new phone and "what a pain in the ass" Archie's parents were, Mullet asked Archie if he wanted "the usual?" Archie said that he did, but also that "Molly is going to be visiting next weekend." Mullet said, "I can do that," and told Archie that he should meet him "at the normal place" at 2:00 pm.

At about 1:30 pm, Archie set off on his bike for Mt. Auburn Cemetery, which was about a mile and a half from Max's house. The cemetery was comprised of over 150 acres of beautiful, manicured land set along hilltops abutting the Charles River. Getting to this location was an easy bike through the streets of Cambridge. Archie had developed the habit of meeting Mullet at the Mary Baker Eddy Monument inside the cemetery's pristine grounds. From the steps and columns of this fifteen-foot-high marble colonnade, Mullet could see anyone approaching from at least one hundred yards.

Mullet arrived on foot, about five minutes after Archie laid his bike down at the side of the brick walkway leading to the Eddy memorial. They sat down next to each other on the marble steps. It was remarkable how little Archie knew about Mullet, other than that he was in his late teens, hung around the square, and often played street chess in front of the Holyoke Center. Archie didn't know if Mullet lived in Cambridge, Watertown, Arlington or Belmont, or whether he was still in school. Normally Mullet wasn't generous about revealing too much information about himself, and Archie didn't ask. But on this breezy autumn afternoon in one of Boston's most bucolic settings, Mullet was more talkative than usual. They sat together for several minutes, just taking in the view and enjoying the weather. Mullet asked Archie if he went to Cambridge Rindge and Latin or "some private school." Archie said he was a freshman at Buckingham, Browne & Nichols. Mullet whistled.

"Wow, that's for rich kids, dude. You like it?"

"It's okay," Archie responded, being totally frank. "I miss my friends in Cambridge."

"I bet there are plenty of drugs available at BB&N. There must be people who party?"

"I'm only a freshman. I don't know too many kids there yet," Archie responded. As soon as he confessed this, he heard how lame it sounded.

"Listen, dude. You want to work with me? Sell some stuff to the rich kids? I'm not talking about anything serious, just some weed and Adderall. Maybe Xanax. High-strung kids at the private schools are totally into that shit. I would pay you. Split the profits."

Archie paused. He didn't want to insult Mullet by saying no. And maybe selling some weed at BB&N might make him more popular with the other kids. So Archie said, "Okay. Sounds great."

Just like that, Archie had secured himself a part-time job. As he gazed out at the cemetery's reflecting pool and the Boston city skyline beyond it, he felt energized by having taken some initiative. Like almost every fourteen-year-old kid everywhere, Archie gave no thought whatsoever to how the decision might impact other members of his family.

10

Monday morning's Criminal Law class focused on one of Mark's favorite topics. The class was discussing the "heat of passion" doctrine, and when an intentional killing could be reduced to manslaughter because the defendant was provoked by the victim. This was a subject that normally evoked a lively discussion among the students.

Under the law in most states up until the mid-20th century, "fighting words" were never considered enough to warrant a manslaughter instruction under the heat of passion doctrine. Reasonable persons were expected to tolerate insults without resorting to violence. Even schoolchildren are taught from an early age, "Sticks and stones may break my bones, but words can never hurt me."

Mark Price always used a Michigan case involving a racial epithet to illustrate the slow erosion of that "words alone are not enough" doctrine. That day he selected a demure and typically quiet female student—Rebecca Olson—to recite the facts of *People v. Green*. An African American male was looking for his dog, who had not come home in over a day. He asked his neighbor, over the hedge separating their properties, if the neighbor had seen his dog. The neighbor exclaimed, "I shot the fucking dog. It's bad enough I have to live next to a fucking nigger, I don't want to live next to a nigger's dog." The defendant, Mr. Green, went into his garage, retrieved a gun, and returned to shoot the victim. The jury convicted Mr. Green on charges of murder because the judge—under then prevailing law—refused to give the jury the option of manslaughter. The conviction was reversed by the Court of Appeals.

Ms. Olson did a nice job reciting the facts of the case and the reasons for the appellate court's decision. The court had written the word "nigger" in its 1974 opinion—just as the neighbor had maliciously invoked it. But Ms. Olson used the term "N-word" in describing the case, as did Mark in his questioning. The class then engaged in a discussion of whether and when the "insulting words" doctrine should be relaxed to take into account circumstances like Mr. Green's, where the victim twice invoked such a highly inflammatory racial epithet.

The class discussed what would happen if the "insulting words" doctrine were abandoned. Some students worried about the slippery slope that such a concession would entail. Would calling someone a homophobic slur suffice to mitigate a murder to manslaughter? How about calling them "fat" or "short?" Several students recommended abandoning an objective reasonableness standard in favor of a subjective standard, focusing on the characteristics of the defendant and whether the inflammatory remark was likely to cause him or her to act from passion or reason.

The conversation seemed to be going well. Just then, Mark saw a tall, well-dressed young man in the back row raise his hand. Mark knew that this student—James Mallinger—was President of the local chapter of the "Federalist Society," a national conservative group.

"Mr. Mallinger, your thoughts?"

"I don't think we should allow any insulting words to mitigate a killing to manslaughter. There would be no sensible place to draw the line."

"So you think that a person whose passions are inflamed by highly offensive racial attack is just as culpable as someone who kills with premeditation?" Mark inquired.

"They may be less culpable, but they are also more dangerous. Anyone who would fly off the handle and kill based on a derogatory comment is a threat to society."

"So, all insults should be treated equally under the eyes of the law?" Mark pressed.

"I think the law should always encourage people to be their strongest and best selves."

"Even when the victim calls an African American a 'nigger' and kills his dog out of racial bigotry?" Mark asked.

"I don't think legal doctrine should capitulate to weaknesses in human nature," Mallinger insisted.

Mark hoped that other students would raise their hands and challenge Mr. Mallinger, particularly his comment about 'weaknesses in human nature.' But he was disappointed—there was dead silence in the room.

Looking up at the clock, Mark realized that it was quitting time. Mallinger was saved by the proverbial bell. Mark gave the students their next reading assignment and dismissed them for the day.

Back in his office, Mark felt unnerved by today's class. What bothered him was not just Mr. Mallinger's rigidity and lack of empathy toward the plight of the defendant in *People v. Green*. It was also the silence that followed Mallinger's remarks. Although Mark could sense other students bristling in the room, no one spoke up.

The glorious October sunshine outside Mark's window beckoned him out of the building. Mark ran at lunchtime at least two or three days per week. Common shower stalls in a unisex bathroom on the fourth floor of LDB's main building served those members of the faculty and staff who, like Mark, exercised during the day.

After changing into his running clothes, Mark stretched lightly on the law school quad to loosen his hamstrings. Running had always been an antidote for Mark's stress—a way for him to clear his head. Today was no exception. Carefully selecting an oldies playlist on his I-Phone and putting in his earbuds, Mark headed out from campus. Before long, Mark felt 'in the zone' as he cruised over the rolling hills and pretty, tree-lined streets of Newton and Waltham. While the temperature was only in the mid-fifties, Mark's perspiration quickly evaporated from his body due to the warming rays of the sun. Mark felt younger than he had in years. Midway through his run, with the melody from the Eagles 'Take it Easy' thumping in his ears, Mark changed course to extend his route. It was too beautiful outside to rush back to work.

Once back on campus, Mark undressed in the fourth floor bathroom and entered the shower stall. Soon, warm water was cascading down his body as he luxuriated in the afterglow of a really good workout. While soaping up, Mark thought he heard the sound of the bathroom door open and close, and the interior deadbolt being slid into its place. "Weird," Mark thought. He felt positive he had locked the door behind him.

Mark was still lathering soap across his chest and abdomen when the shower curtain pulled back, and third-year student Julia Hoffman appeared at his side. Naked, Julia's taut, athletic body and iridescent skin acted as a familiar siren to Mark.

Before Mark could speak, Julia entered the shower and began to move her hands across Mark's torso. She cradled one hand behind Mark's neck and pulled him down for a warm, passionate kiss. Their lips parted, and Mark soon greeted Julia's kiss with familiarity and longing. Julia soaped and caressed

Mark's genitals with her free hand. When he was erect, Julia knelt down in the shower and expertly took Mark's penis in her mouth, gliding her tongue over its soft underside and using her hand to stimulate the scrotum. Mark lifted Julia up by the elbows and pressed her against the cool, smooth tiles of the shower's interior. With one hop, she straddled his hips and they pressed together against the corner of the shower. Julia cupped her left hand behind Mark's head as she used her right hand to guide Mark gently between her legs. Soon, they began a rhythm of rocking back and forth, in and out of the warm shower jets, stifling their moans to avoid being heard in the law school corridor just fifteen feet away. Within minutes, they climaxed together.

Toweling off on the locker room bench after their shower, Mark and Julia spoke in soft whispers to avoid being heard in the corridor.

"I thought we weren't going to do this anymore?" Mark asked, almost in a plaintive tone.

"I saw you stretching in the quad in your running shorts and t-shirt," Julia explained. "I got turned on. You might as well have been an ape baring your backside."

"Seriously, Jules. We agreed to stop seeing each other. I could get fired."

"You agreed, Mark. I didn't. And besides, you didn't seem to have any objection just a few minutes ago."

Mark was at a loss how to respond. Julia had been Mark's student in Criminal Law during her first year of law school. She was clever, poised and extremely confident, qualities that only magnified her beauty. Julia had visited Mark during office hours more often than most students during her first year. The two had wide-ranging conversations about politics, books, movies and even music. Mark could tell that Julia searched for an excuse to come see him, but he didn't mind. Although she was highly intelligent, Julia was also light and breezy. Almost reckless. She made Mark feel young.

At the end of that first semester almost two years ago, Mark was taken aback when Julia Hoffman received the highest score on his Criminal Law exam. It was Mark's practice to ask the top-rated student in his course to be his teaching assistant for the following year. Despite reservations, Mark followed his normal protocol and invited Julia to serve as his TA, an invitation which she eagerly accepted.

That turned out to be a huge mistake. During the fall semester of Julia's second year, the two met regularly to talk about her duties in Mark's Criminal Law course. Their attraction intensified. Mark knew it was a violation of University policy for a faculty member to have a sexual relationship with a current student or a student employee. For the whole semester Mark strove to keep his attraction to Julia in check, notwithstanding her increasingly flirtatious behavior.

It almost worked, until exam period finished for the semester. Mark and Julia met in a coffee shop near campus to discuss final grades in the class. Julia claimed to have left a spreadsheet on her desk in her apartment. She invited him back. One glass of wine led to a kiss, which led to sex.

It was hard to assess in retrospect who had seduced whom, but Mark and Julia's intimacy marked the beginning of an intense, six-month affair. Julia and Mark met several times per week, mostly in the afternoons and mostly at her apartment. Both the romance and the sex were exciting to Mark, filling a void that had been growing in his relationship with Susan.

This past summer, the University—like many across the country—had revised its sexual harassment policy. After much study and debate, faculty were now forbidden to have intimate relationships with any student who was studying in the faculty member's department, regardless of whether there was an ongoing employment or student-teacher relationship. Even though Julia was no longer serving as Mark's teaching assistant, their relationship was now expressly forbidden.

Two months ago, during orientation week at the end of August, Mark invited Julia on a noontime run during their lunch period. He thought, perhaps naively, that being outside and in public view might hedge against drama and recrimination. On their run, Mark told Julia about the new University policy. He told her about the possible ramifications to him if their affair were discovered. And, he told her that he couldn't see her anymore.

Suddenly a soft squeeze on Mark's shoulder jolted him back to the present. Looking up, Mark saw that Julia was already dressed and had slung her stylish gym bag across her shoulder.

> "Stop thinking with your head," Julia whispered. Mark could tell from the devilish glint in her eyes that she was flirting. "You spend your entire life wrapped up in that brain of yours. It's okay to think with your dick once in a while."
>
> "Jules, I can't. It might sabotage my career. It could ruin my family."
>
> "Mark, this is what drives me crazy about lawyers. It was okay for you to cheat on your wife, but now it's not okay for you to violate some written University policy? You need to let it go."

With that, Julia pecked him lightly on the cheek, unbolted the locker room door, and left.

11

Susan had planned her day Tuesday around picking Katie up from a home field hockey game at BB&N. She needed some private time to talk to Katie—uninterrupted—about the compromising texts she had found on Katie's phone. She knew Katie would be belligerent and fly into a rage, so she decided that the best way to approach the subject would be in the car, where Katie could not escape. Susan had told Katie that she was working at home in the morning, attending a meeting at Harvard during the mid-day, and then coming to watch Katie play field hockey in the afternoon. Perfect. She gets credit for being a good mother before she is forced to lower the boom.

In fact, Susan had scheduled a hearing on a student disciplinary matter at Harvard for 10:00 am. Although Susan's expertise was in criminal law, she was frequently called upon to represent children of the firm's corporate clients when they were threatened with suspension or expulsion from college. Susan called this subspecialty her "rich college kids in trouble" cases. Universities had become increasingly aggressive about enforcing sexual conduct codes in order to comply with Title IX of the Civil Rights Act. Because Susan had substantial experience prosecuting rape cases when she worked for the government, her expertise was often utilized by students accused by their institutions of sexual misconduct.

Susan's client today was a good looking kid—well spoken, athletic, conservatively attired. She thought he would present well to the disciplinary committee. But he was also a hockey player and a member of an elite "finals" club at Harvard—two characteristics that might reinforce the panel's stereotypes about sexual entitlement. The incident occurred in the boy's dorm room one night after a party at the Spee Club. Both students had been drinking beer and tequila shots. The victim complained in her statement that the male student had forced himself on her despite her verbal protests. The boy told Susan that the alleged victim had been a willing participant, and in fact had initiated some of the intimate acts leading to intercourse.

Susan had seen these types of cases a hundred times, both as a prosecutor and a defense attorney. She would argue that the female student willingly engaged in sex, that her memory and judgment were clouded by alcohol but that she was not too drunk to legally consent, and that the girl's claim to Student Affairs after the encounter was motivated by regret. But, she would have to be careful not to demonize the complainant or try to paint her client as a saint. Either could backfire. Susan had to present this as a regrettable mistake, pure and simple. They were drunk kids.

The young man held up well at the hearing, both in his presentation and his questioning. He took instruction well—probably after years of being coached hockey. He was poised and direct, but not argumentative. He answered the questions clearly and succinctly, but did not offer any information beyond the question asked. Susan was glad she had spent hours preparing him. His testimony came off as careful, but not rehearsed. The young man was aided at the hearing by text messages he had received from the female student both before and after the event, which were flirtatious and suggestive. "Save the phone" was one of Susan's guiding principles in these types of cases. Technology often provided a key source of evidence.

Leaving the Student Affairs office, Susan met the boy's father in the lobby. An investment banker from New Jersey, Dad had made a special effort to find business in Boston that day so he could see his son. Susan walked them to the Tatte coffee shop across from Harvard's Widener gate, where they sat outside and discussed the case. A big part of Susan's role in these types of cases was to explain the proceedings to the nervous parents and assure them that everything possible was being done on their child's behalf. In this instance, the father's company was an important firm client, so there were, in fact, two relationships at stake in the representation.

"It is typical," Susan explained, "for the hearing panel to take a few months to render a decision. They may find the complaint not substantiated, which means he is exonerated. Or they may impose discipline, but in my experience in cases like this it would likely be a short suspension and not expulsion." Before they left the coffee shop, Susan warned her client to "stay away from the complainant and have no conversation with anyone about the case."

Susan said goodbye to her client and his father in Harvard Square and walked her normal route home, up a short distance on Mass. Avenue and then turning left on Church Street toward Brattle. The bustle of activity in Harvard Square and the exuberance of young people going about their days energized her. During weekday hours, the vibe of Cambridge always felt different to her than Boston. Fewer stressed-out professionals and homeless panhandlers. More Zen. Susan reminded herself that maybe she should work from home more often.

At home, Susan grabbed a quick yogurt and piece of fruit from the kitchen and then jumped into her car. Her thoughts turned quickly to the task ahead of her with Katie. Lawyering was something Susan was good at—she knew the craft. Parenting often made her feel inadequate.

The incongruity of today's two primary assignments was not lost on her. On the one hand she was representing a young man charged with sexual assault, and using the complainant's social posts and text messages against her. On the other hand, she was about to chastise her daughter for sending sexually explicit material on line. She harmonized these two challenges by convincing herself—without a hint of self-delusion—that one job of a good mother was to teach your daughter strategies to avoid becoming a victim.

The playing fields at BB&N were alive with activity when Susan arrived half way into the first period. She sat amid some familiar faces on the bleachers who she knew to be BB&N parents—mostly mothers, with a small scattering of dads. Susan had forgotten most of their first names; internally, she rationalized that failure by reminding herself that she was one of the very few mothers in Katie's social group who worked.

BB&N played well and won the game convincingly, 6-2. Katie secured almost forty minutes of playing time, scoring two goals and three assists. She should be happy with this performance, although you could never be certain with seventeen-year-olds.

Lately Susan felt that parenting Katie was like petting a porcupine. You knew you were going to get pricked, you just didn't know when. She cautiously waited for Katie in the parking lot while the team debriefed with their coaches after the game.

Once they were in the car and driving home, Susan cautiously broached the subject of texting with Katie. She had carefully rehearsed the conversation in her head throughout the field hockey game, as if she were about to cross-examine a hostile witness.

"Honey, I need to talk to you about something important. And I need you to listen. It involves your own safety," Susan began.

"What is it, Mom?"

"I have told you how dangerous it is to take photographs of yourself and send them to other people on your cell phone."

"Mom, that's what kids do. It's how we talk to each other. Have you heard of Tik Tok?"

Even though she was facing forward, Susan could almost feel Katie rolling her eyes. That sarcasm unnerved her.

"I'm talking about *compromising* pictures. Explicit pictures. You have no control over what other kids will do with those photographs after you send them."

"Mom, I'm not twelve. I get it."

"Who is Stickhandler?" Susan asked.

"What?!" Katie's reaction was immediate and high pitched.

"You heard me. Who is 'Stickhandler?' I saw a text exchange with someone named 'Stickhandler' on your phone."

"Oh my God, Mom. How did you get on my phone? That's such an invasion of my privacy!"

"Don't change the subject. I'm your mother, and I pay for that phone. And you are seventeen years old. Who is 'Stickhandler?' You clearly sent him nude photographs."

Susan regretted how quickly the conversation was escalating. Katie was nearly hysterical now, successfully fighting back tears but not the urge to raise her voice.

"I can't believe you disrespected me by going on my phone. What kind of role modeling is that? Do we live in some kind of totalitarian state?"

If Susan was going to be able to get anywhere, she would have to bring the temperature down and reason with Katie. But it might already be too late.

"Either you tell me who 'Stickhandler' is and what you sent to him, or there will be consequences. Not only for your phone, but also for the next several weekends."

"You don't have any proof that I sent anybody nude photos. And I'm not going to tell you my friends' nicknames just so you can embarrass me and stick your nose into something that is absolutely none of your business!"

They had reached the driveway. Katie jumped out of the car and slammed the door before Susan could put the car into park.

"Well, that didn't go well," Susan admitted to herself. She breathed deeply and tried to get her head straight before entering the house. Susan knew that taking the cell phone away from a junior in high school was not a plausible punishment—they needed to know where Katie was at all times, and she needed to get ahold of them for safety reasons. Technology had become a crutch upon which they all depended. Susan also knew that Mark would not be supportive of her position if she re-opened the discussion inside the house. Mark would side with Katie about the invasion of privacy. Katie—ever intuitive—would be able to sniff out a rift between her parents and use it to her advantage.

If Susan was going to get to the bottom of this, she would have to do it herself. She had ways of figuring out who 'Stickhandler' was that did not require either Mark or Katie's cooperation.

12

Archie had only been home from school for about twenty minutes on Tuesday when he received a call on the landline from his friend Max. Nobody except telemarketers ever called the landline anymore, so Archie seldom picked it up. But since his phone had been confiscated by his parents due to the pot smoking incident, this was the only way for his friends to get ahold of him. To Archie, that seemed like living in the dark ages.

"What's up?" Archie asked.

"I'm in the square at Holyoke Center. Get down here now, dude. It's important."

It wasn't like Max to be so secretive. But then again, neither he nor Archie were accustomed to talking over a landline. Archie dropped his backpack in his bedroom, grabbed his skateboard from the garage, and headed out of the house. He could use some fresh air and exercise before he started his homework.

The square was bustling with activity, but Archie found Max quickly in their favorite corner of the outdoor plaza. The look on Max's face told Archie that something serious was afoot.

"What's going on?" Archie asked Max.

"I came here after school to hang out and play some chess. I ran into Mullet. He's really pissed at you."

"What did I do? I haven't seen him since Saturday."

"That's just it," Max explained. "Mullet said he was arrested right after he met you at the Mt. Auburn Cemetery. He's convinced that you are a snitch for the Cambridge cops. He thinks you set him up."

"Holy shit."

Archie sat down on a nearby bench to compose himself and think this through. The timing looked awfully suspicious. But other than that, Mullet had no reason to distrust him.

"Why would I do that? I don't owe the police anything. It would just make me look bad."

"Mullet was hinky about the whole cell phone thing. Remember, you called him on Charlie's cellphone on Saturday to set up the deal? He thinks that was a cop's phone, and you were doing it with the cop standing right next to you."

"Did you show him Charlie's number from your phone?" Archie asked.

"Honestly, I didn't think about that," Max admitted sheepishly. "And I didn't have time. He was totally furious. Said 'you screwed him over royally.' And then he stormed off."

"What did the police find on him?"

"I have no idea, Archie. The whole conversation lasted about two minutes. He left, and I called you."

Archie and Max sat together for another thirty minutes hashing through ideas. Max did not have Mullet's phone number on his cell, so they couldn't call him from the plaza. They didn't know where Mullet lived, so they couldn't skate by his house. Damn, they didn't even know what court he was charged in, or for what crime. It might have helped them to talk to a lawyer, but Archie couldn't possibly get his parents involved without telling them what had happened.

They were fucked.

13

Although Mark Price was an attorney and not a historian, when he looked back on his unraveling from the perspective of hindsight, he would pick Wednesday, October 20, 2021, as the day his life started crashing down around him. Certainly there were indications of trouble earlier, and causal connections that had already been set in motion. But Wednesday, 10/20, was the date Mark's proverbial ship hit an iceberg. Everything after that was just an attempt to prevent himself from drowning.

Mark was sitting in his office, returning emails. He saw a red flag next to an earlier email sent to Brandon Gould indicating it had not been returned. So he decided to make one more attempt to extend an olive branch to the student. Mark sent Brandon a second email asking him to come visit him in his office to discuss last year's Criminal Procedure course. He even went so far as to "apologize" for any misunderstandings. That was the limit of what Mark could bring himself to do under the circumstances.

As he was finishing typing, Mark saw a shadow in his office doorway and looked up. It was Julia. She looked stylish in designer jeans, ankle boots and a V-neck t-shirt that accentuated her trim figure. Smiling, Julia closed the door behind her and came over to his desk. Without waiting for an invitation, she sat on Mark's lap and gave him a warm and gentle kiss on the lips.

"I've missed you," Julia began.

"Jules, we can't."

"Can't what?" Julia asked, running her hand up Mark's trousers and letting it rest on his crotch.

Mark began to grow hard, despite his best intentions. But he had to put an end to this. He picked Julia up by the torso and stood up from the desk chair, planting her firmly on her feet beside his desk.

"Julia, I'm sorry. I've tried to explain this to you. We can't keep seeing each other. Susan has some big things going on right now professionally. A scandal would destroy our family. Please don't make this any harder than it has to be."

At the mention of Susan's name, Julia's entire visage became dark. In a split second, she turned sour, from seductress to woman scorned.

"Interesting, Mark. I don't recall you worrying about your family all those afternoons in my apartment last year when we were fucking each other's lights out."

"Julia, please."

"I thought we had feelings for each other, Mark. I thought this was something more than the standard cliché of a professor using his student."

"What are you *talking* about, Julia? I didn't 'use' you. You came on to me. And you weren't my student last year."

Mark was whispering now, desperate to keep the conversation on an even keel and to avoid being heard in the corridor.

"What happened to you, Mark? You used to be one of the few people around here who had any balls. Now you're behaving like a coward, afraid of your own shadow."

Mark moved Julia toward the office door, opening it just as she finished that accusation.

"I'm sorry, Julia, you have to go."

There was a tear forming in Julia's eye. She was clearly struggling with her emotions, between anger, sadness and longing. As she walked out the door, Julia said over her shoulder:

"This isn't goodbye, Mark. You can't just dismiss me. I'm not some sixteen-year-old schoolgirl."

Mark closed the door gently and leaned against it. He crouched to his knees and held his head in his hands for several minutes as he replayed the conversation in his mind. "That really backfired," he thought to himself. Mark regretted ever starting the relationship with Julia. He should have been stronger. He should have foreseen the consequences.

A ringing phone jolted Mark from his stupor and brought him back to his desk. It was the Dean's office.

"Hi Mark. It's Judy. Sydney wants to see you."

"Sure, Judy. How about tomorrow afternoon? I'm struggling with a deadline right now."

"She wants to see you today, Mark. It's important. She has an opening on her schedule in half an hour. Can you come down at one o'clock?"

"Okay, Judy. I'll see you then."

"Mark, this is serious." Judy was whispering now. "Have you looked at the student blog page today? If not, find time to read it before you come down. She's on a rampage about it."

As soon as he hung up the phone, Mark opened a browser on his computer and clicked on the Law School homepage. Navigating to the student blog "Impressions," Mark saw today's headline. "Professor Price's Use of N-Word in Criminal Law Class Indefensible." The story was written by none other than Brandon Gould.

A dreadful, sinking sensation spread over Mark as he scanned the brief story. It was a hatchet job—completely one-sided and taken entirely out of context. The story recounted that Mark had repeated—in full—a racial epithet in class while discussing a Michigan opinion on heat of passion. The story also quoted by name several students in class—both white and African American—who said the use of the term made them feel "uncomfortable" and "numb," and that it temporarily silenced the class discussion. The story did not mention that the judicial opinion itself used the racial epithet, or that Mark invoked it only when challenging a student who did not think the use of such an egregious racial slur was grounds for reducing a charge from murder to manslaughter.

Mark was outraged. How could the Law School allow a student to smear a professor's reputation like that on a school-run website? Where was the oversight from administrators? Why hadn't they demanded that Gould write a more balanced story, or, at a minimum, seek out a quote from Mark? All of these questions were swirling in Mark's head as he re-read the story one final time and focused on the last sentence: "The Law School must take immediate action against Professor Price to remove him from the classroom."

Mark was furious as he rushed down to the Dean's office. He could actually feel his blood pressure rise and his face flush.

He avoided looking directly at any students and colleagues as he passed them in the corridor. On a stairway landing, he saw a small group of students engaged in conversation suddenly stop talking and stare at him as he bounded down the stairwell. Mark doubted that this was paranoia. By mid-day, most of the campus had probably read Gould's accusatory post.

Mark entered the Dean's suite ready for battle. He needed to convince Sydney Taylor to make a strong public statement supporting him. After all, he was a full professor with an unblemished record of twenty years of distinguished service to the institution. He deserved better.

The Dean's secretary ushered Mark in without making him wait in the outer office. He could tell from the conspiratorial look in her eye that she was both concerned and sympathetic. After all, they had been friends for decades. Judy patted Mark invisibly on the back as she guided him past the threshold of the Dean's office and closed the door.

Sydney Taylor stood up as Mark entered the room and gestured toward an upholstered seat in front of her desk. The Dean's countenance did not bear the same level of sympathy or fondness as that of her assistant.

> "Mark, have you seen today's student blog? It describes an incident in your Criminal Law class yesterday."

> "Yes, I saw it. But..." Mark could not finish the end of his sentence before the Dean interrupted.

> "Did you use the 'N-word' in your class?"

> "Yes. But not at first. I..." Once again, Mark was interrupted before he could finish.

> "There is never any excuse for using that word in class, Mark. Period. It conjures up deep and dark corners of bigotry in our society. It is traumatizing to many of our students."

Mark was suddenly placed on the defensive. He had stormed down to the Dean's office prepared to argue that *he* was the victim here. He had underestimated how difficult it would be to take that position in front of an African-American Dean. Mark had simply misjudged his audience. Now he needed to recalibrate, and quickly.

"Sydney, you don't understand...."

"What exactly don't I understand about the use of the 'N-word,' Mark? What do I need a white male to explain to me?"

Mark was stung by Sydney's level of acerbicness. Although not exactly friends, they had always been cordial to one another. At least until now.

"I didn't mean 'understand.' I meant that you need to appreciate the entire context of the classroom discussion. And the subject we were studying. I didn't use the 'N-word' when first discussing the case, even though the court itself used the word in its written opinion. I only brought it up while challenging a student who thought that the use of the epithet was *not* grounds for reducing murder to manslaughter. Actually, I was being supportive of the defendant in that case, and African Americans in general. I needed the shock value of the word to make the point to that particular white student. You should listen to the tape of the class so you can see the entire picture."

"I have listened to the tape of the class, Mark. I did so this morning. I had the IT department send it to me right after I saw the blog post. And there is never any excuse for using the N-word in a classroom environment. It's triggering."

Mark was flabbergasted. This wasn't a trial; it was an execution.

"If you had already listened to the tape, why did you ask me at the beginning of the conversation whether I had used the 'N-word?' You knew that I had."

"I wanted to see what your response would be, and how you would justify it."

"That was a little duplicitous, Sydney. Plus, I thought law school policy required my authorization to release videotapes of my own classes, even to you."

Sydney ignored the accusation and just stared at Mark, who was struggling to avoid his rising anger. But he continued:

"Now that you know the context, you can appreciate that Brandon Gould's blog post is completely unbalanced. For Christ's sake, Sydney, this is an official law school website, open to the public. Why didn't somebody in a position of authority exercise any editorial control? Why don't you take the posting down now?"

"The damage is done, Mark. Half or more of the people at this school have already seen it. So have prospective students and their families. I wouldn't be surprised if it appeared in the local or national media later this week. The school needs to react strongly and decisively. I am taking you out of Criminal Law for the rest of the semester. Cindy Rodriguez will finish your class."

Mark was shocked. Cindy Rodriguez, of all people. She was a new faculty member and an extreme leftist. Her writings were highly critical of both the police and prosecutors. The symbolism of this move would not be lost on the community—"conservative-leaning, white male professor replaced with Latina progressive."

"Sydney, I have tenure. That ensures me academic freedom, both in my scholarship and in the way I teach my classes. There was a sound pedagogical reason why I framed the discussion the way I did in that class. You can't remove me because some student with an axe to grind doesn't like the way I taught the case."

"First year classes are different, Mark. Students don't have a say in who their professors are. They are assigned to sections randomly. I can't force students who feel triggered and insecure in your class to ride it out with you for the rest of the semester."

"Did you actually talk to any of the minority students who were in my Criminal Law class Wednesday?"

"I didn't have to. Several were quoted in Brandon Gould's blog post."

"So you are trusting his accuracy?"

"Those quotes don't need to be accurate to support my decision. Under the circumstances, I think that any objective student might feel uncomfortable learning from you for the rest of the semester."

"I'm going to the Provost on this, Sydney."

"Feel free to call him Mark," Sydney replied. "I spoke with him an hour ago and he supports my decision."

At that, Sydney stood up from behind her massive desk as if to indicate that the conversation was finished. Mark's mouth was agape, still searching for words to explain himself.

"You will continue to get paid for the rest of the semester, Mark. And I can't kick you out of your office. But it might be better if you work from home until this controversy boils over. You will be allowed to teach your electives in the spring."

Mark walked out of the Dean's suite like a convicted prisoner being led to jail. He glanced at Judy behind her desk in the outer office; she seemed to be holding back tears. Judy offered Mark a thin smile of encouragement, but did not attempt to start a conversation.

Mark bounded up the stairs two at a time, determined not to meet the gaze of passing students or colleagues. At one point, one of his friends on the faculty traveling down the stairwell called out to him and tried to take his arm. Mark brushed him aside, saying, "Can't talk now," and raced to the sanctuary of his private office.

Behind the safety of a closed door, Mark slouched at his desk and cradled his head in his hands for the second time that day. He had to carefully consider his options. He had to think clearly. Mark could call the Provost and try to reason with him. He could hire an attorney who specialized in employment discrimination and threaten a lawsuit against the University. He could bring this matter to the Faculty Grievance Committee, although by the time they made any decision the semester would be over.

Replaying the conversation with Sydney in his head, one of her comments suddenly struck Mark squarely in the face. This may make "the local or national media," she had said. "Shit," Mark thought. He hadn't considered Susan, and how this might affect her judicial nomination. He had to call her immediately.

Mark tried Susan on her cell phone, but she didn't pick up. Frustrated, he called Susan's office, but her assistant told him that she had just left for the day to attend to a "personal matter."

At 2:15 pm? Where *was* she?

14

Wednesday started out like most ordinary days for Susan. As an inveterate planner, she really didn't like surprises. Susan's goal for the day was to sit in her office and prepare for a deposition the following week in an employment discrimination case brought against one of her corporate clients. But she could have never expected the twists that awaited in the next twelve hours.

Throughout her 5:30 am spin class, Susan felt preoccupied about her conversation with Katie. They hadn't really talked since Katie had stormed out of the car. Susan was still furious about the conversation, but in her mind she was trying to separate anger in being challenged by her teenager from concern for Katie's safety. She knew both feelings were at work, but she couldn't pinpoint which sentiment was bothering her the most.

As she wiped down her bike at the end of the workout, Susan spotted Tony Garcia at the back of the studio. An idea popped into her head so suddenly that she did not have time to sort through its repercussions. She approached Tony and asked him if he had time to grab a quick cup of coffee at Peet's on Brattle Street before they headed off to work. He happily agreed.

Harvard Square was just starting to wake when they

grabbed two soy lattes at Peet's and sat in a quiet corner of the coffee shop to chat. Tony still wore the look of a schoolboy with a crush—he couldn't take his eyes off Susan. That initial awkwardness was broken somewhat when Susan insisted on paying for coffee, telling Tony that "she needed some advice."

After catching up briefly on their kids and jobs, Susan jumped right into it.

"Tony, I need some advice about cell phones. I spotted a sexually suggestive message on Katie's phone that worries me. I need to find out the identity of the caller. He's in her contact list as 'Stickhandler.' I tried several reverse look up searches on the internet but came up dry. He must have it blocked somehow."

"What exactly are you worried about, Susan?"

"From the context of the message, I think Katie may have sent him a sexually explicit photo. But she must have deleted that text because it did not show up on her history. I am worried she's in over her head. I have no idea how old this person is or where he lives. This is how teenage girls can get abducted or raped."

"Have you talked to her about it?"

"I did, but it went horribly. She accused me of invading her privacy and refused to tell me a thing."

"What cell phone provider do you use?" Tony asked.

"Verizon."

"Give me Katie's number and Stickhandler's number, and I will see what I can do. I have a friend at Verizon who will usually help me 'off the books.' Try not to worry, it's probably just some crush at school."

Susan reached out and touched Tony's hand softly before she got up to say goodbye.

"Thank you so much, Tony. I'm really grateful. I hope you never have to deal with anything like this with Anna as she gets older. Parenting is just a constant source of worry."

Showered and at her desk at Wright & Graham by 8:30 am, Susan began to review hundreds of pages of documents that she needed to read and commit to memory before next week's deposition. She asked her assistant to hold all calls unless they were urgent. The rain and wind coming off the harbor were now slashing against her office window. They created a cozy, almost tranquil feeling in Susan's corner office. Not a bad day to hunker down and consume a file. Susan kicked her shoes off under her desk, brought one leg up underneath her thigh in a runner's stretch, and dug into the task at hand.

Susan had lost track of time when her assistant interrupted her for the first time almost three hours later.

"Susan, Governor Jeffries is on the line."

Susan's assistant could hardly contain her glee as she said this. By now everyone at the firm probably knew that Susan was a finalist for the Supreme Court position. A call from Jeffries could only mean one thing. If it were bad news, he would have had one of his aides convey it. Susan swallowed hard and tried to steady her nerves.

"Governor Jeffries, Susan Price here."

"Susan, I really enjoyed our conversation last week. You're just what I am looking for in an Associate Justice of our high court. Intellect and Grit. I was impressed. I plan to nominate you today to the Governor's Council."

"Governor, I'm speechless."

"Say you accept!" Jeffries teased.

"Of course I accept," Susan responded. "This is the honor of a lifetime."

"Great. I'm going to have Bridget Moore call you later today about scheduling your hearing before the Governor's Council. It is usually a formality, but you never know with these proceedings. Sometimes things come out of left field. Maybe we can get it wrapped up by next week. We plan to announce the appointment to the media this afternoon."

"Thank you, Governor. I hope I can make you proud."

With that, perhaps the biggest phone call of her career was disconnected.

Susan was left to the silence of her own thoughts. She was euphoric—almost giddy—with her accomplishment. But it didn't take long for these feelings to be replaced with a burgeoning "to do" list. She needed to contact close friends and legal colleagues to get them to write or call their Governor's Councilors on her behalf. She would have to talk to her clients about transitioning pending cases to new lawyers in the firm. She would have to figure out who to bring to the confirmation hearing, and even what to wear.

Susan was still processing the call and mentally arranging her task list when her assistant interrupted her for the second time in an hour.

"Detective Tony Garcia is on the phone from the Middlesex County District Attorney's Office. He says it's urgent."

"Okay, I'll take it."

"That did not take long," Susan thought to herself. She was not surprised that Tony would spring into action quickly when she asked him for a favor. He clearly still held a candle for her. Given that attentiveness, Susan felt guilty that she now seemed mildly annoyed by the interruption.

"Hi Tony. What's up?"

"My contact at Verizon was able to look up that number for you. Also to get me a text history between the caller and Katie. I would have waited until I saw you at the gym, but I thought it was important."

"What did you find out?"

"Do you know someone named Heidi Wilson?"

Susan had been expecting a male name. She was completely taken aback and unable to focus when she learned the gender of 'Stickhandler.' Heidi Wilson? Heidi Wilson? Then it hit her like a punch in the stomach. Katie's assistant field hockey coach. Wilson had been a star field hockey player at BB&N six years ago and then went on to play field hockey at Smith College. She had returned to Boston after graduation and secured a job as a teacher's aide and assistant coach at her alma mater.

"Yes, I know her," Susan almost whispered into the phone. "She's Katie's coach at BB&N."

"How old is she?" Tony asked.

"Twenty-three, twenty-four," Susan responded. "Why?"

"They've clearly been having an intimate relationship for a few months," Tony replied. "Depending on her age and Katie's age at the time it started, this may be statutory rape."

Susan's head was spinning. What she thought had been a suggestive photograph now turned into a relationship—maybe even intercourse. And, she had never for a moment expected that her daughter might be attracted to other women.

> "How do you know they have been intimate?" Susan asked, half hoping Tony was wrong.

> "Susan, you can tell from the context of the messages. Katie clearly deleted them from her phone, but Verizon showed them to me. Plus the photo. I'm sorry to tell you this, but Katie is naked and stimulating herself."

Her mind racing, Susan had to decide on next steps. She should know how to deal with this—she had prosecuted hundreds of sex crimes. But this was her own daughter. And the timing could not be worse. A big story was coming out in the Boston Globe tomorrow about her judicial appointment. Why had Susan ever started down this rabbit hole?

> "Tony, I have to think about this. If we don't know that the relationship started when Katie was under sixteen, we don't know that this is a crime. It may be an employment matter that is best handled by BB&N."

> "That's true, Susan, but I'm a bit out on a limb here. Even if this wasn't statutory rape, disseminating and possessing sexually explicit photographs of a seventeen-year-old is a crime in Massachusetts. Under that statute, I'm considered a mandated reporter. Now that I know, I just can't sit on the situation and do nothing."

> "Tony, I appreciate your help. I really do. But this is a lot to process. And at an incredibly difficult time for me—I just found out that Governor Jeffries is nominating me to the State Supreme Court. It is going to be

all over the newspapers tomorrow. My head is swimming."

"Susan, that's fantastic. I'm very happy for you. But it doesn't change the fact that a crime may have been committed against a vulnerable young person in Wilson's care. She could be doing it to other girls on the team. Plus, Verizon gave me the messages without any kind of administrative subpoena from the DA's office. My contact is expecting to receive a subpoena to cover his own ass."

"Tony, can you just put the materials in an envelope and bring them to the gym on Friday? I need a couple of days to think about this."

"Okay Susan. I'll see you Friday. But I can't sit on this too long."

Susan felt numb when she hung up the phone. In a span of just thirty minutes the quality of her day had gone from the highest of highs to the lowest of lows. What kind of mother was she that she did not have any idea what was going on in Katie's life? And that she had not spotted any clues about Katie's sexual preference?

A light switched on in Susan's head. Katie had not played in the Milton game two weeks ago. Was that some sort of punishment or threat from Heidi Wilson? Was she using her authority as a coach to sexually manipulate a teenage girl? Where was the head coach when all this was happening? Where was the *headmaster*? This was not only a crime; it was a colossal failure by the school.

Suddenly, she knew what she had to do. Susan packed her briefcase and told her assistant that she was gone for the rest of the day. On the way to the parking garage, Susan remembered that she had not told Mark about the call from the

Governor. Terrific. "Shitty mother, shitty wife," Susan thought to herself.

Susan dialed Mark's office number as she got into her car. Mark usually turned his cell phone off when he went into the classroom in the morning and often forgot to turn it back on when class was finished. Susan knew that the desk phone would be the best way to reach him at this time of day. But she got voice mail instead. "Mark, it's me. I just got a call from the Governor. They offered me the job!" Susan tried to sound upbeat as she left the message. She was not ready to fill her husband in on the Katie situation. Not until she had played her next card.

The field hockey field at BB&N was one of the school's older athletics fields, situated off Fresh Pond Parkway, part of the Buckingham School's property before the private all-girls high school had merged with Browne & Nichols in 1974. It was 2:30 pm, and the athletic field had not yet come to life with players. Susan knew from experience that she had about thirty minutes before the girls arrived after their last classes. She parked next to the white athletic van blazoned with the BB&N logo and scanned the field. As predicted, she spotted Heidi Wilson across the field in the process of setting up line cones and goals.

Susan walked across the field to confront her daughter's aggressor.

"Coach Wilson. It's Susan Price. Katie's mother. May I have a word with you privately for a moment?"

Heidi Wilson used the palm of her hand to block the late afternoon sun as she stared up at the approaching figure. At the sound of Susan's name, her entire visage changed. Panic spread across her face.

"I'm kind of busy getting ready for practice," she answered lamely. Even Wilson could hear how pathetic her own voice sounded as she struggled to retain composure.

"This is really important," Susan insisted. "Ten minutes. I think it's best if we talk in my car."

As they walked back to the car, Susan assessed Heidi Wilson's appearance. Even wearing warmup pants and a baggy sweatshirt, she was strikingly beautiful. Wilson was about 5'6" tall, thin but not bony, even curvy for an athlete. She had strawberry blonde hair tied back in a ponytail and bright blue eyes that shone back at Susan fiercely in the fading October sunlight. Her skin was gorgeous. It was readily apparent why any seventeen-year-old might be infatuated with her.

Susan had prepared her strategy on the car ride to Cambridge. She would treat Wilson just as she had treated hundreds of defendants over the years when she was a prosecutor. She would 'brace' the defendant by presenting her with all the facts she knew (as well as some she merely supposed) without revealing too much detail about how she knew them. She would lay the possible consequences of the defendant's behavior out before her in stark relief. Then she would present her with a simple choice: cooperate or go to jail.

As they sat in the front seat of Susan's Volvo, the doors were barely closed before Susan began her lecture.

"Heidi, I know that you have been having an inappropriate sexual relationship with my daughter. I came here to talk about what we are going to do about that."

"Mrs. Price, I don't know what you are...." Wilson could not finish her own sentence before Susan raised her hand and interrupted.

"Please, Heidi. The girls and other coaches are going to be here in ten minutes. I don't have time for your pathetic denials. I have your text messages to my daughter. I also have an explicit photograph that she sent to you and you commented upon. They all come back to your cell phone number. And you go by the handle 'Stickhandler.'"

Heidi Wilson went ashen as she listened to the invocation of her nickname. She was still naïve enough to believe that text messages and images went away once you deleted them from your cell phone.

"You misread them. We never had sex. Flirtations maybe, but not sex." Wilson was stammering now, a surefire tell.

"Heidi, please," Susan responded. "Don't insult me. I worked as a prosecutor for decades and handled hundreds of rape cases. The context of some of these text messages is very graphic. As is the photograph that you asked her to send to you."

At the sound of the word "rape," all of the remaining color drained from Wilson's face and her jaw went agape. She felt trapped, and wanted desperately to get out of the car.

"My daughter turned seventeen years old last month. If your relationship with her started before she was sixteen, that's statutory rape, and you are looking at a life felony. Even if the relationship did not start until more recently, you clearly abused a position of authority as a coach at BB&N to lure her into it. You could be fired for sexual misconduct with a student, and no school or university would ever hire you again. And then there's the photograph. You encouraged my daughter to take and send you a suggestive photograph through a computer device. Even if she was seventeen years old at the time, that is a separate crime in Massachusetts—

'dissemination of sexually explicit depiction of a minor.' That's a five year felony."

Crying softly now, Wilson had her hand on the car door and was ready to jump out. As young as she was, she was smart enough to know not to make any damaging admissions against herself or to argue with a seasoned attorney.

Susan placed a hand softly on Wilson's arm, as if to guide her back to the conversation.

> "So here's what's going to happen, Heidi. I will take this to Cambridge Police and the BB&N headmaster if I have to. I'll do whatever it takes to protect my daughter and the other girls on this team. But I would prefer not to put Katie through the humiliating experience of giving a statement to the police. And right now, Katie has no idea I know about your relationship. I would like to keep it that way. So, you are going to end your relationship with my daughter immediately. No personal contact other than on the hockey field, no private meetings, no intimacy. You will break up with her, however it takes. And at the end of the field hockey season next month, you are going to resign from BB&N. You can give them whatever excuse you like. But you are going to leave the school. And if you do both of those things, I will not report this conduct to the authorities."

Wilson stared blankly through the windshield, wiping away tears from the side of her face. She had no response—Susan had played her cards deftly. Wilson quietly reached for the door handle and opened the door.

> "Oh, and Coach Wilson. Do not tell my daughter we had this conversation. I'll know if you do—a mother can tell. If you say anything to Katie, our deal is off."

With that, Wilson climbed out of the car and lumbered back across the athletic field. With her shoulders slumped and her head bowed, Wilson looked inches shorter than she had just ten minutes earlier. Susan was fairly certain that Heidi would comply with the terms of the arrangement. She had too much to lose otherwise.

On the short drive back to their house on Brattle Street, Susan contemplated how and what she was going to tell Mark about this confrontation. She knew Mark would be furious at her for defying his recommendation and engaging an investigator to track the 'Stickhandler' number. He would be even more enraged if he knew that Susan had asked a favor from her old lover, Tony Garcia. Then, there was the more substantive issue. Mark would be upset that Susan had made an important decision about their daughter's wellbeing without consulting him. It was going to be a very difficult conversation.

The likely media attention tomorrow about Susan's judicial appointment should feel like a highlight of her career. Why couldn't she feel more elated about *that* development? The question gnawing at the back of Susan's mind during the short drive home was whether the way she had just taken Heidi Wilson down was in Katie's best interests, or her own.

16

As she pulled into their driveway, Susan noticed that Mark's car was parked on the street in front of their house. She was surprised that he was home already. Maybe he had gotten the message about her judicial appointment and come home to surprise her?

When she entered the kitchen, there were no flowers or champagne anywhere in sight. Susan could tell immediately something was wrong. Mark was dressed in jeans and a t-shirt, staring vacantly out the picture window into the back yard. It was not typical of Mark to be so aimless in the afternoon. Mark was always active—if he came home early, he cleaned or fixed something, or got dinner started. Today there were no signs of purpose or exertion of any kind.

"You're home early, hon," Susan began on a cheery note.

"We have to talk," Mark began. "Something bad happened at work today."

"Me too," Susan replied. "Did you get my voice message?"

"No. I left the office early."

"Where's Archie?" Susan asked. She wanted to be careful not to share difficult news within earshot of the kids.

"He just went upstairs to do his homework."

"Good. Katie should be at field hockey for another hour and a half. Let's go out on the back patio and talk."

Once Susan had changed out of her work clothes, the couple grabbed light jackets and headed out to the back patio. The sun was beginning to set over the tops of the trees, and a light breeze felt cool upon their skin. During the Covid pandemic, the Prices had bought propane heaters for their back patio. Mark lit one of them now as they got situated, each with a glass of red wine in hand.

"The Governor called me today," Susan began. "I got the job."

"That's great news, Susan. I'm really happy for you."

"You don't sound happy."

"My thing at work today might complicate your confirmation."

"What is it?"

"The LDB student blog published a piece saying that I used the 'N-word' in my Criminal Law class. It was totally one-sided and devoid of context. Written by none other than Brandon Gould. But the Dean called me into her office and said she was taking me out of Criminal Law for the rest of the semester. Cindy Rodriguez is going to finish out my section."

"That's outrageous. She can't just do that without any kind of hearing, can she? Doesn't it have to go through the Provost?"

"She said she already ran it by the Provost," Mark explained.

"Have you called him?"

"Not yet. I'm still processing it and assessing my next moves. I just found out a few hours ago."

"You should have made peace with that Brandon Gould. Now he has a vendetta against you."

"I tried, Susan. He never returned my emails."

"Clearly you didn't try hard enough."

"Really, Susan? Instead of being supportive, you're going to point fingers?"

"I'm just saying. Sometimes you have to play along to get along. Is the blog post still up there?

"Yes."

"Well, then you need to respond to it and tell your side of the story. Which is what, by the way? It is not like you ever use the 'N-word.'"

"We were discussing a case. I was actually being sympathetic to an African American defendant accused of homicide. I was trying to make the point to a conservative student that the use of that term might be grounds for mitigating a murder to manslaughter."

"You probably could have made the point without repeating the entire word."

> "Why are you taking the school's side, for Christ's sake? I'm your husband."
>
> "I'm just trying to solve a problem with you, Mark."
>
> "Well, it doesn't sound like it. And sometimes empathy is more important than problem-solving."
>
> "What time did the blog post go up?" Susan asked.
>
> "This morning sometime. Why?"
>
> "I'm just wondering whether the Boston Globe or the local media stations will see it before they publish news of my appointment."

Mark's face contorted in anger. He had to look away. He knew it was natural for Susan to be concerned about her career. But his wife was so self-absorbed that she couldn't pretend—even for one moment—to separate her own interests from his problems.

Susan sensed Mark's hostility and tried to redirect the conversation ever so slightly.

> "The reporters are lazy. They will just take the Governor's press release and run with it, plus a little filler from my firm biography and a few quotes from friends. I doubt that they had time this afternoon to look into your background before their 4:00 pm deadlines. So we have a day to get in front of this. Have any of the legal education blogs got hold of the story?"
>
> "Not that I know of," Mark almost whispered.
>
> "Good. So this is what you have to do. Email the provost now and tell him that you would like to speak to him tonight or first thing in the morning. Give him your cell phone number. See if you can convince him

to reverse the Dean's decision before it gets communicated to the students. Then, work on a letter to the community explaining what happened in class. Don't apologize exactly, but recognize the complexity of the issue and say that you regret how the conversation unraveled. Also, note that the author of the blog post is not a class member and has no direct knowledge of the classroom dynamic. Play up everything you have done for minority students at the school throughout your career."

Mark felt completely demoralized. He knew Susan was right. She was a savvy public relations strategist—most ambitious people are. But somehow it seemed to Mark that Susan was not fully on his side. And being given a "to do" list in this situation felt patronizing.

"I'll email the Provost right now," Mark said, picking up his phone. "I feel like my professional reputation is being assassinated. How does somebody come back from that?"

"That's why you have to take the offensive. In your letter, say that it is unfair to the students in your Criminal Law class to have the course finished and the exams evaluated by another instructor. Say that the administration did not conduct any type of investigation or talk to your students directly to see how they felt. Say that none of your students even lodged a complaint to the administration!"

"Okay Susan. I'll write the letter first thing in the morning. But honestly, I feel like you are more worried about the effect of this on your judicial appointment than my career."

"I'm worried about *both*, Mark. We have one day to get in front of this before the media picks it up. You need to tell your side of the story. If the ACLU is going to oppose me at my confirmation hearing, at least I want them to know the full context of what happened."

"Susan, my academic career may be going down the shitter. You have a great job at the law firm, whether or not you're confirmed to a seat on the Court. This isn't about you. It's about me."

"Mark, we're a team. What affects you affects me. And our family. I'm just trying to look at the big picture."

Mark sipped his wine and stared at his cell phone as if by positive energy he could will the Provost to respond to his email. It was getting dark. They should think about ordering something for dinner. Katie would be voracious when she got home. Then something occurred to him.

"You said you had a shitty day at work, too. What happened?"

Susan braced herself. She had driven home prepared to tell her husband all about Katie and Coach Wilson. Susan owed him that. But given what a bad day Mark had at school, Susan was now unsure that he could handle the conversation.

"I got to the bottom of Katie's 'sexting,'" Susan began gingerly. "I know who 'Stickhandler' is."

"How did you figure it out?"

"An investigator worked through his friend at Verizon."

"Susan, I specifically asked you not to hire an investigator. What are we, mother Russia?"

"You asked me not to *hire* an investigator, Mark. I didn't hire anyone. Somebody did me a favor."

"That's splitting hairs and you know it. Who did you the favor?" Mark asked.

"What does it matter, Mark? You know our firm has several private investigators on staff." Susan was skirting the truth now—not outright lying, but clearly leaving Mark with a false impression.

"That's setting a horrible example. First nosing around her phone, now cutting corners on the phone company. Katie may never forgive you."

"Mark, you're missing the most important point. Our daughter's safety is at stake. Don't you want to know who 'Stickhandler' is?"

"Okay, who is it?" Mark asked, exhaustion creeping into his voice.

"Her assistant field hockey coach. Heidi Wilson."

Mark was dumbfounded. He had assumed 'Stickhandler' was a boy. Thinking of Katie with another woman—a more mature woman at that—was momentarily paralyzing.

"Oh my God. Do you think they had sex?"

"My investigator tells me that the nature of the photograph and some texts that Katie deleted from her phone suggest that they were likely in a relationship. An intimate relationship."

"That's abuse of a minor," Mark insisted. "It explains so much. Katie's anxiety and her sour moods. Her fallout with her friends. The coach not playing her during the Milton game. Wilson was probably extorting her for sex. We have to tell the school and go to the police."

"Mark, it's all taken care of. Katie never has to know that we know."

"What are you talking about? She's our daughter. We have to get her to open up about it. She's probably been traumatized."

"I confronted Heidi Wilson at the BB&N field this afternoon. I told her she was going to break up with Katie and resign from the school at the end of the season, or we would go to the police."

Mark could not believe his ears. Why would Susan take this step without discussing it with him? His voice was rising now:

"What the hell, Susan? You did that without consulting me? Just a second ago you said we were a 'team'!"

"This is the most sensible solution, Mark. It gets Wilson away from our daughter and separated from the school. And, we don't have to further traumatize Katie by submitting her to an interview with the police."

"Katie might have been the victim of a crime. For all we know, Wilson is doing this with other girls on the team—maybe some girls even younger than Katie. We can't just brush it under the rug."

"I had to make a decision quickly, Mark. And I think this was the best decision for our family."

Mark's eyes narrowed and his jaw slackened. Suddenly it occurred to him why timing was so critical for Susan. The media was on the brink of announcing her judicial appointment. The upcoming weeks would bring scrutiny of Susan during her confirmation hearing in front of the Governor's Council.

"You didn't do this because it was best for Katie. You did this because it was best for you. You didn't want any family drama to get in the way of your judicial appointment. That is why you confronted Wilson today. That is why you didn't take the time to consult with me."

"Please, Mark..."

"Don't spin this as anything other than what it is, Susan. Your career. The shitshow going on in Katie's life doesn't fit squarely into your tapestry—a perfect family living an idyllic life. That's why you wanted to put a lid on the situation so quickly."

"That's not fair, Mark. I've dealt with hundreds of sexual assault cases in my career. I know that prosecution is not always in the victim's best interest."

"Maybe so, Susan. But you didn't sit down with Katie to see what happened or how she feels about it. You haven't considered Katie's interests at all—or the inner turmoil she is probably going through."

"Mark, it's done. There's no sense arguing about it. We'll find a way to encourage Katie to open up to us about her sexuality another day."

"Just what you wanted, Susan. Check the box—problem solved. The package is all tied up in a neat little bow. Except, that's not how life works."

"You may disagree with how I handled this, Mark. But don't you dare question my devotion to Katie."

"Susan, we've all become bit players in your life story. You call the shots, and you do what's best for you. Always. I'm outa here."

Mark put down his drink and picked up his jacket.

"Where are you going?" Susan asked.

"For a walk. I've got a lot to process. Not that you give a shit about how I feel."

Mark walked around the house and out to the street without saying goodbye to Archie or waiting for Katie to get home from practice. He needed some space. He needed time to think.

The walk down Brattle Street to Harvard Square felt liberating. Mark knew he could not leave his troubles behind. But getting out of the house and away from Susan allowed him to check his anger, even if momentarily.

At the intersection of Brattle Street and JFK Avenue, gravity and habit pulled Mark left toward Massachusetts Ave. Mark passed familiar haunts like the Hong Kong and Mr. Bartley's Burger Cottage that brought back memories of his days as a law student. At twenty-five years of age, he had felt like he had the world by the tail. Now his career, his relationship with Susan, and his family life had taken a dark turn.

Suddenly Mark knew where he was headed, and he walked further down Massachusetts Avenue toward the 'Plough 'n Stars.' This Irish bar had been his favorite local watering hole in law school, and for several years thereafter. A haunt of politicians, writers and visiting musicians, the small corner establishment had a reputation and history that greatly overshadowed its diminutive size and musty odor. Mark knew that the 'Plough 'n Stars' dark interior and its long walnut bar would provide him with just the privacy he needed to have a pint and think things out.

The bar was busy, but not yet so crowded that Mark couldn't find a seat. There would be some musicians playing a session in an hour or so, but the live music had not yet started. A small group of twenty-somethings were playing darts in the corner. Even though Mark didn't know a soul in the place, it felt intimate and safe.

Mark realized he was famished—having skipped lunch and barely eaten any breakfast. He hunkered down in front of a chiseled bartender named Seamus and ordered a pint of Guinness and a burger. The first sip of the draft calmed Mark, the taste buds tricking his brain into remembering happier times.

Mark opened his phone to see if the Provost had responded to his email. He had. But it was short and to the point. "I will be in the office at 8:00 am tomorrow if you want to call me on my direct line—(617) 552-4006." Mark was disappointed. He knew that if the subject were truly open to negotiation, the Provost would probably have called him at home tonight—before the Dean had a chance to announce her decision to the student body. The Provost was throwing him a bone by giving him an audience before Sydney's hammer came crashing down.

A text from Susan popped up on Mark's phone.

"Where are you?"

"Having a beer," Mark responded. He did not feel like telling Susan his location.

"You shouldn't have left while you were angry. Come home," Susan pleaded.

"I can't be in the same room with you right now," Mark responded. "Don't wait up."

Mark turned his phone over on the bar and started to mentally compose the letter he would write to his Criminal Law class tomorrow morning. Susan was correct about one thing—Mark had to take affirmative steps to salvage his reputation. He would have to explain the heat of passion doctrine and why the inflammatory nature of the word was so important to the context of the case he was teaching. He would have to explain that he uttered the word only in response to a student who thought that it was *not* sufficiently inflammatory to warrant mercy toward the defendant. And, he would have to put Brandon Gould in his place—suggesting without revealing any confidential information that the blog host had an axe to grind against him. After emailing the letter to every student in the class, Mark would post it on the 'Impressions' webpage and send it to any media outlets that later picked up the story.

Playing these steps out in his mind was not calming for Mark. In fact, it had the opposite effect. It made him feel more anxious and depressed. When he came back to school in January, would any students sign up for his classes? Would he continue to receive invitations to conferences? Would publishers boycott his scholarship?

Mark hadn't felt this annoyed with Susan in years. He had always been attracted to her energy, her focus and her ability to tackle tough problems. But she had really steamrolled over other people this time. And Mark knew that it was personal ambition that had gotten the better of her.

Sipping his third pint of Guinness, he turned over his phone and succumbed to an impulse. He texted Julia.

"I miss you."

"Really, Mark? WTF?"

"I'm sorry about this morning."

"You should be," Julia replied.

Less than two minutes passed before Julia sent another text.

> "Come over. Maybe all will be forgiven. " Julia ended that text with a happy face and a heart emoji.
>
> "I can't," Mark responded. "Way too complicated. You'll understand when you read the newspapers tomorrow."
>
> "Why are you texting me then?" Julia responded.
>
> "I just need a shoulder," Mark answered.
>
> "Whatever. GN."

Mark regretted those texts as soon as he had sent them. Like a drowning man, he was flailing—his arms searching wildly for something, anything, to keep him afloat.

17

When Mark got home that evening the house was quiet. A light was still on in Katie's bedroom, so Mark knocked softly and entered. She was in her bed reading a history book, a yellow highlighter suspended in her hand and headphones cradled in her ears. Mark walked over softly and kissed her on the cheek.

"How was your day, kiddo?"

"Okay. Killer practice. I'm really tired. But I have an AP history quiz tomorrow."

"Did you talk to Mom after dinner?"

"Yea, she told us the big news. I'm happy for her. Huge changes coming up for the family, though. Are you on board with this whole 'judge' thing?"

"Your mother will be a terrific judge. I'm really proud of her. You know, this is a prominent appointment. There will probably be some stories in the media."

"That's fine. Mom's a master manipulator. They'll say nice things about her."

"Be nice Katie. That's not what I meant. I was just saying our family is going to be in the spotlight. Are you okay with that?"

"I'll be fine, Dad. Besides, Mom could not possibly work longer hours as a judge than she does as a lawyer. Maybe it will humanize her a little bit."

"Katie, you know that you can always talk to me about anything. You know that, don't you?" Mark whispered.

"Yes, Dad," Katie said, rolling her eyes. "But I really have to study now. Goodnight."

Mark was way too wound up to go straight to sleep. Back downstairs, he grabbed his laptop and began composing a letter to his Criminal Law class at the kitchen table.

Mark worked on the letter for over two hours. It had to be perfect. Mark understood that his audience was not just seventy-five law students, but also the university community, the professoriate at other law schools, and likely the local media.

After recounting the exact events that transpired in class, the context of the murder case they were discussing, the second-hand nature of Gould's complaint, and the hastiness of the Dean's decision, Mark concluded his letter with the following paragraphs:

> "I have spent two decades of my life training empathic and compassionate lawyers. I have been recognized with countless awards from my students for doing so. It has always been my goal to create a classroom environment where all students can flourish, including those students who traditionally have been underrepresented in the legal community. However, it is also my duty to accurately present and discuss the realities

of the world around us, including the facts as presented in the legal cases we are studying."

"Eleanor Holmes Norton, an acclaimed civil rights lawyer before she became a Congresswomen, once used in a legal brief the very same word that I used in class on Monday. She was using the word to describe racism and discrimination, just as I was using the word to describe racism and discrimination. What transpired in my classroom was no different, and the administration should not treat it differently because I am white and she is black, or because this is a classroom and that was a courtroom. Facts are facts, and what we need to do at this law school is to train lawyers to apply law to facts."

"It does not do anybody any good to cover up facts, no matter how unsettling or ugly those facts may be. A broader issue is at stake here—if facts of a case must be alluded to only in code, what is to prevent other students from curtailing classroom speech about horrific events they find triggering? Cross burning may be offensive to Catholics, Holocaust discussions may be triggering for Jews. No one is served when we re-write history to avoid the ugliness of our past. Preparing tough lawyers who are both passionate and brave requires that we confront rather than shrink from our society's history, even its racist history."

Mark proofread the letter closely—twice—and then pressed 'send,' shooting it by email to his Criminal Law students. Mark also uploaded the essay to the Law School's online Impressions forum.

It was a cathartic essay to write. Deep down, Mark was not sure whether he was hoping to salvage his academic career or his wife's judicial appointment. Even more disturbing, he was not sure that his wife deserved any help under the circumstances.

18

Tony Garcia was sitting at his cubicle in the District Attorney's office scanning the local police blotters from the night before. There had been a beating of a middle-aged man in Danehy Park in North Cambridge. A jogger found the victim's dead body on a run after work at about 7:00 pm. No signs of struggle or robbery—the victim's watch, wallet and cell phone were still on his person. The victim was a 50-year-old single man apparently walking through the park on his way to his rental apartment in North Cambridge after getting off the subway in Porter Square. Computer programmer. Initial examination suggested that the victim died of multiple blunt force trauma to the head. No weapon was recovered.

Tony wanted this case. He *needed* this case. Feeling like his career as a homicide detective had plateaued, Tony sought something substantial to re-excite his passion for police work. Plus, having a high-profile case on his assignment list would allow him to reduce the brass's pressure on him to get back into uniform.

Suddenly, it occurred to Tony that the State Police were not mentioned anywhere on the Cambridge Police blotter for the Danehy Park murder. Normally, when there was a potential homicide scene, the locals would call the District Attorney's CPAC unit immediately to send a detective. Why didn't Tony

get a text last night to respond to the crime scene?
Tony bolted into Emily's office to figure out what was up.

"Hey Captain. Has there been an assignment on the Danehy Park murder yet?"

"Yea, I assigned it to Ray Jones."

"Ray Jones? He's practically brand new. This looks like it may be a tough case."

"Tony, we all started somewhere. Ray needs to cut his teeth just like you did. Besides, I was hoping you would mentor him if he needs any help."

Emily had laid a gut punch. "Mentor" was police speak for "back seat." If Cronin had really valued Tony's expertise, she would have assigned him as lead detective, and asked Ray Jones to assist him on the case.

Garcia's fragile relationship with Captain Emily Cronin seemed to have reached an inflection point. He harbored resentment about Cronin getting promoted over him. Cronin felt threatened that Tony had more violent crime experience than her, and probably commanded more respect from their junior colleagues. She undoubtedly wished that Tony would leave the DA's office and accept the offer in Athol—solving both of their problems.

"Shit," Tony muttered to himself as he left Cronin's office.

19

Katie couldn't stand it. Heidi hadn't returned any of her texts in over a week. She avoided her at school and on the hockey field. And Katie knew she wasn't imagining it. No casual brushing of the hands during team huddles, no soft touch by Heidi on the small of Katie's back, no stolen glances.

Something was definitely up. It was torturing Katie inside. Heidi Wilson had been Katie's first sexual partner. They had explored each other's bodies in ways that Katie had never imagined could bring her such joy. And now, Katie was left confused and doubtful—not only about her own sexual orientation, but also about Heidi's intentions.

Katie found time to confront her coach after the Noble & Greenough game. Katie was helping Wilson load some equipment into the back of her car while the other girls were boarding the bus. Katie has been rehearsing her words for days. She only hoped she could get them out without breaking down.

"Why aren't you returning my texts?" Katie whispered.

"Sorry, I've been really busy."

"You weren't too busy last month."

"Look, Katie, you and me is a bad idea. You're still in high school. And I could lose my job."

"But I thought we...."

"There is no 'we,' Katie," Wilson hissed. "It was just a little fun. I regret it ever happened."

Katie's eyes were misting up. She couldn't let the other girls see her like this. The team bus was just a few hundred feet away.

"I thought you had feelings for me."

"Don't be a child, Katie. Oh, and please delete any text messages between us," the Coach ordered. "It's not a good idea to leave your phone laying around."

20

Friday was sunny and unseasonably warm in Boston for a late October day. Archie had been crippled socially when his parents confiscated his cell phone last week. But he knew he could find his friends at Holyoke Plaza in Harvard Square as soon as BB&N was dismissed for the day. Walking away from his locker toward the front doors of school while all the jocks walked to the field house in the opposite direction, Archie felt a little bit like a salmon swimming upstream. He tried to avert his eyes from their judgmental stares.

Bursting out the front door and jumping on his skateboard felt like a rush of freedom for Archie after what had been a soul-crushing week of school. He hadn't seen his friends, Max and Charlie, for several days. He knew he could count on them to be in the square on a beautiful Friday afternoon.

Archie bought a Gatorade at the nearby CVS and started glancing around for his friends as soon as he entered the plaza. He spotted the usual chess players and a broad assortment of undergraduates milling about and sipping coffee. And then Archie felt some eyes penetrating him like a laser from across the plaza. Looking up, he saw Mullet staring him down. Their eyes locked. Mullet knew Archie had spotted him—turning around and pretending otherwise would just be seen as an admission of guilt. Archie had no choice but to confront his accuser.

"Hey, Mullet," Archie whispered warily as the two approached one another. "Max told me that you got arrested leaving the cemetery. I was sorry to hear about that."

"What a bunch of bullshit, Price. You set me up."

"Mullet, I've never spoken to the police about us. I was just as surprised as you were. Honest."

"There is no 'us,' Price. My biggest mistake was ever selling to you and your dipshit friends."

"At least they let you out," Archie responded lamely. He regretted those words as soon as they left his lips.

"Cost my family two grand to a bail bondsman. That's a lot of money for us. My father is out of work. We aren't rich like you. Now my public defender is trying to get me to plead guilty for holding the junk they caught me with. Says he can get me off on 'mere possession.' But somehow you biked away from that cemetery totally in the clear. Wonder why that was?"

Mullet's eyes were red and swollen. Archie couldn't tell if he was high or on the verge of crying. Archie suddenly felt incredibly sad for him.

"I swear to God, Mullet, I had nothing to do with it."

"Funny, I was reading the Boston Globe over there," Mullet said, pointing to a pile of already-perused newspapers on a table in the corner of the plaza. "I saw your Mom just got awarded some fancy judge title or something. Says she used to be a DA. I'm sure that had nothing to do with you turning me in to the cops."

Before Archie could respond, Mullet brushed past him, butting shoulders as if to impart a blow.

"You and your perfect family better watch their backs," Mullet sneered as he barreled away.

Watching Mullet leave, Archie stood dumbstruck with his mouth draped open. Within seconds, Charlie and Max appeared on either side of him.

"Dude, that looked really awkward," Max said. "We didn't know whether to interrupt or call for help."

"God, he's pissed," Archie whispered. "But I didn't do anything."

"Let's get out of here in case he comes back," Charlie replied. "We can go Xbox at my house."

21

The Massachusetts Governor's Council—eight men and women elected from across the state to confirm judicial nominations and review the Governor's pardon and commutation decisions—met every Wednesday afternoon while the legislature was in session. Under the Massachusetts Constitution, the Lieutenant Governor presided over Council Meetings and voted in cases of a tie.

Their chamber sat on the third floor of the Massachusetts State House on Beacon Hill, right outside the Governor's suite of offices. Room 360 was essentially an oversized conference room decorated in antiques, with ornate wainscotting framing the walls and plush red velvet curtains framing the oversized windows. In the corner of the room was the stately "Royal Governor's Chair," embedded with gold leaf and meticulously refurbished to approximate the same chair that the King's Governor sat in to preside over the Colonial Council 350 years earlier, when the room served as the nerve center for the British Empire in America.

On Wednesday, October 27th, Susan and Mark were seated in chairs lining the hallway outside the Governor's Council chamber, waiting patiently for Susan's nomination to be called. Bridget Moore had joined them from the Governor's Legal Counsel's Office to ease their anxiety and answer any questions they had about the process. But mostly she was there to make small talk and help pass the time.

Both Mark and Susan were dressed in impeccable business attire. While they undoubtedly made a striking couple, Mark's appearance that day was just for show. Given what was going on with him at the Law School and the emotional distance between Susan and Mark over the past several weeks, Susan did not ask her husband to make any formal statement on her behalf. Bridget Moore had advised Susan that the Council just liked to get a "visual picture" of a candidate's family support.

Seated next to them on the hallway chairs were Katie and Archie. They looked like they were awaiting a firing squad. Indeed, negotiating their attendance today had been very difficult. Katie had been distant and diffident around the house for weeks, likely still seething with her mother about the phone incident, even though Susan was confident that Katie did not fully appreciate the extent of Susan's involvement. Archie was, well, Archie. He was a disheveled, distracted and sullen fourteen-year-old boy who didn't see much sense in anything. Both children put up opposition to coming to their mother's hearing—"a Chemistry quiz," "missing Field Hockey practice," etc. etc., until Mark snapped at the dinner table and said, "Enough! You don't have to speak; you just have to sit there and smile. Given every God damn thing your mother has done for you over the past seventeen years, that is not a lot to ask!" That uncharacteristic outburst had ended the conversation, but only partially to Susan's satisfaction.

Normally, candidates for judicial office invite two or three legal colleagues to make formal statements on their behalf and answer any questions the Councilors might have. Susan had invited her former District Attorney, now Attorney General David Thompson, to make a presentation supporting Susan's nomination. Although he was of a different political party than the current Governor, his stature and democratic bona-fides would appeal to certain left-of-center members of the Governor's Council. Susan had also invited the head of the litigation department at her law firm—Marcia Blackwell—a long-time friend and colleague who could address more directly Susan's recent cases and clients.

Susan's nomination was called at 10:30 am, and the group entered the Chamber. Mark, Katie and Archie sat in side chairs arranged at the back wall for spectators. Susan, Attorney General Thompson, and Marcia Blackwell took seats at the formal conference table. The Lieutenant Governor called the meeting to order with a smile and pleasant thanks to everyone for attending the day's events.

Susan spoke first. She thanked the Governor for his confidence in her in making the nomination, and assured the panel that service on the State Supreme Court would be both an honor and a privilege. She then briefly went through her background—education, legal training, and career highlights. Susan spoke briefly about her judicial philosophy; without revealing any political leanings or preconceptions on specific legal issues, she said she would decide each case based on the law and the facts, with deference to the legislature if she was interpreting or applying a statute.

Attorney General Thompson was impressive, and commanded the rapt attention of the eight Council members when he spoke. He commented on what a terrific prosecutor and public servant Susan was when she served under him, how skilled a courtroom advocate she had become, and the incredible work she did with victims and their families in several high-profile murder and rape prosecutions. Thompson opined that Susan had a keen intellect and a capacious appetite for work, and soon became a leader in the office and a trusted confidant and advisor to him.

Marcia Blackwell had rehearsed her comments with Susan before the hearing. Rather than going through all the cases Susan had handled and clients Susan had served, Blackwell focused on how well Susan had transitioned into civil practice after leaving government work, and how much service Susan had given to the Massachusetts legal community through her bar association activities, pro-bono cases and numerous volunteer commitments. This seemed to help round out Susan's biography and make her appear to be someone devoted to the profession rather than to just making money.

After about thirty minutes of prepared statements, it was the Councilors' turn to ask questions. The first questioners prefaced their remarks with pleasantries about Susan's impressive credentials and experience. They then peppered her with "soft ball" questions that Susan had anticipated and prepared for. "Why do you want to become a judge?" "What was the most significant trial of your career?" "Do you think it will be difficult for you to serve as a neutral arbitrator after you have been a zealous advocate for over two decades?" Susan answered each of these questions with aplomb, somehow managing to convey confidence and humility simultaneously.

Susan's first tough question came from Councilor Marilyn Tucci, a bombastic woman in her mid-seventies who was one of the longest serving members of the Council. Tucci resided in Watertown and represented a largely working class district of Massachusetts. She was known for inviting controversy by taking far-right populist positions. Tucci barked at Susan, barely in the form of a question, "I see from your list of trials that you represented Jose Vasquez, an undocumented immigrant accused of murdering a Watertown police officer after an armed robbery. Why should this Council put someone on the Court who defended a cop-killer?" Susan was not entirely prepared for this question or its argumentative tone, but she answered it with skill. She reminded the Council that all persons accused of felonies were guaranteed the right to counsel under the Sixth Amendment, and that she took the case because she volunteered on the bar advocate list and was appointed by the court.

"Even those accused of the most heinous crimes deserve a fair trial," Susan explained. Yet Tucci was not mollified.

"Aren't you also on the Board of Directors of the Massachusetts ACLU? Isn't that the same organization trying to curtail the ability of police to use facial recognition technology to protect public safety?"

The next question came from the far left, specifically an African American Councilor named Louis Charles, a criminal defense attorney from Brockton who specialized mostly in drunk driving cases and made a lot of money representing people in the immigrant Haitian community. Charles clearly had prepared for the hearing and researched Susan's background, or at least asked a staffer to do so. "I see that your husband is on leave from his Law School because of a racial incident in one of his classes. Could you please explain that to us?"

Susan took a deep breath. She had suspected this question was coming and prepared for it. First, she tried to clarify several erroneous assumptions implicit in Councilor Charles' question. "Mark is not on leave. He is still a full time tenured faculty member at the law school. He was asked to step back from his Criminal Law class this semester due to an incident not entirely of his own making. The class was discussing a case involving the heat of passion doctrine and whether insulting words could be sufficiently provoking to reduce a murder to manslaughter. The facts of the case involved a bigoted neighbor who called the defendant the 'N-word' after the neighbor shot the defendant's dog. One white member of the class thought that this racial insult was not sufficiently provoking to justify the legal mitigation. Mark pressed the student to put himself in the defendant's shoes, and in doing so used the actual 'N-word' to illustrate the powerful effect of the insult. Nobody in the class—including the students of color—complained about the way the class was conducted. The only person who complained was a white male—a former student of Mark's not in the class—who entertained a grudge against my husband for reasons I am not at liberty to discuss under

Federal Educational Privacy laws."

Susan was awaiting a follow-up from Councilor Charles when she was saved by the bell. The Lieutenant Governor looked at the clock, noted that it was 11:30 am, and decided to conclude the hearing. "Ms. Price, we thank you for your presence today, your willingness to serve the Commonwealth, and your excellent presentation to the Council. Our normal course is to vote on nominations on the Wednesday following the candidate's hearing. So we should have more news for you next week." With that she banged the gavel and called the next matter on the agenda.

When the Price family left the front door of the state house, they were greeted by picketers holding signs that read "Blue Lives Matter" and "Support the Police." Some heckled Susan with chants of "No friends of cop killers!" and "Citizens first!" Clearly, Councilor Tucci had planned her questioning of Susan and alerted 'law and order' groups to make their positions known in front of the media. Susan was taken aback that Tucci had used the confirmation hearing to grandstand in such a manner.

The Prices' walk down the hill from the State House to the Boston Common parking garage was brisk and silent. Nobody wanted to talk about the hearing or how it had concluded. They dodged skateboarders in the park and wove between young lovers holding hands and walking dogs. All four of them were quiet and detached, soaking in the events of the day as they strode several paces apart from one another.

Susan didn't know how she would explain the hearing to her children. The Governor's aid, Bridget Moore, had whispered to Susan as she left the chamber, "I'll call you later," and given her a warm squeeze of the arm. Susan did not know whether to interpret that gesture as reassuring or patronizing.

Once they were in the car and headed back to Cambridge, Archie was the first to break the silence.

"Why did the witchy lady with the red hair hate you so much?" he inquired.

"She didn't hate me. She was just doing her job. Whenever you represent criminal defendants there will be some unpopular cases," Susan explained.

"But you spent so many years working as a prosecutor. Was she saying you're soft on crime?" Archie asked.

"Archie, grow up. That was political theater," Katie intoned. "It's just lame people posturing for their constituents."

A small smile spread across Mark's lips. Katie was getting more and more like him every day: smart, savvy, and just a little too cynical. He didn't know whether to be proud or concerned.

"What was really gross, though, was that black Councilor trying to throw Dad under the bus," Katie continued. "What has that got to do with Mom's application? And even if it matters somehow, what's the point? Mom is somehow both too liberal and too conservative? She fights for the underprivileged, but she is married to a bigot? The whole thing was a farce."

Susan felt a powerful urge to try to put the kids at ease. It was tough for any parent to watch their children worry. Even more troublesome, Mark's situation at work had now become a raw subject at home.

"Most of the hearing went really well," Susan interjected. "Remember, those were only two votes out of eight. Let's all stay positive."

22

When they pulled into the driveway, the kids bounded out of the car and went straight to their rooms, ostensibly to start their homework. Mark and Susan knew that Katie would spend at least the next hour on her cell phone catching up with her friends. But they didn't care. The family needed a little space from each other right now. Susan grabbed her briefcase and headed to the desk in the kitchen to catch up on emails.

Mark stayed in the driveway and chatted briefly with their mailman, Sam, who was just getting into his truck after canvassing the neighborhood. Small neighborly interactions like this provided Mark with a sense of normalcy during a difficult time. He had no classes to teach, no papers to grade, and no mental focus to concentrate on research. Mark felt untethered, and simple routines like this had helped ground him over the past couple of weeks.

After waving goodbye to Sam, Mark emptied the contents of the Price's mailbox at the end of the drive. Mark remembered vividly when Susan had purchased this faux antique at Restoration Hardware. She thought it provided a "nice accent" and some "country charm" to the front of their small driveway. Mark had cursed those words under his breath one steamy summer day when he had borrowed a neighbor's pole digger and mixed concrete to secure the beamed pedestal.

Mark was sorting through the mail in his hands as he entered the kitchen. Standard fare—utility bills, charitable solicitations, alumni mailings. Then his eye caught an envelope without a stamp, a postmark, or even a return address. It was just a simple white envelope with letters on the front spelling out "The Prices." The two words were not handwritten or typed—they were cutouts of random letters from a newspaper or magazine. The envelope had not even been sealed—its flap was loose and unfastened.

Mark's stomach sank as he leaned against the dining room table and deposited the mail. After two shitty weeks, what menacing news could this envelope possibly bear? He tried to calm himself down by thinking maybe it was a themed invitation to a Halloween party—one of their neighbors was quite the practical joker. His hopes were quickly dashed when he pulled the correspondence out of the envelope.

You Better Watch out for that Precious Family of Yours

The warning contained the same form of lettering as the front of the envelope—cutouts of letters carefully fastened with glue to an otherwise clean $8\frac{1}{2}$ by 11 piece of white paper.

Mark quickly tucked the letter and its envelope into his vest pocket and determined to wait until later that evening to show it to Susan. The conversations and recriminations about who could possibly be telegraphing this warning to the Price family were too intense to expose the children to right now. It might scare them. He and Susan would have to hash out a plan, together.

Mark tried to occupy himself in the family room by reading the day's newspapers on his tablet. Yet his mind kept coming back to the ominous letter. "Who could possibly be threatening them like this? And why?" His first thought focused on

Julia Hoffman. She hadn't taken their breakup well, and certainly was headstrong. But Julia was too smart and too independent to do something that craven for attention. Sure, she was high strung and impulsive, but he didn't think she was crazy.

Mark's next thought focused on Katie's field hockey coach. Possibly Heidi Wilson was still reeling from Susan's threats of exposure and sent the letter as a way to act out her frustrations. Like Julia, Coach Wilson would have access to the family's address through school records. But Mark didn't understand what the coach could hope to accomplish by sending this letter. It wouldn't save her job. It wouldn't alleviate the difficult predicament Susan had placed her in.

Then he thought about Brandon Gould. The law student certainly had a vendetta against Mark. But Gould had already exacted his revenge by writing that essay on the school website. Mark's reputation had taken a pounding, and he had been removed from his Criminal Law class. What more did Gould hope to accomplish? No, Gould was a poser and a narcissist, but he was not so stupid as to jeopardize his admission to the bar by threatening a professor's family.

Mark was just finishing scanning an article in the New York times when Susan entered the family room and sat down on the sofa next to him.

"Bridget Moore just called me," Susan began. "It's not great news."

"What did the Council do?" Mark asked, somewhat taken aback.

"Well, they didn't '*do*' anything. They decided that they were concerned enough about certain issues that they are going to continue taking further testimony next Wednesday. They won't vote until two weeks from now."

"Is Governor Jeffries going to stick with your nomination?"

"Bridget assured me that he was. At least she didn't seem to be hinting that I withdraw. But Bridget had a couple of suggestions on new witnesses I could call next week."

"Like who?" Mark asked.

"Well, Bridget thought that maybe I could call a junior associate at the firm who has worked extensively with me. Somebody who could describe me as a mentor and a role model. But also somebody who was one of your former students and could describe you as a teacher and rebut today's accusation of racism."

Mark was frustrated that a momentary classroom incident now seemed to be affecting his family so profoundly. Yet he also understood that he needed to help Susan confine the damage.

"I think that's a great idea," Mark replied. "White & Graham is full of young lawyers from my school. If you want to run by me a list of associates who you have worked with, I'd be glad to recommend one or two who would say nice things about me."

"Great. But that's not all," Susan continued. "Bridget thinks I should call a police officer who worked closely with me when I was a prosecutor, to rebut the notion that the Vasquez case proves me to be anti-police."

"Also a good suggestion," Mark said.

"I was thinking of Tony Garcia."

The name hit Mark like a slap on the face. It had been almost twenty years since Mark and Susan were married; still, Mark would never forget that during a brief period before their engagement, Susan and Tony had had an affair. Although Tony was once a friend and colleague to both of them, Mark knew that Tony had been smitten with Susan since the day they had all first met. It had always made Mark feel insecure.

> "You've worked with dozens of great cops over your career, Susan. Why Tony Garcia?"
>
> "Well, he's a homicide investigator and well regarded in the State Police. Plus, he goes to my gym. It would be very easy to ask him. I see him at spin class pretty frequently."
>
> "You've been seeing Tony Garcia?"
>
> "I haven't been *seeing* him, Mark. He belongs to my gym."

Susan felt bad omitting reference to her coffee with Tony, or to his help on Katie's cell phone. Those details would only confuse the matter.
Mark lowered his voice now.

> "Do you worry the press might have a way of finding out about your prior relationship with Tony, detracting from his objectivity?"
>
> "I doubt it Mark. We were very discreet around the office. And, the fling only lasted a few months. I told you about it when we got back together only because I wanted to be completely honest with you."

Mark made another quick decision that he would soon regret.

> "Do whatever you have to do, Susan. I want you to get this job. You deserve it."

23

Dinner that night was more than a little strained. Archie reminded his parents that his punishment was up and that he was due to get his cell phone back the following morning. Katie asked her mother to come to the mall during the upcoming weekend to help pick out a dress for BB&N's homecoming dance. When Mark asked who she was going to the dance with, Katie immediately shut him down. "Just a group of kids, Dad." Clearly there was lots of work left to be done in the communications department.

The children had gone to bed and Susan was putting away dinner dishes when Mark approached her about the mysterious letter that had arrived in the mailbox earlier that day. He showed it to her and explained where he had found it.

"What do you think this means?" Mark began.

Susan examined the letter and its envelope carefully, and then shrugged.

"Could it have something to do with what's going on at the law school?" Susan asked.

Mark explained that he doubted Brandon Gould or any of his Criminal Law students would have a motive to try to intimidate him like that.

"What about the field hockey coach?" Mark asked. "We don't know what is going on in Heidi Wilson's head since you threatened her. Maybe we should come clean with Katie and let her know what we know. Show her the letter. It might be a relief to Katie to be able to talk to us about it. Maybe something else is going on since you last talked to the coach."

"Mark, I would prefer not to discuss Katie's sexuality with her in the context of these text messages. She is just going to throw a wall up against us, claiming invasion of privacy. I want to wait until after the field hockey season is over and after the coach resigns."

"Why don't we just show the kids the letter tomorrow night at dinner, and ask them generally if anything is going on with either one of them at school that might cause someone to do this? One of them might know something we don't know," Mark pressed.

"I would prefer not to alarm them. Things are pretty tense in the family right now. I don't want them to worry unnecessarily."

Mark was frustrated. If there was a problem that Susan couldn't fix quickly, she preferred to sweep it under the rug.

"What if it's related to your judicial appointment? Should we show it to the police or to the Governor's office? Someone could be trying to intimidate you."

"The letter was in the mailbox when we got back from the State House," Susan replied. "Even a crackpot who was following the State House news service couldn't have gotten here so quickly."

"I don't know. I don't think we should just ignore it."

"Mark, the odds are that it is either some kind of school prank by one of the kids' classmates, or somebody at the law school. I think you should show it to your Dean."

"Why would I do that?"

"They have treated you horribly. Not coming to your defense on the web forum. Taking you out of a pending course. You should put them on notice that their actions have consequences! Tell them that the whole controversy has caused you lots of emotional distress. Show them the letter. They will be afraid of a lawsuit; that will put them on their heels going forward."

Always the wise legal strategist, Susan had a good point. But Mark still felt very uneasy about not showing the letter to the kids or bringing it to the police.

"If there's a real threat out there, shouldn't the Cambridge police know about it?"

"Mark, if we bring it to the Cambridge Police right now, we have no control over whether it will be leaked to the media. A story could make its way into the Globe that a high level judicial candidate has been threatened. I just want to get through the vote without any more controversy."

There it was. Self-interest. Mark felt downright weary arguing with Susan. She had an answer to everything, even if it wasn't always an honest one. Her lack of self-awareness was extremely frustrating.

"I'll go to school tomorrow and show it to my Dean," Mark concluded in compromise.

Privately, Mark assured himself that going to campus tomorrow would also give him a chance to track down Julia and smoke out how she had been feeling since their last text exchange. He knew it was risky, but he desperately needed to see her.

24

Walking across campus Thursday morning, Mark felt like the place had changed. He had only been away for slightly more than a week, but the law school looked tired and worn. The leaves had changed from their vibrant orange to a dirty red, and were beginning to clog gutters and walkways. The manicured lawns had morphed from a brilliant green to a dullish brown. The plants that had once flowered spectacularly had now shed their blooms. It was as if Mark had put a filtered lens atop his glasses to darken the view.

Mark had intentionally driven to campus early to avoid seeing people on his way to his office. He didn't feel like making desultory small talk with current or former students, or answering the probing and simultaneously patronizing "how *are* you?" questions from his colleagues. No, he was a man on a mission today. He had two things to accomplish, and he wanted to get them done quickly and leave.

Seated behind his desk with a cup of coffee, Mark fired off two quick messages. The first was an email to his Dean telling her that he needed to see her for a few minutes today about a matter of some urgency. The second was a text to Julia. Mark asked cryptically, "I am on campus today and would love to see you. Coffee in the cafeteria?"

As he awaited their responses, Mark fired up his computer

and scanned the day's news. He began with the New York Times and the Washington Post. It was an occupational hazard, but Mark's eyes were trained to focus on stories relating to law and politics. Fights on Capitol Hill, newly released opinions from the Supreme Court, indictments of government officials. Then, Mark turned to the Boston Globe for his local news. A short story on the front of the Metro Section immediately caught Mark's attention:

SJC Nomination Hits Snag at Governor's Council

The article was accompanied by an attractive photograph of Susan borrowed from her law firm's website. Yet the photo was the only flattering thing about the story.

> The nomination of Susan Price for the Supreme Judicial Court hit a snag Wednesday at her hearing before the Governor's Council. After receiving testimony from witnesses supporting Price, two Councilors grilled Price about perceived professional and personal limitations. Councilor Marilyn Tucci asked Price about her controversial representation of a defendant tried and convicted in 2019 for the murder of a revered Watertown Police officer, Kevin O'Meara. Councilor Louis Charles pressed Price about her husband's alleged discrimination against black students in his law school classroom.
>
> The Council took the unusual step of continuing their hearings on Price's nomination for another week. They will not vote on the matter until November 10th, assuming the nomination proceeds. Asked whether the administration still supports Price's nomination, Lieutenant Governor Marjorie Cunningham responded, 'We are confident that Attorney Price will eventually

be confirmed, notwithstanding this delay. She possesses outstanding qualifications and will make an excellent jurist.'

Mark clicked off the website in disgust. Somehow his repetition of a racially-charged term in class had become an instance of "discrimination" against black students, without providing the reader with any context whatsoever. That type of lazy reporting angered him.

Even more troubling for Mark was the Governor's office hiding behind a statement from the Lieutenant Governor. If they really intended to stand by Susan, Governor Jeffries would have made a statement himself. Asking a subordinate to respond to the Globe was a common trick to insulate the Governor from embarrassment should he ultimately decide to pull the nomination. That was not a good sign.

An email from the Dean's Office snapped Mark out of his despair. "Mark, I have a few minutes before my 9:00 am meeting. Feel free to come down if you are available. Best, Sydney." Mark grabbed his coffee and made his way downstairs to the Dean's suite.

Mark wanted to keep the conversation cordial and professional. Driving to work this morning he had vowed not to lose his temper with the Dean. So he was somewhat taken aback when Sydney began the conversation with what Mark perceived as a jab.

"Hi Mark. I'm surprised to see you here."

"I haven't been banned from campus, Sydney. I have every right to be here."

"Of course. I only meant that you seem to have a lot going on at home. I figured Susan's nomination might be keeping you busy."

"So much for pleasantries," Mark thought. Clearly, the Dean had read that morning's newspaper.

"While we're on the subject of family, that's why I wanted to talk to you," Mark responded. "We received a threatening letter in our mailbox yesterday."

Mark passed the envelope to Sydney and gave her time to inspect its contents. After she had handed it back to him, Sydney said:

"I'm sorry, Mark. I understand why this would cause you concern. What can I do for you?"

"Sydney, this whole incident in Criminal Law has gotten out of control. Nasty postings on the law school website. Me being yanked from my class. Now my family is being threatened."

"What makes you think that letter is connected with the law school, Mark?"

"I can't prove it came from a student at LDB, Sydney. But I don't think the timing is a coincidence, either. I am showing you because I want you to know what a devastating impact this event is having on my reputation and on my emotional state. The university is partially to blame by letting the matter get out of hand and not backing me up."

Mark had chosen his words carefully to insinuate the basis for a possible legal claim. Sydney chose her words equally carefully in response.

"Mark, absent any evidence that this letter came from a member of the law school community, I don't think there is anything I can or should do about it. It could have come from one of your children's schools, or one of Susan's clients, or someone who followed Susan's hearings yesterday and is protesting her nomination. I simply don't see how it is the University's problem. I strongly suggest you take it to the Cambridge police if you believe your safety is at risk."

Sydney stood up from her desk, signaling that the meeting was over. On his way out of the Dean's suite, Mark received a cordial smile from Judy. But he was far too self-conscious to stop and chat with her.

When Mark got back to his office, there was a text message on his cell phone from Julia.

"I have a class at 10. Meet for coffee at 9:30?"

"Great," Mark responded. "Cafeteria?"

"No. Adirondack chairs outside the library."

It was a little chilly to sit outside for coffee. The sky was gray and the wind was up. Nevertheless, Mark welcomed the relative privacy that the outdoors would bring compared to the cafeteria. Mark was grateful to meet in a quasi-public forum where there were limitations on how emotional Julia would allow herself to become.

Mark stopped at the cafeteria to buy himself a black coffee before heading outside. He also bought Julia a latte with skim milk—just how she liked it. A peace offering might get their conversation off to a good start.

Julia had already arrived and saved him a seat on the quad when Mark got there promptly at 9:30 am. She looked gorgeous in a pair of tight black jeans and a light gray cashmere sweater.

"Hey, Mark. I've been worried about you."

"I'm okay. I've been worried about you too, though. How are classes going?"

"The clinic is great. Federal Courts sucks though. I don't understand a word that dickhead says. And the readings are incredibly boring."

"I'm sorry about those texts I sent you last week," Mark confided. "I was really down. I just needed somebody to talk to."

"I get it, Mark. But I can't be your scratching post when you're drunk or feeling sad. We're either together, or we're not," Julia whispered. "There is no in-between."

"I've tried to explain it to you, Jules. We can't be together. I can't risk my family or my job. My life is imploding around me. I can't afford any further complications."

"Now I'm a 'complication'?" Julia asked.

"You were never just a 'complication.' You were a relief and a respite. But the *situation* is very complicated. And it's not fair to you. You're young and you have your entire life in front of you."

"I'm sorry your life sucks right now, Mark. I mean it. I read the Globe this morning. You are getting absolutely crucified over this Criminal Law fiasco. And you don't deserve it. But you also need to grow a pair when it comes to your personal relationships. You either want to be with Susan, or you want to be with me." Julia was tearing up now, barely keeping it under control.

"I really care about you, Julia. But my family comes first. I thought you always knew that."

"What I *knew*, Mark, is that I was a good fuck at a time you really needed a good fuck. And now you have other priorities. I get it."

"Jules, it's not like that."

"It's *exactly* like that, Mark. At least be honest with yourself if you can't be honest with me. I have to get to class."

With that, Julia grabbed her backpack and headed into the building. Mark's mouth hung open. He hadn't expected the conversation to fall off the rails like that. And he never had an opportunity to show Julia the letter.

25

Mark wished he had known that Monday, November 1st, would be such an eventful day in his life. He would have paid more attention to every single detail—where he went, what he did, who he saw, what they said. But he didn't know any of that would matter when he woke up that morning. Once Susan went off to work and he drove the kids to school, the day stretched out ahead of him like a blank canvas.

Mark remembered that he read the newspapers and drank several cups of coffee in front of the television. The FED had raised interest rates again, and the President's approval ratings were way down due to record inflation. There was no local television coverage of Susan's confirmation hearings or his classroom probation.

He remembered that at mid-day he took a long run on the Charles River. The temperatures were only in the fifties, but the sun shined warm upon his face, and he felt healthy and vibrant as he glided the four mile loop between the Anderson Memorial and Western Avenue bridges. After his run, Mark bought a latte at Peet's Coffee Shop and chatted with a couple of patrons before returning home.

Mark tried to concentrate for a few hours on a research project, but got nowhere. His research assistant had written him a memo comparing sentencing reform initiatives in several states, but Mark could barely concentrate as he tried to parse the differences in statutes. His eyes glazed over and he nodded off for a short nap on the couch.

At about 2:00 pm Mark vowed to fix his family a nice dinner. They had been eating way too much take out recently, often devouring it at separate times of the evening in separate spaces of the house. He drove to the Whole Foods on River Street and found parking easily—a task not typically accomplished for professionals who arrived between 5:00 and 7:00 pm. Mark bought all of the ingredients for a nice pasta Bolognese and salad. He didn't remember seeing anyone he knew.

After unpacking the groceries, Mark remembered that Katie had a home field hockey game against Dana Hall that afternoon. This was the last week of the season. So he drove down to BB&N to watch her play. That also gave Mark an opportunity to scope out Coach Heidi Wilson and see if he could read anything from her body language. He couldn't.

Katie saw lots of playing time and scored twice. She even agreed to ride home with Mark after the game rather than hitching a ride with one of her teammates. That gave the two of them a chance to talk. Katie seemed fairly buoyant, given the incredibly sour mood she had been in for the past three weeks. Mark desperately wanted to find a way to get Katie to open up to him about her sexual explorations, but they were conversing pleasantly and enjoying each other's company. Mark didn't want to risk breaking that fragile détente by overstepping any boundaries.

Archie was home when they arrived, playing video games. Mark couldn't get more than three words out of him about his day. "Fine," "Okay," "Nope." After exhausting every conceivable line of inquiry, Mark gave up. "Why don't you both run up and start your homework while I get dinner ready."

"I have a team dinner tonight, Dad," Katie replied.

So much for Mark's vision of family togetherness. He tried not to display his frustration.

"Where is it?" Mark asked. "I'll give you a ride."

"It's at Sarah Gottlieb's house on Lexington Avenue. I can walk."

With that, both kids took off for their bedrooms, leaving Mark alone once again in the kitchen.

He poured himself a bourbon while starting dinner prep. Mark knew he had been drinking too much lately, but he rationalized it as stress relief. His situation at school and his tension with Susan had put him in a huge funk. And, the mysterious letter had only added to his anxiety.

Mark opened up his texts. A colleague from the Law School had reached out. "How you holding up, pal? You're totally getting a raw deal on this Criminal Law thing." Mark knew that he meant well, but he couldn't bring himself to respond right now.

Mark decided to text Susan and find out what time she would be home from work. Susan often tried to take the subway into Boston on Mondays and Fridays to avoid traffic on Storrow Drive. Her car was in the garage, so Mark knew she would be commuting home on the redline tonight.

"Running a little late. Probably not home 'til about 7. Go ahead and start dinner without me."

Great. And then there were two.

Katie ran out of the house around 6:15 pm. Mark and Archie sat down to a rather lonely dinner around 6:30 pm. Mark tried to ask Archie about his friends, his classes, his band. Little response. He tried to make inroads on the subject of winter sports. "Are you planning to go out for the ski team?" Even worse. "Dad, I'll decide when I decide. Stop trying to turn me into you."

Was Mark this sullen when he was a teenager? Maybe he was, but he couldn't remember treating his own parents that disdainfully.

Mark made Archie wash the dinner dishes, partially as a punishment for his anti-social behavior. Susan seldom made the kids do chores around the house, other than picking up their bedrooms. This had been a source of tension in their parenting for over a decade. But with Susan out of the house, Mark got to call the shots.

While Archie cleaned the kitchen, Mark texted Susan again.

"You on your way?"

"Just getting on the T," Susan responded. "Leave something for me on the stove."

Mark switched on CNN after Archie retreated upstairs to his room. Erin Burnett, 'Out Front.' Had she changed her hair color again?

Seven thirty came and went, and there was still no sign of Susan. Mark began to grow impatient. It was weird how worry about your spouse's whereabouts somehow morphed into annoyance after twenty years of marriage.

At about 8:00 pm, the doorbell rang. Mark assumed that Susan had misplaced her keys. He rolled off the couch and approached the door languidly in stocking feet. Upon opening it, Mark was surprised to see two uniformed Cambridge police officers on the stoop, one male, one female. They couldn't have been more than thirty years old.

"Mr. Price?" the female officer began. "I'm officer Morgan. There's been an accident involving your wife. We need to get you to Mt. Auburn Hospital."

26

Had Mark been thinking more clearly, he would have run upstairs and dragged Archie with him to the hospital. Or, at least told him where he was going. Mark thought about it fleetingly, but decided to send Archie a text from the hospital. After all, it was less than a half mile away. Mark could never have anticipated that this omission would be a source of resentment by his son in the months to come.

After they got in the squad car and took off down Brattle Street with blue lights flashing, Mark finally summoned the courage to ask the officers what had happened. He was sure that Susan had been struck by a bicyclist on her way home, or fallen off the curb and twisted an ankle. Mark was stunned when the male officer responded, "Mr. Price, your wife has been stabbed. Happened between the Harvard Square T Station and your house, off of Church Street. They are working on her now."

When they arrived at the hospital, the officers took Mark to the emergency room and sat him down. They told him snippets of what they knew. "A stabbing on Church Street." "Susan was cutting through the cemetery." "No immediate description of the assailant." "Passerby found her." "Lots of blood."

As Mark sat head in hands, trying to comprehend how

this had happened, he heard one of the officers radio their supervisor, "The husband has arrived at the hospital."

Mark looked up. "I need to see her," he told them.

"You can't," the female officer replied. "She's in the operating room. We'll ask one of the residents to come out and brief you on her condition." With that, the two officers approached the emergency room receptionist, chatted briefly, and left.

The next hour or so was a complete fog. Mark was not processing things clearly. He felt like he was viewing events from a distance, disassociated from reality. People and events were appearing like shards of glass in a shifting kaleidoscope. Some brief snapshots of those images would stick in his memory forever. The receptionist at the admitting desk snapping her gum. The drunk college-aged boy holding an ice pack to an eye socket that looked bruised and bloody. The machine-brewed coffee that tasted bitter and strong.

Mark remembered texting Katie to see if she was home.

"I'm at the hospital with Mom," he texted. "She's had an accident."

"OMG, is she okay? I'll come right down."

"I don't know anything yet. Can you please stay home and watch Archie?"

It seemed like hours, but it was probably only thirty minutes or so after Mark first arrived that a young surgical resident named Dr. Singh came out and spoke to him. She was tall and angular, sporting long, thick black hair tied back in a bun. The doctor located Mark in the waiting room and approached him with compassion.

"Mr. Price, I'm Dr. Singh. Our chief vascular surgeon asked me to come out and brief you on your wife's condition."

"What's happening in there?" Mark jumped in.

"She suffered multiple stab wounds to the abdomen. She lost a lot of blood before someone found her and called an ambulance. One of the wounds punctured the mesenteric artery. Dr. Driscoll is seeking to repair that artery and other damage that was done in the attack."

"Can I see her?" Mark asked.

"I am afraid that's impossible," Dr. Singh explained. "It's a sterile operating room. And she's not conscious in any event. Her blood pressure is extremely low."

"Is she going to make it?" Mark almost whispered.

"I'm afraid I can't predict that. The situation is very grave. We'll keep you posted as soon as we get more information."

As Dr. Singh walked away, she suddenly turned and added:

"There is a chapel in the Needham Lobby on the first floor. You might find that a comforting place to wait."

Mark felt certain that the young doctor had been taught to say that in medical school. Although it was intended to convey empathy, in the circumstances it felt incredibly jarring. God was not going to save Susan, only science could.

As he paced through the emergency room, Mark saw two nondescript but serious-looking men walk through the revolving doors. He could pick them out as plainclothes Cambridge police detectives immediately—shiny shoes, frayed dark pants, shabby jacket, no-iron dress shirt open at the collar. Years of prosecutorial experience had taught Mark to spot a plain-clothes police officer a mile away. Plus, he saw the strap of a shoulder holster on one of the officers as they strode into the hospital.

Mark approached the pair, looking for information.

"I'm Mark Price. Are you investigating the attack on my wife?"

"Yes, we were called to the scene by the responding officers. Let's sit down."

The three of them huddled in the corner. After the officers offered their initial condolences, Mark pressed them for answers.

"What happened to her? Was it a robbery?"

"Doesn't appear to be a robbery," the more senior of the two detectives responded. "No jewelry, pocket book or cell phone taken."

"Is anybody in custody?" Mark answered.

"No. It doesn't appear that anybody saw or heard the attack. The church bells were ringing on the hour at 7:00 pm, which would have muffled any screams. A passerby found her body at about 7:10 and called 911. There was a lot of blood."

The use of the word "body" sent chills down Mark's spine.

"Where exactly did the attack happen?" Mark asked.

"By the First Parish Church on Church Street."

Mark knew the area well. Its adjacent cemetery, the Old Burial Ground, was a frequent cut-through for Susan as she threaded her way from Massachusetts Avenue to Brattle Street.

"Any weapon recovered?" Mark's mind was racing like a lawyer's now.

"No," the younger detective responded.

The senior detective glared at his junior colleague as if to chastise him for revealing too much information.

"Mr. Price, was your wife coming home from work?"

"Yes, Mark explained. She had texted me from the office. She took the T. Left her office in Boston sometime around 6:30 pm."

"Was she traveling alone?"

"As far as I know," Mark explained. "Unless she encountered a neighbor and was walking with her on the way to the house."

"What is her normal path from Harvard Square?"

"Mass Avenue T station to Church Street to Brattle Street," Mark explained.

"Where were you at the time?" one of the detectives inquired.

Mark was stunned. Did they think he was a suspect? They were clearly in the information gathering stage, but Mark was in no mood to be handled.

"I was at home making dinner for my family."

Their conversation was interrupted by the appearance of a doctor. Mark stood up and shook hands with a tall, white-haired man wearing scrubs and a surgeon's cap.

"Mr. Price, I'm Ted Driscoll, chief of vascular surgery here at the hospital. I'm terribly sorry. Your wife didn't make it. Our team did everything we could to save her, but the wounds were just too severe. They punctured multiple organs and a major artery. She bled out during the surgery."

Mark felt the floor falling out from beneath him. All he could do was steady himself and blurt out the first words that came to mind.

"I want to see her."

27

One of the operating room nurses escorted Mark down to the hospital mortuary. She patted him on the arm and told him that she would wait outside.

The Mt. Auburn Hospital mortuary was a small, cold room in the basement with six or ten drawers for the deceased. They didn't stay here long—usually the funeral home or the coroner's office would pick the body up from the hospital within twenty-four hours.

Susan's body was on a gurney at the center of the room. They had cleaned off the blood and put a crisp fresh sheet over her. Only Susan's face was visible. She looked oddly serene. Her thick brown hair flowed almost luxuriously over the stark white sheet. Her penetrating green eyes were still open and stared unfocused at the ceiling. The jewelry that Susan had put on that morning—jade and silver earrings and a simple matching necklace—was still in place. Even her lipstick was not smudged. Mark had seen dead bodies before, but this visage was enough to take his breath away.

What struck Mark so acutely as he stared down at his Susan's lifeless body was something that a stranger would never have noticed: her lack of power. Throughout her life Susan had been a powerful figure; she commanded every room she entered with authority and grace. This was one of the qualities that had attracted Mark to Susan when they first met. As Mark stared helplessly at his wife's corpse, he felt both angry and saddened that someone had robbed Susan of that gift.

Mark felt overcome with loss, but somehow helpless to express it. He could not bring himself to lower the sheet and look at Susan's abdomen. Mark knew the ugly scars that lay underneath, and he was certain that if he looked at them now, he would never be able to force that image out of his mind.

Mark had been staring silently at Susan's corpse for about five minutes when a thought suddenly struck him like a lightning bolt.

"The kids. I have to get home to the kids."

When Mark opened the door and entered the quiet hallway, he came face-to-face with Tony Garcia. They had probably only seen each other two or three times since they worked together decades ago—mostly at retirement parties and similar events. But Mark would recognize Tony anywhere—handsome, chiseled, olive complexion. He had a few gray hairs around the temples and some burgeoning crows' feet around the eyes, but he was still the same Tony Garcia who had once been his friend. Except that Tony's eyes were watering now, and he himself was fighting back tears.

"Tony, what are you doing here?" Mark felt an inexplicable anger rising inside of him. He was not thinking clearly.

"Mark, I've been assigned as lead detective on Susan's case. Let me drive you home."

28

Mark had no excuse not to accept the ride home. He thought of calling an Uber, but the concept seemed ludicrous considering the lead detective on his wife's homicide investigation was offering him a ride.

When Mark settled into the passenger seat of Garcia's undercover vehicle, Tony was the first to speak.

> "Mark, I'm so sorry for your loss. This is gut-wrenching. We will do whatever it takes to catch whoever did this to Susan."

> "Thank you Tony. She was an incredible person. I know you knew that."

Mark was choosing his words carefully now. He needed time to think clearly, and he was in no position to do that in his current state.

> "Tony, under the circumstances, do you think you are the appropriate person to lead this investigation?"

Garcia's response was equally measured, if not reassuring.

> "Mark, I will not let Susan and my friendship twenty years ago get in the way of me being objective. If

anything, it will motivate me to find her killer. So many people loved her. I hope you can understand that."

Mark sat in silence thinking for a couple of moments as they pulled up to the house. Garcia interrupted:

"Mark, do you know anyone who would have a motive to hurt Susan?"

As he paced the hospital waiting room that night, Mark had been thinking over and over about the threatening letter they had received in the mailbox. He told Tony about it.

"It's sitting in my briefcase in the house. I can run in and get it for you."

"That would help," Tony said. Then he added, "Given Susan's prominence in the legal community and her pending nomination, the District Attorney wants to hold a press conference about the attack first thing in the morning. Several of the local outlets have already picked up the story through police logs. The DA wants to get in front of it. The Governor and Lieutenant Governor may also want to be there."

Mark hadn't yet told the kids about their mother's death and Tony Garcia was asking Mark to think about the media. He didn't know whether Garcia was asking for permission or just notifying him out of courtesy.

"I, I'm not sure. I don't think I could make it through a press conference. I need to be with the kids. Are you asking me to attend?"

"No Mark, under the circumstances I think it is better if the family of the victim is not present. Just officials."

They were in Mark's driveway now, and Mark could see lights coming from the family room and two upstairs bedrooms. He looked at the clock on his phone for the first time in hours. 11:30 pm. Six missed calls from Katie and Archie. He took a deep breath.

> "I'll run in and get you that envelope. Wait here."

Mark darted into the mud room and grabbed his briefcase. As soon as he opened the door he heard Katie jump up from the family room couch.

> "Dad. Oh my God, I have been trying to reach you! Where's Mom?"

Mark's heart wrenched as he thought about how he was going to tell the kids.

> "Wait here for just a second, honey." Mark was choking back tears now. "There's a police officer in the driveway and I have to give him something."

Mark ran the letter out to Garcia, who was waiting for him in the driveway. Passing it through the driver's side window, Mark whispered:

> "Someone left this in our mailbox about a week ago. We have no idea where it came from."

Garcia was all business now, relying on both habit and years of training.

> "Mark, here is my business card. It has my cell phone number on it. We are going to need to talk at length tomorrow. I'll be in touch to set up a time. But if you think of anything else tonight that might be important, please text me."

Mark shook Tony's hand and thanked him for the ride home.

"Will do. You need my cell phone number?" Mark asked.

"No, I got it."

29

As Mark walked into the house, Katie was standing at the back door and Archie was rising out of slumber from the family room sofa. Seeing the concern on their faces and knowing they were now without a mother brought forth a wave of emotions that had been building up inside Mark for over an hour. He sat down on the couch, gathered them into his arms, and began to weep.

Between gulps of tears, Mark told them that Susan had been attacked with a knife on Church Street on her way home from the subway. The stab wounds punctured several arteries and the doctors were unable to save her during surgery. She was gone.

Katie's reaction was one of furor. She jumped up from the couch and paced around the family room. "I don't believe it," she wailed. "Who would want to do this to Mom?"

Mark ran after Katie and tried to wrap her in his arms, caressing her hair and repeating:

"I know Katie. She loved you so much."

Archie sat with his head in his hands, weeping quietly. When he finally looked up from the couch, Mark saw a look of pure anguish on his face.

"It's all my fault," Archie whispered.

"What are you talking about?" Mark asked. "Don't be silly."

"No, Dad, I have to tell you something. It's really bad," Archie croaked between tears.

With that, Archie told his father about buying drugs from Mullet, Mullet's arrest, and his threat at Holyoke Plaza that Archie should "watch out." Archie felt so guilty that he spilled the narrative in gushes, beginning all the way back with first buying pot with his friends, seeking to buy some Molly for a concert, and agreeing to sell drugs for Mullet at BB&N. Mark was having trouble following the whole story through his son's heaves and sighs. Archie kept repeating, "I hate myself. It should have been me."

"Wait, *did* you turn that kid in to the police?"

"No Dad, I never did. He just thought I did because he was stopped and arrested holding drugs right after I met him in the Mt. Auburn cemetery."

"What exactly did he say to you that day in Holyoke Plaza?"

Archie tried to compose himself and slow down. He recited the threat to Mark as best he could remember it. "You and your perfect family better watch their backs." To Mark, it sounded eerily similar to the letter.

"Did you tell him where you lived? Has he ever been to this house?"

Mark didn't like interrogating his children, especially during a time of anguish, but it was clear that Archie was in pain and was trying to get something out.

"No Dad, he's never been here. I never thought he would do anything like this."

"Archie, I doubt a minor drug arrest would be a motive for murder. I'll let the police know about it. Do you know Mullet's name and where he lives?"

"He lives in Arlington, that's all I know. He's about eighteen."

Just then Katie interrupted. She had begun to compose herself during Archie's story, but was wiping away tears while leaning on the couch across her father's shoulder.

"Dad, who would possibly want to do this to Mom? Was she robbed?"

"No, it doesn't look like it."

"Could it have something to do with the whole judge thing? Or with what is going on with you at school?"

Mark could not rule those motives out, although he didn't consider either of them a strong possibility. He wanted to calm his children down as much as possible, but he also knew that they were teenagers and would be seeing things about the case in the media tomorrow. So he had to be up front with them.

"Your Mom and I received a threatening message in our mailbox about a week ago. No handwriting, just cut out letters from a magazine. It said, 'You better watch out for that precious family of yours.' I gave the letter to the police."

"That could have been Mullet," Archie offered.

"It could have been *anybody*," Katie argued, surprising Mark.

Mark scrutinized Katie carefully. He wanted to raise the subject of Susan discovering sexting on Katie's cell phone and her confrontation with Heidi Wilson. But he did not want to broach that sensitive topic in front of Archie. So he opted for a more subtle line of inquiry.

"Katie, do you know of anybody in your life who would want to hurt our family? Is there anything going on with you at school?"

That strategy backfired. Katie melted into another torrent of tears.

"With all the shit surrounding Mom's judgeship and your crap at work, you think someone at BB&N would stab Mom? That is so fucked up!"

Mark backed off. His primary role as a father right now had to be to comfort his children. He would talk to Tony Garcia about potential leads another time.

"Dad, why didn't you take me to the hospital?" Archie gulped a few minutes later. "I could have said goodbye to Mom."

"I didn't know it was that bad, buddy. When the police came to get me, they just told me there had been an accident. Turns out I never got to say goodbye either. They wouldn't even let me into the operating room."

The three of them stayed on the couch rocking in each other's arms until well past 2:00 am, when the kids finally fell asleep. Mark kept whispering to them, like a mantra:

"We'll get through this, I promise."

30

Mark jolted awake about 4:30 am when a numbed right arm began to tingle under the weight of Archie's torso. He wriggled himself free of the couch and stood up to get his bearings. It was dark outside, but the lights were on inside the house. For a moment he felt disoriented and confused, until the realities of the prior evening came rushing back to him.

Upstairs in his bedroom, Mark tore off his clothes and entered the shower. He closed his eyes and let the pulsating hot water stream over his body for several minutes. The steam cleared his head and allowed him to relax somewhat. After getting out of the shower, Mark threw on a t-shirt and a pair of boxer shorts and sat down on the edge of his bed. Their bed.

The enormity of what happened engulfed Mark like a tidal wave. His career was in the shitter. His life partner was gone. Scandal and controversy would pursue the Prices relentlessly as the police tried to solve the murder. And now, Mark was the sole source of support for two bereaved teenaged children. He had to get his crap together.

Mark wanted to get in touch with Tony Garcia. There was a murderer on the loose. Mark needed to alert the police before the killer destroyed evidence or struck again. Mark texted Tony.

"We need to meet for coffee. I talked to the kids and I may have some leads."

Mark then confronted the difficult task of notifying Susan's family and her law firm. Susan's older sister lived in New Jersey. She had never married herself, and was devoted to Susan and the kids. Mark didn't want her to hear about Susan's death from the media. Mark called her cell phone and she answered on the second ring. When Mark conveyed the news of what happened, Anne broke down in such powerful tears that Mark was at a loss for how to comfort her. After fifteen or so minutes, his only way of escaping the phone call was to tell Anne that he had to call the funeral home and make arrangements.

Next, Mark called Marcia Blackwell, Susan's best friend from Wright & Graham. Marcia was extremely organized and structured, just like Susan. Mark knew that she would be getting up early anyway, probably to exercise. Mark needed somebody inside the firm to take care of administrative matters like notifying colleagues and clients, and postponing court proceedings. He did not have the cell phone number of the managing partner, and would not have wanted to talk with him about such a personal matter in any event. Marcia was the perfect choice—she would take care of everything out of loyalty to both Susan and the firm. Like Anne, she received the news with stunned horror.

Clearly, there would be no school for Katie and Archie this week. Mark called the principal's office at BB&N. Thankfully he got a message machine and briefly explained the kids' absence in a tone that was clinical and detached.

Mark wandered downstairs to check on the kids. They were still stretched out languidly on the family room sectional. He tiptoed into the kitchen and started a pot of coffee. Suddenly Mark remembered that Tony had said there would be a press conference. It was still barely daylight, but Mark knew that the Boston Globe evening desk would at least have gotten an initial story out on their web edition from the police blotter. Mark clicked open his tablet and pulled up the paper:

High Court Nominee Stabbed to Death in Cambridge

The story included a photograph of Susan and a brief description of the location of the attack. "Attorney Price died at Mt. Auburn hospital after life-saving measures by a team of surgeons were unsuccessful." The article went on to state that no arrests had yet been made in the case. "It is unclear at this time whether the motive for the attack relates in any way to her judicial nomination. The victim's screams were likely muffled by the ringing of church bells at the scene. The Middlesex District Attorney's Office and the State Police are pleading with any passerby who may have been in the vicinity and seen something relevant to come forward. They will hold a press conference at 9:30 am on Tuesday."

31

Tony Garcia sat in his state police cubicle at the District Attorney's Office nursing the fifth cup of coffee of a very long night. There would be no sleep for him today. The District Attorney and the Governor were holding a press conference in just a couple of hours, and Tony was on the hotseat. This might be the most important case of his career. Yet he was also grieving the loss of a beautiful woman who, in many ways, he still loved. He had to clear his head of emotion and focus on the tasks at hand.

Tony was gratified that his boss had assigned the case to him. There was no ignoring the highly public nature of the crime. The brass had to assign the case to the best homicide detective in the office. And that was Tony. This meant that his career as a detective was still on track. It would, for now, eliminate the pressure on Tony to take on a new assignment back in uniform.

Garcia had thought about telling Emily about his brief relationship with Susan when she called him last night to assign him the case. Maybe he should have. But very few people other than Tony and Susan knew about the affair—perhaps only the two of them, and maybe Mark. They had been very discreet. Tony really didn't think it would interfere with his judgment. Perhaps he was rationalizing. Or maybe he put his own career ambitions and drive to find Susan's killer ahead of the department's bests interests. In either event, Tony felt like he was the best person for the job, so he accepted the assignment and said nothing.

Tony had been at the crime scene both before and after going to the hospital. He met with the first responders and heard their version of events. He marked off the area with tape, flagged locations of recovered items with number tents, and had the state police photographer take pictures of the scene. Forensics came in and took samples of blood on the sidewalk and grassy areas.

If they got lucky, there would be blood left from the perpetrator at the scene. But Tony was not feeling lucky. The nature of Susan's wounds did not suggest that she could have been able to put up much of a defense. The stab wounds were vicious and mortal. The first penetration to the abdomen probably crumpled her to the ground. The additional wounds—likely inflicted while Susan was already down—were motivated by pure hatred. Tony saw no signs of defensive wounds on Susan's hands or arms.

At his desk, Tony turned his attention to the paper aspect of the investigation. Without any eye witnesses, he desperately needed to figure out a motive. Records would be key. He had Susan's cell phone. He had used her right index finger in the morgue to unlock her phone, and he was now scanning her texts and charting her history of calls made and received. The family was on the same cell phone plan. Tony started work on a subpoena to the carrier for a history of calls and texts made and received from those three phones as well. Tony would have one of the junior troopers in the office hand deliver the administrative subpoena to the phone company offices when they opened. Tony's friend in the security division would prioritize that search and get him calls for the last several months by the close of business. Assuming they established any incriminating patterns, Tony felt certain he could convince a judge to issue a search warrant to have the cell carrier turn over the contents of their text messages, too. But they would have to hurry because most carriers only kept the contents of text messages for a few days, if at all.

Tony already knew that the Assistant District Attorney assigned to the case would be Camille Jones. Aggressive and competent, she was now the most experienced trial lawyer in the office. Tony felt assured that the government had brought in their "A" team. He had already spoken with Camille, and she told him that she had scheduled time in the grand jury for Thursday. That meant that they could start building a paper case by issuing grand jury subpoenas. Tony had Susan's bank and credit cards from the purse recovered at the scene. He typed up subpoenas for bank account and credit card records going back one year. Maybe that would show any unusual transactions. If Susan's Venmo account was linked to either her bank or credit cards, Tony would also get those records.

Tony's phone buzzed and he saw a text from Mark Price. Mark wanted to meet and share some information. Tony had to handle this request very carefully. Massachusetts law required the recording of all interrogations of suspects in homicide investigations when they were in custody. Tony had not yet ruled Mark out as a suspect. In fact, Susan had intimated last week when she asked Tony to testify on her behalf at the next Governor's Council meeting that there may have been some trouble in the marriage. It was more of a hint than a bald statement, but Tony had picked up on it. Mark was more likely to be forthcoming if Tony kept the conversation casual. Still, Tony did not want to screw up the investigation and taint any possible confession or damning statements if Mark made admissions in a coffee shop. No, he needed to play this by the book as much as possible. He texted Mark back:

"Can you come to my office at 2:00 pm? We'll have coffee here."

For the next hour or so, Tony gave his team various assignments and answered their questions. He wasn't great at delegation, but this case would test his abilities. There was lots of leg work to be done, and Tony only had two legs himself.

Tony wanted his colleagues to track down membership in extremist groups in Boston to see if anyone who was picketing on the steps of the State House after Susan's hearing could be identified. Maybe there was video footage of them from the Harvard Square subway station on the night of her murder. It may have been a long shot, but it wasn't out of the question that Susan's killing could have been the work of the Proud Boys or the American Freedom Party.

At 8:30 am, Tony bolted from his desk and ran to the locker room in the basement of the building. He would have to shave, shower, and make himself presentable by the time of the press conference. Tony kept a spare jacket, dress shirt and tie on a hanger in his locker for sudden trips to court or unexpected events such as this.

Arriving at the executive suite on the fifth floor of the District Attorney's office at 9:00 am, Tony was led to the press briefing room by the DA's communications secretary. District Attorney Kevin O'Sullivan was already there, standing at the front of the room talking to Camille Jones. Tony knew that there had been a lot of back and forth during the night about whether to hold the press conference in the Governor's Office or the District Attorney's Office. It was settled to do it on the DA's home turf, to send a signal that this investigation was a judicial matter and not a political one. Major Martin Kelly from the State Police was in full uniform and greeted Tony warmly. "I guess we'll have to put that transfer to the Athol Barracks on the back burner," he whispered while shaking Tony's hand.

Governor Jeffries strode into the room at precisely 9:29 am, surrounded by an entourage of security and aides. With that, District Attorney O'Sullivan called the press briefing to order. Even though a pool camera was videotaping the event, almost every reporter of the fifty or so present had their cell phones fully engaged on video.

The significance of the packed room was not lost on Tony, who suddenly felt a huge pit swell in his stomach. Although he had no formal role in the briefing except to stand on the stage behind the speakers, Tony was paying rapt attention to every single word.

District Attorney O'Sullivan described the knife attack on Susan Price as "senseless and disturbing." The time of death was listed as 10:35 pm at Mt. Auburn Hospital. "No personal valuables were taken, so it is unlikely that this was an attempted robbery, although we have not yet ruled that out. We are not going to speculate at this time about any motive or any possible connection to Ms. Price's pending judicial nomination." O'Sullivan added that the investigation would be spearheaded by ADA Camille Jones and Detective Lieutenant Tony Garcia, "perhaps the finest homicide team in the state." In conclusion, the District Attorney urged cooperation from the community. "We are trying to ascertain whether there were any eyewitnesses to the crime other than the perpetrator. If anyone was in the vicinity of the First Parish Church in Harvard Square last night between 6:30 pm and 7:30 pm and saw or heard something unusual, please contact the State Police in our office."

Governor Jeffries wrapped up the press conference by praising Susan as "an exceptional lawyer and a tremendous public servant." His words of praise were genuine and effusive. "She would have brought tremendous energy, unparalleled experience and practical wisdom to the high court if her nomination were affirmed, which I am confident was only a matter of days away." Jeffries noted that "above all, Susan Price was a pragmatist and a believer in good government—she would not have wanted for one moment to have the state's judiciary delayed or impeded in its work by the cowardly acts of one criminal. The wheels of progress must not be stymied, even for an instant. For that reason, and in honor of Susan Price's memory, I have decided to announce today my replacement nomination to fill the vacancy on the Massachusetts Supreme Judicial Court, Appeals Court Justice Carter Ellis."

32

Mark Price walked into the reception area of the Middlesex County District Attorney's Office feeling very self-conscious. Were people giving him conciliatory stares, or was that just his imagination? He still hadn't had time to process Susan's death, but the media coverage about it had been widespread and intense. Mark had switched off the radio on the ride over to the DA's office because even NPR was covering the murder.

The receptionist was kind enough to escort Mark back to the State Police unit in the building, even though Mark knew exactly where it was and could have walked back there himself. Mark felt weird finding himself on the "other" side of crime as a victim and a witness, when he had spent so many years as a prosecutor. It was also very eerie to wander through the very same office building where he and Susan had first met, and where they had spent many long hours together during their younger days as lawyers. Not much about the building had changed, including most of the furniture and the dust balls in the corners of the linoleum flooring.

Tony Garcia met him at the entry vestibule to the State Police unit and shook Mark's hand, again expressing his deepest condolences. Tony brought Mark by the break area and poured them each a cup of coffee before directing Mark into a small private conference room used for interviewing witnesses.

"Thanks for coming by Mark. Is it okay if I record this interview?"

Mark was taken aback. He didn't know this was a formal "interview." He and Tony had approached each other last night like former colleagues, if not exactly friends. Mark thought he was just coming by to fill Tony in on his conversation with Archie.

"It doesn't bother me, but why would you do that?"

Tony paused and chose his words very carefully. He did not want to spook Mark and cause him to "lawyer-up" very early in the investigation. Once a lawyer became involved, the subject of the investigation often declined to speak. So Tony wanted to continue to make Mark feel comfortable cooperating.

"State Police protocol in homicide investigations, Mark. I'm sure you understand."

Mark was familiar with criminal procedure and Massachusetts protocols. He knew Tony did not have to record the interview unless Mark was both a suspect and in custody. Mark wasn't in custody because he had voluntarily come to the station. Was he a suspect? If not, why in God's name was Garcia being so cautious?

"That's fine, Tony. Whatever. I wanted to come over to tell you about a teenager in the neighborhood who threatened Archie. Archie told me about him last night. Archie thinks he may have wanted to get back at our family."

With that, Mark told Garcia everything he knew about Mullet—age, town, cell phone number, general appearance.

Mark also related how Archie had bought drugs from Mullet before Mullet's arrest by the Cambridge P.D. and that Mullet suspected he may have been set up.

Tony took careful notes, before interjecting:

> "We will find him and check him out. We have his cell phone number. Shouldn't be hard to get an address. Mark, do you know anyone else who would want to hurt Susan or your family?"

Mark thought carefully before responding. Susan had threatened the field hockey coach at BB&N. That may have provided Wilson with a motive to harm Susan. Even though the story did not paint Susan in a particularly flattering light, Mark thought it was important to share with Tony. So he did.

After Mark finished, Tony scrutinized Mark carefully. Did Mark know that Tony had been the one who had used his contacts at the phone company to retrieve Heidi Wilson's identity? Tony could not be sure. It was possible that Susan revealed this to her husband, but somehow Tony did not think so. It might have provoked jealousy. So he declined to take the bait.

> "Thanks for sharing that with me Mark. We will check out Heidi Wilson, too. Have you spoken to Katie about their relationship?"

> "No. Not yet."

Mark didn't like how this conversation had focused exclusively on his family. So he felt like it was his turn to fish for some information.

> "Did you find anything at the crime scene last night that might lead to a possible motive?"

> "Not yet Mark. But we are still processing everything."

Typical cop speak, close to the vest.

Mark got up to leave. He had been away from the house for too long already. As he was headed toward the door, Garcia put his hand on his shoulder.

> "Mark, please sit down for just another second. Tell me what is going on with you at school. All I know is what I read in that one Globe article about the confirmation hearing, and what I could glean from a quick glance at the student blogs this morning. Is there anyone at school who would want to harm you or your family?"

With that, Mark told Garcia the entire story of Brandon Gould's campaign against him. Then he added:

> "I don't think that's a motive to kill, Tony. Gould is angry, but I don't think he's crazy."

Tony eyed Mark carefully and decided to cast one more line in the water while he had Mark's cooperation.

> "Mark, whose cell phone is (202) 258-8793? We ran the calls to and from your family's cell phone lines this morning. This one came up repeatedly connected to your phone."

Mark felt like he had just received a powerful blow to the stomach. That was Julia's number. There was no sense lying about it. If Tony had traced his phone, he might have already received the subscriber information from the phone company.

> "That's Julia Hoffman, my former teaching assistant."

33

Susan's memorial was held on Saturday. They needed almost a full week to get the body released from the medical examiner's office and to make arrangements for the service. Susan had always wanted to be cremated—so there was no rush from a logistical standpoint—but Mark knew that the kids needed closure. Their raw emotions over the past week had run the gamut from anger, to worry, to acute sadness. Unfortunately, the three of them were not always demonstrating the same symptoms at the same time, so consoling Archie and Katie in the past five days had tested Mark's parenting skills like nothing before. Susan had undoubtedly been the leader of the Price family—its CEO, its driving force, its tour guide on the travels of life. Mark sensed that the kids' primary concern was what would happen to the three of them now that she was gone.

The Price family held the memorial at Marsh Chapel at Boston University, a beautiful gothic structure located right on the Charles River. Mark had thought about holding it in Cambridge, but the proximity to the crime scene would have been too jarring for everyone, including the kids. And Mark could not stomach asking permission to hold the service on the LDB campus, given the tensions between him and his Dean. Boston University had been a sensible compromise. It was close to Cambridge and close to downtown Boston. Susan was a prominent graduate of its law school and had been very generous with her time and talents, including teaching part-time courses and serving on their Board of Advisors. Getting Marsh Chapel on short notice was not a problem given Susan's prominence in the community.

The attendance list was a "who's who?" of the Boston legal establishment. Although the mid-size chapel held only 250 visitors comfortably, so many people came to pay their respects that they were lined up on both sides of the aisles and in the entryway on the expansive Marsh plaza. Mark was gratified by the attendance, knowing that it was important for the kids to see how many lives Susan had touched in less than five decades.

Mark delivered the eulogy. Although he was an experienced public speaker used to lecturing hundreds, this was undoubtedly the hardest talk he had ever given in his life. As he spoke, Mark focused his gaze just over the heads of the attendees at the vaulted beamed ceiling and stained glass windows at the very back of the chapel, knowing that if he looked directly at Katie or Archie in the front row he would completely break down. Mark had spent many sleepless nights this week jotting on index cards to outline his remarks. But he didn't need them. Mark spoke from experience, and he spoke from the heart. He talked about the sources of Susan's power and strength—her passion, her intellect, her energy, and her incredible gift for bringing people together. When he was finished, there was not a dry eye in the house.

Katie read a poem from Pablo Neruda about life and death entitled "When I Die I Want Your Hands on my Eyes." She was radiant that day in a simple black dress and her mother's pearls. Mark choked back tears as Katie delivered the following lines:

> I want for what I love to go on living and as for you
> I loved you and sang you above everything, for that,

go on flowering, flowery one, so that you reach all that my love orders for you, so that my shadow passes through your hair, so that they know by this the reason for my song.

Mark had helped Katie pick out the poem as they huddled together on the family room sofa this week discussing the service. Neruda had been Susan's favorite poet, and she was delighted last year when Katie's Spanish class had taken up some of his work. The two of them had read Neruda together. That had provided Susan with a rare opportunity to bond with an otherwise distant sixteen-year-old daughter.

Archie had fretted all week about whether to try to do a reading at the service. Fourteen-year-old boys were typically self-conscious, but Susan's murder, coupled with Mullet's threats, had made Archie spiral into a deep, inward loathing. Archie told Mark there was no way he could get through a reading without breaking down. Archie asked, "Will people think it is weird if Katie does a reading and I don't?" Mark felt so bad for him, all he could do was wrap his arms around Archie and assure him that "Mom would not want you to do anything you are not comfortable doing. People will understand your grief," Mark explained. "Lots of family members don't speak at funerals." In the end, Susan's sister Anne agreed to read a passage from the third chapter of Ecclesiastes in the Old Testament.

> "There is a time for everything, and a season for every activity under the heavens: a time to be born and a time to die, a time to plant and a time to uproot...."

The minister had suggested that Anne stop after the eighth verse. Given Susan's murder, there was no need for the congregants to hear, "God will bring into judgment both the righteous and the wicked," although the significance of that omission was not lost on Mark.

The Prices hosted a reception at the Boston University Faculty Club following the service. The caterer served light hors d'oeuvres, pastries, wine, and coffee. Mark has prepared the kids for the long line of mourners they would be required to greet at the entrance. "Just shake their hands, look them in the eyes, and thank them for coming," Mark explained. "They don't expect you to engage beyond that."

For himself, Mark felt like he was somehow outside his own body, hovering above the reception, watching from afar. There were so many different people, so many small groups, so many whispered conversations. Although some of the guests were ghoulish enough to ask about the murder investigation, most just offered their condolences and expressed warm thoughts about Susan. To almost all of them, Mark responded with the same words: "Thank you for your support. Somehow we'll get through this."

Soon after the last of the stragglers had entered the club, Anne took Mark aside for a brief, private conversation. "I want to stay for a while and help with the kids," Anne whispered. It was more of a demand than a request. Mark and Anne had forged a somewhat edgy relationship which dated back well before Mark had married her sister. Anne still resented Mark for the brief "pause" in Susan and Mark's relationship twenty years earlier, which Mark had instigated and which had temporarily devastated Susan. Anne had been circumspect around Mark ever since, almost as if she suspected he might someday hurt her sister again. But Anne was Susan's only living family member. Childless herself, she had been a doting aunt and surrogate mother to the kids for almost seventeen years. As much as Mark would have liked to protect his family's privacy, he did not see any room to maneuver on this issue. They had a spare guest room, and the kids would benefit from her support. So he responded simply, "That would be great."

After the reception, Mark, Katie, Archie and Anne drove

back to Cambridge in near silence. They were completely exhausted. Katie wept quietly in the front passenger seat. Archie stared out the window in the back, his forehead literally pressed against the glass. All Mark could find the strength to say inside the car was, "Mom would have been very proud of both of you today." Anne added, "It was a beautiful service."

She was right about that. The beauty, dignity and grace of the memorial had befitted Susan perfectly. Mark was in awe at how many people had attended, from all walks of Susan's life. Neighbors, Dartmouth friends, judges, politicians, and legal colleagues all came to pay their respects. Many of Mark's colleagues from the law school also showed up. No doubt some of them—the small handful of Mark's true friends on the faculty—were sincere in their concern for Mark and his family. Mark suspected that others were mere gawkers, witnessing the spectacle of somebody else's misery.

34

When they got home Saturday night it was very difficult for anyone to think clearly. The enormity and finality of their loss had suddenly sunk in. Anne unpacked. The kids scrolled their phones in front of the television. None of them really had a chance to eat much at the reception, so Mark ordered pizza.

Everyone went to bed early that night except Mark, who stayed up scrolling the news on the television and his tablet. Inflation, a contentious ruling from the Supreme Court on gun rights, stock market decline, tornadoes in the Midwest. The state of the country seemed both devastating and inconsequential at the same time. Mark's life was an utter disaster, and it was hard to worry about the world when one's place in it seemed so precarious.

At around 10:00 pm, Mark tired of pacing the house. He was fatigued to the bone, but somehow not tired enough to sleep. There were too many thoughts rolling around in his head. Mark realized that he had not checked the mail in several days. Maybe reading some sympathy cards from friends would console him. Mark walked outside to the end of the drive and retrieved a huge pile of mail.

He was sorting through correspondence and making piles on the dining room table when he came across an envelope addressed only to "The Prices." The appearance jarred him because the name was fashioned with cut out magazine letters, just like the warning letter they had received before Susan's death. Mark's heart stopped. There was no return address. No stamp or postmark. The envelope was not sealed.

Without thinking, Mark opened the envelope. Inside was a single piece of paper, just like before, with letters cut out from magazine print.

FOR IT IS THE BLOOD BY REASON OF THE LIFE THAT MAKES ATONEMENT. LEVITICUS 17:11.

Mark's hands were trembling. He dropped the paper on the table, staring at it in terror. Then Mark realized this was critical evidence. He had to tell the police.

Mark found his phone on the family room sofa and immediately dialed Tony Garcia. Garcia picked up on the second ring.

"Tony, I just received another anonymous letter. In our mailbox."

"Leave it where it is. Don't handle it any further. We will need to look for prints and DNA. I'm coming right over."

It took Tony only ten minutes to drive from Watertown to Harvard Square. Mark met him at the back door. They whispered to avoid waking anybody up.

"It's on the dining room table."

Tony carefully pulled on latex gloves before picking up the letter by its edges. He stared at it carefully to digest its contents before placing it in a clear plastic evidence bag. Tony put the envelope in a separate bag and then turned to Mark.

"Mark, I need to talk to you again. It's about Mullet. Can you come to the office tomorrow afternoon around 1:00?"

35

Early on Sunday afternoon, Mark made an excuse to Anne about running some errands and drove over to the District Attorney's Office in Woburn. The parking lot was desolate, as he knew it would be. There was no public access to the building on weekends. Mark texted Tony Garcia when he arrived, and the detective came down to the front door immediately to let him in.

Had Mark been thinking clearly, he would have realized how reckless it was to go down to the DA's Office without having an attorney with him. Only a very foolish lawyer represents himself. Mark knew that detectives weren't in the practice of giving out information, their job was to gather evidence. In telling Mark that they "had to talk about Mullet," Tony was just casting a piece of bait to try to lure Mark back into the office for another interview.

Garcia led Mark to the upstairs conference room. When they entered, Mark was shocked to see ADA Camille Jones already seated at the table. It was not unusual for a prosecutor to sit in on important witness interviews in a murder investigation. But seldom on a Sunday. And not unless there was a lot at stake.

Because he was nervous, Mark tried to keep it light:

"Ms. Jones. I am surprised to see you. The Commonwealth is well represented. Do I need a lawyer?"

"Completely your choice, Mr. Price. I understand you have come down to the office of your own volition, but you can cancel the meeting and come back with a lawyer another time if you wish."

All business. Mark was taken aback. Tony filled the silence.

"Just like last week, you understand that this interview is being recorded."

"Yes, Tony. I came over to find out what you learned about Mullet. You said we needed to talk."

"Mullet is Ben DeCicco. Eighteen years of age. Lives with his parents in Arlington. He has a solid alibi for the night of Susan's murder. He was in the lockup at the Cambridge Police Department. DeCicco got caught dealing weed again that afternoon in Holyoke Plaza, which was in violation of his bail order."

Mark was disappointed, but not surprised. He had seriously doubted that a minor drug pinch would motivate anyone to murder. Archie would be relieved and stop blaming himself.

"Did you talk to Heidi Wilson?"

"She lawyered up. Attorney won't let us talk to her. But he did tell us where she was that night. She allegedly was with her head coach following practice on Monday, having coffee at the Starbucks in Watertown. After that, they stopped at the Gottlieb's team dinner on Lexington Avenue. We checked with the head coach— she backs Wilson up on the alibi. Plus, the headmaster at BB&N told us Wilson submitted her notice in early

October. In fact, he had already served as a reference for Wilson's new head coaching job out of state. So, it doesn't look like there was any real motive either."

"Unless she hired somebody," Mark interjected. "She may have been concerned that Susan would renege on the deal and disclose the sexting after she was gone."

"Possible. We are looking at her bank accounts."

"Did you find any touch DNA on Susan's clothing?" Mark asked.

"Still processing," Garcia responded. "But it doesn't look promising. Killer probably wore gloves."

Garcia paused and observed Mark's reaction to these details before continuing.

"Mark, we want to talk to you about something else today. Julia Hoffman. Can you tell us about your relationship with her?"

Garcia was good. He had shifted the conversation in a steady, almost comforting tone. But Mark nonetheless felt blindsided. He glimpsed at Camille Jones and saw her straighten, almost imperceptibly. She leaned over the table, focusing on the notepad in front of her. Camille had been expecting the question.

Mark bit the inside of his cheek to steady himself. He had to get this right. If he lied and they caught him in a lie, it would be evidence against him. The problem was, he didn't know what they knew.

"Julia and I had a brief relationship. An intimate one. But it was over."

"When did it end?" Tony asked.

"At the beginning of the school year," Mark fudged.

"Did Susan know?," Tony asked.

"No. At least I don't think so."

"Who ended the relationship?"

"I did. Lots going on at school, and I didn't want a violation of university sexual harassment policy used against me."

"How did Julia take it?"

"Fine. Well, not exactly fine. She was disappointed. But she's not a killer, if that's what you mean."

The three seasoned criminal investigators stared at each other, waiting for someone else to blink. Mark did not want to give up any more information than he had to. Camille and Tony did not want to tell Mark what they knew from cell phone records, or who they had already spoken to.

Camille ended the stalemate.

"Mr. Price, we would like to talk to your children, Archie and Katie. They might have something that could advance our investigation."

"They are still devastated. It would really shake them up."

"Mr. Price, it's possible that Archie was involved in drug purchases with someone other than Mullet. And, Katie was not at the team dinner for the entire evening last Monday night. The hosts said that she came briefly, but then left early."

That last sentence took Mark's breath away. Katie had not come home until well after Mark had left for the hospital.

"Give them a few days to calm down, and I will make them available for an interview. I want to be there, of course."

"Mr. Price, I don't think that would be a good idea. They might be influenced by your presence."

Mark was not going to be bullied on this point. Especially if Katie was hiding something. His first obligation was to his children.

"They are still under eighteen. Under state law, a parent has the right to be present whenever minors are interviewed by the police."

"That's true," Camille Jones replied. "But we are trying to do this the easiest way possible for the sake of the victim's children. If that is not possible, we could subpoena them to the grand jury and ask the court to appoint a *guardian ad litem* to represent them there rather than you."

"Why would any judge allow that?" Mark protested.

"I'm sure a judge would not want a possible suspect to enter the grand jury room to advise his own children."

That was it. The word "suspect" was all Mark had to hear before he stood up to leave.

"This interview is over. I'm getting a lawyer."

36

The Monday commute from Cambridge to Boston was heavily congested, even at 7:00 am. On Sunday afternoon Mark had called Finn Cummings in a panic and asked to see him as soon as possible. Finn told Mark to come to his office in the financial district at 8:00 am and he would squeeze in a meeting before he had to be in court. Mark made a point of getting downtown early, picking up a coffee from Dunkin Donuts for both of them as he trudged to Finn's small office on Franklin Street.

Theodore J. Cummings V was one of Mark's oldest and dearest friends. He was the fifth in a long line of Theodore Cummingses. Since the nicknames Ted, Ned, Ed and Theo were already taken by men further up in his paternal lineage, the only moniker left for Theodore was the street jargon for a five dollar bill. Everyone in the Boston legal community knew Theodore by his eponym "Finn." The only time Finn used his formal name was when he announced himself in court, and even then judges tended to look up from their benches with a smile.

Finn and Mark had worked together at the District Attorney's office in their late twenties and early thirties, forming a deep bond. They had served as groomsmen at each other's weddings, and were present for all the other major milestones in each other's lives. Mark thought that Finn was one of the finest criminal lawyers in town. They had always joked that if either of them ever got into legal trouble, they would look to the other for representation. Well, life had now found a way to call upon that promise.

Finn Cummings came from an extremely wealthy family in Winchester, Massachusetts. They had made their fortune in commercial real estate. Finn attended Brown University and Columbia Law School. With his intelligence and Ivy League connections, he could have worked at any major law firm in Boston or New York. But he was passionate about criminal justice and decided to start his career at the District Attorney's Office. Finn soon proved himself to be one of the smartest lawyers in the office, and a brilliant trial strategist.

Notwithstanding Finn's pedigree, he preferred domestic beer to bourbon, the Boston Bruins to the New England Patriots, and food trucks to fancy restaurants. He had light brown curly hair and a beard that could definitely use a trim. Stout and solid, Finn Cummings' appearance could fairly be described as "shabby." He had two or three wool blazers that he paired unthinkingly with black slacks almost every weekday. His fingertips were stained brown from nicotine.

Finn Cummings loved to tell and hear a good joke—the raunchier, the better. And he dropped the f-bomb frequently, both in his personal and his professional life. In short, he was a very down-to-earth person who found it easy to relate to the average man or woman. That's why juries loved him.

When it was time to leave government work, Finn chose to start his own criminal defense practice rather than go into the family business or put up with the administrative headaches of a large law firm. He rented an old, run-down office in the financial district that was constantly cluttered with papers, old coffee cups, and boxes of possible trial exhibits. But the physical disorder of the surroundings did not fool anyone—Finn had the facts of every case at his fingertips, and could recite case law from memory. Although he frequently hired bright young lawyers to work with him right out of law school, typically they cycled out after a few years, probably because Finn was an extremely hard task master and a perfectionist.

At 8:00 am precisely, Finn greeted Mark in the office lobby of "Theodore J. Cummings & Associates" and wrapped him up with a great big bear hug. Although the two had seen each other briefly at Susan's memorial service, Mark really hadn't had any time to process his wife's murder with his best friend. Finn expressed his fondness for Susan and his horror at her death. Then, he led Mark into a small conference room, where the two of them got right down to business.

Mark told Finn everything he knew about the DA's investigation to date—the wounds, the lack of physical evidence at the scene, the threatening notes left in his mailbox, Heidi Wilson, Julia Hoffman, Mullet, and his meetings with Tony Garcia. Mark also told Finn what was going on with him at school, including his removal from class and Brandon Gould's vendetta against him. Finn let him talk for almost twenty minutes before interrupting.

"Did they really use the word 'suspect'?"

"They said I couldn't go into the grand jury with my kids because I 'may' be a suspect."

"Okay, first and foremost, from this point on you do not talk to anybody from the prosecution team without me being present. You understand? Even if Garcia calls you on the phone or casually stops by your house. Nothing."

"I understand."

"I am surprised that Tony Garcia is taking the lead on this murder case. Weren't he and Susan very close in the old days?"

Mark paused for a moment before answering. He was not particularly comfortable talking about Susan's sexual history with Finn, but he also knew that it was not smart for a client to withhold information from his lawyer, especially when the stakes were so high.

> "Yes, they were close. In fact, when Susan and I took a break for four months or so in the early two thousands, they had a brief fling."

Finn chewed on that information for a few moments before responding.

> "I think we should keep that tidbit in our back pockets for now. We both know Tony. He likes us—or at least me. Our personal history together could help us to stay close to the investigation. If I try to get him removed from the case he may be replaced by someone not nearly as cooperative. If any of this goes to trial, I can always use that information on cross-examination to discredit his objectivity."

Finn stared at his friend sympathetically for a moment before probing another critical point.

> "Tell me what they know about Julia Hoffman."

Mark smiled. Like any good defense lawyer, Finn did not necessarily want to hear the complete truth from his client because it would ethically constrain what testimony he could present in court. He just wanted to hear what the government could prove.

> "I told them we had a brief relationship. I didn't go into details."

"Good. But you should assume by now that they have all your texts with Julia over the past few years. Is there anything in those texts that could incriminate you?"

"For adultery, but not for murder. I think it would embarrass me, but that's all. Susan and I had a fight a few days before her death and I texted Julia about it from a bar."

Finn scowled. He didn't like where this was heading.

"They may think you had a motive to kill Susan to continue your relationship with Julia. Or that she did. Or both of you. Don't talk to Julia from now on. They may have already interviewed her. She may be cooperating. Let us find out what she knows, if anything."

Hearing the word "us," Mark glanced through the glass partition of the conference room at Finn's unkept, empty offices, and wondered secretly how he was set for resources.

"Finn, who are you using for private investigators these days?"

"A couple different guys. Mostly retired cops. You may know some of them. Why?"

"The situation with Katie is very sensitive. I want to make sure you use somebody with a lot of discretion."

"Don't worry. I get it. Remember Paul Troy? He worked with us on a task force in the nineties. He recently retired from the Boston Police Department. Spends most of his days fishing in Megansett on the Cape. But he needs part-time work. I have used him on a few cases. I'll try to get him."

"I like Paul. He would be great," Mark agreed.

With that, Mark steered their conversation to his most immediate concern—the kids.

"Camille Jones is trying to talk to Archie and Katie. Says if she can't do it informally, she will subpoena them to the grand jury. Can she do that?"

"There is a privilege in Massachusetts that protects minors from having to testify against their parents at trial or in the grand jury. But it's complicated. There is an exception for when the victim of the crime is a family member. Arguably, that exception applies here. But, you are not yet a defendant and the crime did not occur inside the household, so I could convince the judge that the privilege still applies. In any event, I doubt Camille Jones is going to want to litigate that issue. It makes her office look bad, turning kids against their parents. I'll talk to her. Maybe when I press her, she'll agree to an informal interview with either you or me present."

Mark felt like there was so much left to discuss, but he knew that his friend had to be in court at 9:30 am. So he confronted the white elephant standing in the corner of the room.

"Finn, how could they possibly think I would kill Susan?"

"Maybe they don't. Maybe they are just trying to eliminate all possible alternatives. They don't have any eyewitnesses or a murder weapon. Remember the old expression, 'it's usually about love or money.' They are testing infidelity as a motive."

The old friends stared at each other in silence. Then Finn decided to give some advice that he knew would not be easy for Mark to hear:

"Mark, keeping ahead of these investigations requires me to know everything the government may know. So you have to tell me. Did you go anywhere that night between 6:00 and 8:00 pm?"

"No. Archie and I were at the house and I was cooking dinner."

"Was Archie with you the whole time?"

"After dinner, he went upstairs to do his homework."

"So your alibi is not rock solid."

Mark received this comment like a blow. Was Finn really suggesting that he could have done this?

"The facts are the facts," Mark almost whispered.

"Do you have a Nest camera on your front door?"

"Yea, why?"

"Do you think Garcia noticed it when he was at your house?"

"I don't know. Both times, it was dark, and it was late."

With that, Finn ran to grab his laptop from his desk and brought it back into the conference room.

"Log into your Nest account. I want to see the video from the night of Susan's murder?"

Together, Mark and Finn reviewed the Nest history for November 1st, now almost one-week old. The camera captured the front stoop and half of the walkway down to the drive. Archie arrived home from school at 4:17 pm. Mark and Katie arrived home from the field hockey game at 5:05 pm. Katie left for the Gottlieb's house at 6:15 pm. Mark left the house at 7:09 pm. The police arrived on Mark's doorstep at 8:04 pm. Katie returned home at 9:22 pm.

Wait, what? Mark and Finn stared at each other. Mark left the front door at 7:09 pm but did not return before the police arrived. How was that even possible?

Finn broke the silence.

"What the hell, Mark? You left at 7:09 pm. Where did you go?"

"I don't remember, Finn. I probably went to get something out of my car. Like my briefcase or my phone. Or the mail. I have no idea."

"Why isn't there an image of you coming back in?"

"Maybe I went through the back door on the patio. Sometimes I go around the house to check on things. Or to do something in the garden. I honestly can't remember!"

Mark retraced the chronology for Finn. Archie did the dishes and went upstairs. He was watching the news. The cops showed up.

"Mark, I have to go to court. This is what I want you to do. When you get home, detach your Nest camera from the door. Put it in an envelope with my name on it marked 'Confidential and Privileged' and bring it back to my office this afternoon. If I am not here, leave the envelope with my secretary."

"What will that accomplish? The police can still access the video digitally through the Nest web account."

"But they would have to get a search warrant to do that. And, they might not know enough to seek a search warrant if they do not know that you have a Nest camera to begin with. Our conversation today is privileged. So is your delivery of the camera to me."

Mark's head was swimming. He had been hoping he would leave today's meeting feeling better. Now he understood how quickly things could turn bad for him.

"I gotta' run," Finn concluded. "We'll meet again tomorrow. Get the Nest camera off your door right away. And, I want you to talk to Katie about where she was between 6:15 and 9:22 pm last Monday."

37

After dinner on Tuesday, Mark suggested to Katie that they take a run on the Charles River. "Just like old times. See if you can keep up with your old man." The field hockey coach had suspended practice for a few days this week due to midterms; post-season play would not start until next week. So Mark had a window of opportunity to talk to Katie and assess how she was holding up.

Father and daughter met at the front door, dressed like twins in running tights, light fleeces and baseball hats. Mark smiled to see Katie in a Williams College cap she had purchased at field hockey camp the prior summer. Maybe that dream still hadn't died.

The moon was bright and it was unseasonably warm for an early November evening. Crew teams were shouldering their sculls back into the boathouse as Mark and Katie traversed the running paths. The lights were glistening from the windows of the river houses at Harvard, casting a warming glow on the picturesque river.

Mark tried to keep the conversation light at first. He knew how tricky this territory would be.

"How did you feel going back to school yesterday?"

"Horrible. It felt like I had the same conversation over and over with all the kids and teachers. 'So Sorry! How are you doing? Do they have any suspects?' It was exhausting. I gave the same stupid answers five hundred times."

"I can keep you out of school for another couple of weeks if you want. Get your midterms postponed?"

"No, Dad. I need something to focus on right now. It will help me keep my mind off of Mom. It's just that I feel like I can't win. If I break down in tears they will gossip and say I'm a mess. If I hold it together, they'll say I'm an ice princess."

"I get it. How do you think Archie is doing?" Mark asked. "Have you seen him around school at all?"

"I worry about him the most. He doesn't have many friends at BB&N yet. If he was with his old friends at the public school he wouldn't feel so awkward."

Mark knew she was right. Wisdom from the mouths of babes. But he wasn't quite sure what to do about it. He would have to talk to Archie about moving back to Cambridge Rindge and Latin next semester.

They finished their run where the Anderson Memorial Bridge meets Memorial Drive. When they got tied up in foot traffic at the crossing signal, Mark pretended to be tired, telling Katie: "Let's walk up the hill." Mark was plenty fit for a man in his late forties. That simple pretense helped stretch out their time together.

As they began their climb up Kennedy Drive, Mark tested Katie's openness to further conversation. "How about an ice cream at J.P. Licks?" He was taking a big gamble here. Katie rarely ate junk food "in season." He was pleasantly surprised when she agreed.

Their favorite ice cream store still had its metal tables and chairs scattered on the sidewalk out front, notwithstanding the change in seasons. 'One positive remnant of Covid,' Mark thought to himself. The Prices purchased small scoops and took them outside, their anonymity protected by darkness and the quickly cooling autumn temperature.

Mark knew that the best way to start a difficult conversation was by deflection. So he put it on Finn.

"I went to see Finn Cummings today to talk about Mom's case."

"Why is Mr. Cummings involved in Mom's case?"

"He's not, yet. I just wanted to get some legal advice from him."

"What kind of legal advice?"

"Well, the investigators want to talk to you and Archie. I wanted Finn to advise me whether I should let them."

"What would we be able to tell them?"

"Well, I'm sure they want to talk to Archie about Mullet and whether there was anyone else that their group bought drugs from. They might also want to see if either of you know of any enemies the family might have had."

"Could Archie go to jail for buying drugs?"

"No, they are not looking to put Archie in jail. They just want to see who he knows."

"I'm happy to talk to them, Dad. But I don't know anything."

Mark tread cautiously now. He didn't want Katie to shut down on him.

"Katie, did you stay at the Gottlieb's for the whole team dinner last Monday?"

"I may have been in and out. It was like a buffet. Kids milling around."

"The state police talked to the Gottliebs. They said you came early and then left."

Katie stared at Mark in disbelief. He held her gaze until she broke the silence.

"What are they suggesting? Like, I killed my own mother?"

"Of course not, honey. It is just standard procedure for the police to try to account for everybody's whereabouts."

"Dad, I met Brian Garrity in Longfellow Park. It's a couple blocks from the Gottlieb's house. He texted me to come outside."

"Who is Brian Garrity?"

"Just a kid in my grade at school."

Mark suddenly felt both relieved and confused. What the heck was Katie doing with a boy in Longfellow Park?

"Are you dating this guy?"

"Dad, don't be weird. Nobody 'dates' in eleventh grade. He's just a boy I've been hanging out with."

"What were you doing with him in Longfellow Park?"

"Dad, gross. I am 100% not having that conversation with you. We were just lying on the grass talking and stuff."

"Did you go back to the Gottlieb's after the park?"

"No, Brian drove me home."

"What time?"

Even though Mark knew the answer, he had to test whether Katie was lying to him.

"9:15, 9:30."

Katie didn't seem to be hiding anything, And she hadn't shut him down yet. So Mark decided to inch just a little bit further out on the limb.

"Honey, I'm a little bit confused. Do you like Brian Garrity in a romantic way? Because before Mom died, she seemed to think that you might be gay. No judgment. We wouldn't care either way."

"What made Mom think that?" Small tears began to well up in Katie's eyes now.

"Apparently you sent some photos to somebody on your phone named 'Stickhandler.' Mom found out that it was Coach Wilson."

Katie stared at him in disbelief for a moment before jolting up from her seat and heading to the curb. Mark rushed after her down Mass. Avenue in the direction of the house. They walked in silence for a few moments. Katie was crying softly, and Mark put his arm around her shoulder.

"Dad, that was a total invasion of my privacy. Mom should never have looked at my phone," Katie hissed. "And then, playing private detective and getting the name of the caller was way over the top."

"Your Mom was worried about you. Scary things happen to teenage girls. You were a victim."

"The only thing I was a victim of was Mom's snooping. Here I am missing Mom and you're telling me something that makes me feel really angry at her. How am I supposed to process that?"

"I need to know, Katie. Did you ever have sex with Heidi Wilson?"

"No, Dad!" Katie insisted. "We made out a couple of times. That's it. At the beginning I thought she was really cool. I was just bi-curious. But I really didn't like it, and that was the end of it. I swear."

Mark was trying to be a good parent at the same time that he was trying to get information. He wanted Katie to know that it was okay to be confused about her sexuality.

"I wouldn't care if you did 'like it,' Katie. But assistant coaches shouldn't be messing around with their 17-year-old students. Who ended the relationship?"

"There was no '*relationship*,' Dad. We just stopped texting and hanging out with each other. That's it."

They were getting closer to the house now. Mark knew that if he didn't finish this conversation, he might not have another opportunity. So he turned Katie around to face him on the sidewalk and gave her a big hug.

"Katie, there is one other thing I haven't told you. Mom confronted Heidi Wilson and told her to stop seeing you and quit BB&N, or she would notify the headmaster and the police."

"How could you let her do that?" Katie whispered, nearly in shock.

"She did it without me knowing. She only told me afterwards."

"That's so fucked up. It's practically blackmail."

"Honey, I don't want you to remember your Mom that way. She was trying to protect you."

"Then why are you telling me?"

"I want to know whether you think there's any way that Heidi Wilson could have been involved in your mother's murder."

38

As soon as the house was quiet and everyone was asleep, Mark called Finn on his cell phone. Finn picked up right away.

"I talked to Katie. She was in Longfellow Park making out with some boy from her class named Brian Garrity."

"That's good news. I will have Paul Troy check it out. Where does the kid live?"

"Boston."

"Okay. Did you talk to her about Heidi Wilson?" Finn asked.

"Yes. She doesn't think Wilson would ever do such a thing. And she doesn't think Wilson has a motive. Apparently she was planning on taking this new job long before Susan got involved. Katie thinks it's a head coaching job."

"That tracks. Troy talked to the Headmaster. He said he served as a reference for her in the job search. He thinks Wilson was really psyched about the move."

"How did Troy explain those questions to the headmaster?"

"I don't ask Paul how he gets people to talk. He just does."

"I don't want the Headmaster thinking the Prices are suspects. People gossip."

"Let me worry about that."

"Did Paul make any progress at the law school?"

"Brandon Gould seems to be out. He was at the law review offices on the 1st all evening working on a manuscript. Fellow students will vouch for him. And, he has time stamps from the document to back him up. Plus, Paul says he definitely doesn't fit the profile. Apparently he's afraid of his own shadow."

"Did Paul talk to Julia Hoffman?"

"Not yet. She's ducking him. For all we know, Julia may be cooperating with the police and they have cautioned her about talking to anybody else."

"What's next?" Mark asked.

"I have a meeting with Camille Jones at the DA's office tomorrow afternoon. I need to try to figure out where they're going with this."

"Want me to come?" Mark offered.

"Absolutely not. I can't give them another free crack at you. I'll call you tomorrow night and tell you what happened."

"One more thing, Finn. It feels risky not having a security camera on my house, given that there may be a bullseye on my family. What should I do now that I have taken down the Nest?"

"Go ahead and subscribe to another service, like Ring or ADT. If the police ask, you can honestly tell them that you were trying to protect your family. Perfectly natural."

When Mark hung up, he stared across the empty family room of the quiet house and felt completely vulnerable. So much of his life had been premised on the search for order: his education, his career, his family. Now, he felt like matters had spun completely out of his control, and he had no idea how to deal with it.

39

Finn Cummings drove out to the District Attorney's Office at 2:00 pm on Wednesday. He was appreciative of Camille Jones' agreement to see him on short notice. They had known each other for a long time, and even tried cases against each other once Finn entered private practice. But Finn knew that Camille's flexibility was only partly due to professional courtesy. He could hear a hint of eagerness in Camille's voice when he called her on the phone. That suggested to him that the state's investigation was moving quickly.

Camille met Finn in the reception area and led him back to her office. As one of the most senior trial lawyers in the bureau, Camille's work area was huge by state standards, with large floor-to-ceiling windows and a comfortable seating area beyond her desk. Her walls we cluttered with tributes, awards and photographs with dignitaries. Camille had led a distinguished career. This case could be another jewel in her crown.

After exchanging pleasantries, Camille and Finn eyed each other warily. If the matter became oppositional, they both knew that the lawyer on the other side of the table would be a formidable adversary. That recognition fostered both respect and competitive energy. They behaved that day like a large fox and a coyote circling each other in a field; each respecting the other's territory but still trying to avoid any misstep that could be used to their disadvantage.

Camille made the first move:

"So, Mark Price has retained counsel. That's a very interesting development."

"You shouldn't draw any negative inference from that. I represent both Mark and his family. Given your request to talk to his children, Mark is doing what any devoted father would do. He wants to understand the family's legal rights."

"Are you going to make them available for an interview, or do I need to subpoena them to the grand jury?"

"No judge would allow that. They would assert their privilege and refuse to testify."

"The privilege doesn't apply when it's an 'intra-family crime.'"

"Now you're putting the cart before the horse. You have no evidence that it *was* an 'intra-family crime.'"

They stared at each other for a few moments, assessing next moves. Finn knew that Camille was not going to tell him all the facts in her possession. That would compromise the investigation. She was trying to gather evidence, not show her hand.

"The statute says a juvenile witness has to have a disinterested party present when they are interviewed by the police. Let us talk to the kids in an informal environment with another family member present. Maybe Aunt Anne."

Finn smiled. The government clearly knew that Susan's sister had moved into the house.

"What exactly are you looking for, Camille? That might help me advise my client on this issue."

"Among other things, I want to find out where everybody was that night. I also want to know what the conditions were inside the house. Whether there was any family discord."

"Camille, I am a little surprised that you are focusing on the family. After all, the Prices were sent two threatening letters. Have you found any prints or DNA on those?"

"Not yet."

"Maybe it wasn't even a targeted crime," Finn lobbed. "It was Halloween weekend. It could have been some gang thing, or teenaged wilding."

"We aren't discounting any possibility at this time, Finn. But the nature of the wounds and the lack of any robbery suggest to us some deep-seated animosity."

"Have you checked for similarities with the Danehey Park murder?"

"Finn, I'm not going to tell you every lead we're chasing. I assure you, our office is throwing all of its resources at this case."

They seemed to have reached an impasse. But Finn could not leave the meeting without casting his client in the most favorable possible light.

"Camille, my client has lost his wife of twenty years. He is devastated. He wants the crime solved as quickly as possible. And he has nothing to hide. But Mark has to protect his family. You need to understand that."

"I can't exclude the kids as perpetrators without at least talking to them."

"Wow. That's a ridiculous theory. But if you think for a moment that one of them may have been involved, that's even more reason I can't have you talk to them without parental supervision."

They stared at each other cautiously, each guarding their respective positions. Finn budged first.

"How about this: You give me a list of questions, and then I let you talk to the kids about those agreed-upon topics with both me and Anne present. I could propose that to Mark."

Camille paused. She did not like the idea of pre-approved questions, but it was better than nothing.

"Let me think about that for a day, Finn. In the meantime, run that proposal by Mark and see if he would agree to it. We can talk again tomorrow."

"Okay, Camille. But I want your assurance that until we have an agreement, no police officers will approach my clients for statements without me being present?"

"That's fine, Finn."

"Tony Garcia is leading this investigation. He's a great detective. But he has a prior relationship with the family."

"I get it. I'll talk to Tony."

Finn felt like he had gotten as far as he was going to get with Camille Jones today. He started to rise from his chair.

"There's one more thing, Finn. We'd like Mark's consent to search the house."

Finn was not surprised by this request. They were almost certainly looking for a murder weapon or blood-splattered clothing. But if they had probable cause to search the house, they would have already applied for a warrant with a judge. The fact that Camille was asking for consent suggested that she was short of having anything tangible on the Prices.

"I'm sorry, Camille, but I can't let you do that. Mark has nothing to hide of course, but there are privacy interests of the kids at stake. They are teenagers, after all. It's a tricky age. And Susan was a practicing lawyer with dozens of active clients. She doubtless has client files in the house that are confidential."

"Your choice, Finn. If we get a warrant, it's going to be ugly in front of the children. And in front of the media, for that matter. I can't control if television crews show up on the street."

"I'll take my chances, Camille. You don't have anything, because Mark Price hasn't done anything. And, if the state or local police do something to besmirch my client's reputation in this community, it will be your bar ticket on the line."

At that point, the fox and the coyote parted company.

40

Mark awoke early Friday morning to the sound of the newspaper being thrown against the front door. The television was still on, but muted. He had fallen asleep on the family room couch, as he had done so many times in the past few weeks. He was staying up too late, and drinking too much. An empty rocks glass and a bottle of bourbon rested on a pile of papers on the coffee table in front of him.

Mark stretched, scratched the three-day stubble on his face, and took stock of his surroundings. He had been restless last night because of a difficult conversation he had with Finn Cummings. Finn had called Mark on Thursday to fill him in on his conversation with Camille Jones. Unfortunately, there hadn't been too much information to report about the search for Susan's killer, which had greatly disappointed Mark. Finn had presented Mark with two difficult choices: whether to let the police interview the kids, and whether to let them search the house. Lawyers are usually adept about advising their clients of options, but often no better than ordinary folks about making difficult decisions themselves. As a husband, Mark wanted to assist the police in their search for Susan's killer, but as a father he was not sure he wanted to give the cops free access to his children. What if there was something going on in their lives that Mark did not know about? He had told

Finn he needed a day to think about it. That turned out to be a fateful decision.

At approximately 7:15 am, Mark heard a rustle in front of the house and the low murmur of voices. As he approached the front door, there was a thunderous bang and a deep voice screaming, "State Police, we have a search warrant!" Before Mark could even open the door, it was broken down with a battering ram. Shards of wood and glass flew everywhere. Mark was lucky to escape injury, but his bodily safety was only temporary. The first officer to enter the house—a 6' 4", 230-pound detective dressed in riot gear—threw him against the entry hallway and twisted his arm painfully behind his back. "Mr. Price, we have a warrant to search your home. We expect your cooperation. How many people are present in the house this morning?"

Mark hardly needed to answer that question. The sound of the door crashing and the commotion of a half-dozen officers entering the house had brought Anne, Katie and Archie to the top of the stairs. "What's happening? What's happening?" they were screaming. At the same time, officers were going from room to room, shouting "Clear, Clear." The bedlam lasted several minutes, until Mark felt a hand on a shoulder. He was turned around to face Tony Garcia.

> "Mark, we have a warrant to search the house. Please bring the family into the living room."

Mark went to the bottom of the stairs and directed everyone to join him downstairs. The house was still filled with the sounds of slamming doors, drawers and cabinets. The four of them gathered in the family room and sat down.

"Mark, are there any firearms in the house?"

"No."

Garcia looked at the kids and Aunt Anne. All of them shook their heads.

"We have a warrant to search the house and all electronics within the house. Where are your computers and your cell phones located?"

Mark waved his cell phone at Garcia, and the kids and Anne pointed upstairs. Katie and Anne were crying. Archie held his head in his hands. Mark was still half asleep, but just starting to get his wits about him.

"I have a right to see the warrant."

Garcia handed Mark a two-sided form issued by the Cambridge District Court.

"Where is the affidavit setting forth the probable cause?"

"The magistrate placed it under seal until the warrant is returned later today."

Mark scanned the document, trying to concentrate. His home address was listed on the front, as were "all persons present," "all computers, tablets, and cellphones on the premises," and all "appurtenances and curtilage" of the property. The document seemed to be in order. Mark had seen hundreds of them.
Mark suddenly realized he needed to contact Finn Cummings.

"I want to call my lawyer," Mark demanded.

Garcia knew better than to object. He led Mark to the back patio and handed him back his cell phone. There was frost on the garden, and the early morning temperature sent a chill down Mark's torso. He was still barefoot, dressed in running tights and an old tattered Princeton t-shirt. The patio furniture was damp, mildewed and scattered with leaves—he should have put it away weeks ago. Mark suddenly began to see himself as the police probably saw him—a man teetering on the edge.

Mark hobbled from foot to foot on the cold stones of the patio as he dialed Finn's number. His old friend picked up the phone on the second ring.

> "The police are here. They have a search warrant. Can you come as soon as possible?"

When Mark got off the phone he was led back to the family room by Tony Garcia. The family clustered around the coffee table as they listened to the shouts and clamor of officers going from room to room.

> "Do my kids really need to be subjected to this? They just lost their mother."

Garcia hadn't thought this through. The bottom floor was becoming very congested as officers scurried from room to room. A forensics van from the state crime lab had just shown up, and technicians wearing protective masks, gloves and smocks had entered the house.

> "We have their electronics and cell phones. As long as we can pat them down before they leave, your sister-in-law can take them to a neighbor's house."

Mark didn't want his children to witness the upheaval of their childhood home, but he also didn't want them to suffer the humiliation of being treated like criminals. Under the circumstances, he had little choice.

"Anne, would you please take them over to the Nicholson's house?"

Katie went to Mark's side and wrapped her arms around her father. "Dad, what's this about? How can they do this?" Mark held back tears as he uncurled his daughter from his shoulders and faced her. "It will be okay. Finn Cummings is on his way. Just go with Anne." At Garcia's instruction, a male and female officer came over to pat-frisk Anne, Katie and Archie before escorting them to the front door.

Mark spent the next several minutes curled up in an overstuffed chair in the family room, trying desperately to process what was going on. What did they expect to find? Who did they suspect? The shouting and banging made it difficult for him to focus.

Finn Cummings arrived at the house within twenty minutes. He immediately cornered Tony Garcia in the kitchen.

"Is my client under arrest?"

"Not at this moment."

"Did you talk to him?"

"All I did was serve the warrant."

"Camille Jones and I were hammering out an agreement. Why did you have to do this?"

"I don't know what agreement you think you had with the District Attorney. You'll have to bring that up with her."

"I want to see the affidavit."

"It's been sealed by the court. You're going to have to wait until the search is finished."

Garcia brushed past Finn Cummings, ordering him to stay out of the way or he could be locked up for obstruction.

Finn sat next to Mark and tried to console him. "It'll be alright. You have nothing to hide. They are just covering all bases." Under the circumstances, this was not even marginally consoling. Both of them knew that there must be something in the affidavit that cast suspicion on one of the Prices.

Finn reached Camille Jones on her cell phone, and Mark could hear only one side of a very heated exchange. "I thought you were going to wait to hear back from me?" "You never gave me a deadline of twenty-four hours!" "We had an agreement in principle!" "This is total bullshit and you know it!"

Mark needed to wake up and think clearly. When Garcia next walked through the family room, he asked Tony, "Is it okay if I make a pot of coffee?"

Tony nodded. "Stay in the kitchen."

Mark and Finn stood at the kitchen island and waited for coffee to percolate, whispering in conspiratorial silence. Mark felt like this whole thing could have been avoided but for an ambitious district attorney seeking to make a name for herself. Finn felt like he had somehow let Mark down. "They must really be worried about the destruction of evidence if they are moving this quickly."

Garcia came back into the kitchen.

"Mark, how long have you had a doorbell camera on the front door?"

"My client is not answering any questions," Finn interjected before Mark could speak.

"That's fine. We are taking the Ring camera off the door. It falls within the category of computing technology."

Finn did not raise any protest, knowing that it would yield them nothing.

The lab technicians seemed to be focusing on carpet fibers throughout the house, undoubtedly looking for traces of Susan's blood. At first Mark was confident that they would not find anything. But then his mind leapt to all sorts of wild speculation. When was the last time Susan cut her leg shaving? Or nicked her toe on a piece of glass in the kitchen?

For the next hour or so, Finn and Mark stood in the kitchen sipping coffee and trying to hold their heads high. It wasn't easy. Mark had practiced or taught criminal law for over thirty years, but he had never suffered the indignity of feeling like a suspect himself. The fact that the crime was so horrific and they were searching for the killer of his wife only made Mark's shame worse. Every time his gaze caught the eye of one of the investigators, Mark imagined what they must be thinking about him—and what *he* probably would have been thinking when he was in their shoes. Mark knew that the presumption of innocence was a legal fiction. It doesn't alter everyday human assumptions, particularly those of police officers.

About mid-morning, Mark and Finn saw through the kitchen's bay window that the State Police canine unit had arrived in the back yard. A rubber-gloved officer was holding a piece of clothing and crouching before a German Shepherd, letting it sniff and giving it instructions. Mark cringed when he recognized the blood-soaked blouse that Susan had been wearing the night of her murder. The dog proceeded to traverse the small back yard, sniffing and pausing, sniffing and pausing. The lot was smaller than a quarter acre, so it did not take long. Back by the property line, the canine sniffed among short evergreen hedges separating the Price's property from their neighbors. Suddenly the dog barked once and assumed an "alert" pose, lying on the ground with his front legs stretched toward its target and its tail in the air. The canine officer rushed to his side and used his radio to alert technicians from inside the house. Mark's heart stopped. He strained to see from the window exactly what was happening.

Within moments the investigators had dug a small hole and retrieved an object. One officer was taking photographs of the scene while a technician carefully placed that object in a large glassine evidence bag. Although struggling to see, Mark heard a transmission on Garcia's radio inside the house. "Lieutenant, we got a knife." Garcia went running out the back door. As the technician outside turned toward the window, Mark caught a glimpse of a bag containing a large, black-handled kitchen knife.

Garcia wasted no time. Within moments he was standing next to Mark in the kitchen, leaning him against the kitchen island, placing him in handcuffs, turning him around, and reading him his Miranda warnings. "You are under arrest for the murder of Susan Price." Mark saw a faint trace of emotion cross Garcia's face. He couldn't tell whether it was satisfaction or remorse.

Mark Price was led handcuffed to a state police cruiser parked in front of the house. The bright sun was in his eyes as he held up his hand to shield his vision. As he walked the short distance from the front door to the car, Mark saw a local WBZ-TV van with a video cameraman and reporter standing outside. The image they caught of Professor Mark Price—disheveled, disoriented, with unruly hair and a three-day growth of beard, wearing a tattered college t-shirt, became the prime feed for the afternoon and evening news in Boston and across the nation.

41

Mark remembered very little about the drive from Cambridge to the Middlesex House of Corrections in Billerica, twenty miles north of Boston. He recalled one of the officers violently pushing his head down into the backseat of the cruiser, ostensibly to protect him from injury. He remembered passing the Nicholson's house and thinking he saw Archie staring disconsolately out of the front bay window. Was Archie really there, or was Mark projecting his own fears? Mark remembered the officers in the front seat attempting to make small talk with him until they received a radio communication from Tony Garcia, shutting down all conversation with the prisoner. After that Mark just stared out of the window, silently watching the surroundings change from urban to suburban to rural. A curtain seemed to have fallen down on Mark's life, without the mercy of ending the play.

Processing at the House of Corrections was degrading and soulless. Mark's belongings were inventoried. He was strip searched and ordered to shower. He was handed pale yellow prison garb and slides for his feet. A male correctional officer watched him change. Someone barked instructions on meals, shower time and exercise time. He knew the drill—in his younger days, Mark had subjected defendants to the same processing; in more recent years, he had taken his students on tours of this very same prison. Still, it felt completely different when you were on the receiving end. Mark felt like he had not only been stripped of his clothes but also of his dignity.

He was assigned to a single cell rather than a dorm. Mark heard one of the C.O.s mutter to another, "Suicide risk." Mark was torn: he felt grateful to be alone, but amazed that anyone in their right mind could possibly think he would take his own life.

Mark's immediate worries were for Katie and Archie. He might have stopped being a husband with Susan's death last week, but he would never stop being a parent. What would their reactions be when they got back into the house this afternoon and saw their childhood home torn apart? What might they be thinking about him right now?

Mark's 10' by 5' cell was sparse and dank. Somehow it smelled of disinfectant and mold at the very same time. There was no window or natural light. A cot, toilet and sink were the only objects in the room. Mark sat on the cot, held his head in his hands, and tried to think. What evidence did the police possibly have against him that would permit them to get a search warrant? Who put that knife in his back yard? Why would anyone try to frame him?

The next four hours felt like four months. Mark was waiting for Finn to show up at the jail and explain what was going on. He had assumed Finn would be following right behind the transport cruiser. Mark felt frustrated with his friend and desperate for answers. The wait seemed interminable.

At about 4:30 pm, one of the C.O.s came to his cell and unlocked the sliding metal door. "Legal Visitor," he announced. Mark exhaled a huge sigh of relief. As he was shuffled, handcuffed, through the hallways and the dining hall, Mark endured the questioning stares of fellow prisoners. A glint of recognition showed in many sets of eyes, doubtless from the mid-day news that they had been watching in the common area. Several inmates murmured to each other and cocked their heads in his direction. Mark was not being paranoid. He felt certain that the media buzz about his arrest had found its way into the House of Corrections. Mark was now a celebrity of the sort he had never wished for or imagined.

Mark was led into a common visiting room and saw Finn sitting at a table in the corner. Since this was a jail and not a maximum security prison, they had the freedom of sitting near each other unobstructed by plexiglass security partitions. But they had to share the space with other inmates and their family members. Fortunately the room was fairly quiet, given the time of day.

Mark sat across from Finn and resisted the temptation to give him a hug. "No physical contact!" the C.O. had barked. Mark desperately craved some human interaction, but he did not want to start out on the wrong foot with the guards.

"What took you so long?" Mark asked.

"I went to the Cambridge District Court to get a copy of the warrant affidavit."

"Did you get it?"

"Yes, but it took a while. The State Police were not in any hurry to make a return. They left me cooling my heels. Finally, I had to make a stink and get the magistrate to intervene. Remember Rich Parsons? He is still there. Said he was sorry for your troubles."

Mark was in no mood for small talk. He reached across the table and took the papers from Finn.

"I had Rich make two copies," Finn explained. "Then I jumped right in the car to get over here. I haven't read it yet either."

The two of them read the document in silence. It wasn't long—three pages, single spaced. The background recounted Susan's injuries and the coroner's conclusions. The type of weapon used. The lack of defensive injuries or robbery. The opinion that it was a targeted crime. They both raced through those sections. The last four paragraphs focused on Mark. One recounted an interview with a neighbor who overheard Mark and Susan fighting on the patio approximately one week before the incident. One recounted texts between Mark and Julia Hoffman in the days preceding the murder. A third paragraph discussed an interview one of the cops had with a law student who overheard Julia and Mark fighting on the quad just days before Susan's death. The student remembered hearing a tearful Julia tell Mark, "You have to choose, Mark, you can't have both of us," or words to that effect. The fourth paragraph was a real punch in the gut. The signatory on the affidavit, none other than Tony Garcia, recounted waiting for Mark outside the hospital morgue on the night of Susan's murder. Garcia wrote that Mark Price was "unusually calm and composed" standing over his wife's body, and did "not shed any tears."

Shit. They looked up at each other at almost the same time. Mark felt like the evidence was powerful. Finn pulled him back from the brink of despair.

> "This is really thin. No eyewitnesses or surveillance cameras. No physical or forensic evidence. Motive only. People cheat. Couples have fights. I can get this warrant thrown out."

"But Finn, where did that knife come from?"

Finn chose his words carefully, mindful of the Nest camera in a sealed envelope back at his office.

"We will have to wait to see what forensic tests reveal on the knife. Do you know anybody who might have put it there?"

"Finn, someone is trying to frame me. I have no idea where that knife came from or how it got there. I promise you . . . ."

Finn cut Mark off. He had heard empty promises from clients before. Every criminal defendant had a reason to lie to their attorney when their back was up against a wall. Why should best friends be any different?

"Mark, they should have the initial results on the knife by the time of your arraignment. We will just have to see what it shows. Did you get a good look at the knife when they seized it? Did you recognize it?

"It looked like a standard kitchen carving knife to me."

"Do you know of any knives missing from your kitchen?"

"I don't think so. Susan bought a new knife set a couple weeks ago on-line. She said the old knives were getting dull. She threw them out."

"What days do you put out your trash?"

"Tuesday mornings."

Finn started to pack his briefcase.

"I have to find Paul Troy and have him do some leg work before the arraignment. I'll bring a suit and tie from your house. In the meantime, try to get some sleep. And focus on the positive. I'm sure Camille Jones is really disappointed that the police didn't find any bloody clothing or shoes at your house today. That leaves a lot of big holes in the government's case."

Mark didn't like the sound of those assurances. "Holes in the case" was defense code for "You may have done this, but the prosecutor can't prove it."

"Finn, I didn't kill Susan. You have to believe me."

42

Because Mark was arrested on a Friday, he had to wait until Monday morning for his arraignment. Over the weekend Mark was despondent that Anne did not bring the kids to visit him at the jail. He was allowed only a few phone calls per day, but with the exception of Finn, nobody picked up. Mark's isolation was driving him crazy. He had too much time to think, and too many conflicting ideas and theories racing around in his head.

Cambridge District Court was already buzzing at 8:00 am on Monday when the Sherriff's office transported Mark through the back garage. Television vans were parked all across the street and in several alleys surrounding the courthouse. The presiding judge needed space to accommodate the media and public spectators, so she switched arraignments that day to a larger jury room.

Finn arrived at about 9:00 am and visited Mark in the lock-up, explaining to him the plan for the day. Mark was not nearly as interested in the evidence as he was in his family. "Are Archie and Katie coming?" Mark asked. Mark was frightened at the prospect of having his children witness the spectacle. On the other hand, he wanted some assurance that they still loved him. Finn told Mark that he had convinced Anne to bring the kids, after considerable argument. "I told her the judge would want to see family support before making a bail decision. I told her it was not an option."

Mark knew that today's arraignment would be fairly pro forma. A judge in Massachusetts was not required to grant bail in a murder case, and few did. The arraignment was mostly an opportunity for the prosecutor to describe the crime and then posture for the public. But Finn would not let Mark's reputation be destroyed in public without some form of rebuttal. Mark knew that Finn would do an excellent job casting aspersions on the strength of the government's case, even if he didn't get him released on bail. It would be enough of a "win" for the defense if the judge and the public were left with lingering questions about whether the government had arrested the right guy.

Judge Veronica Lee took the bench at 9:45 am and had her clerk call the case. Mark was led into the dock in handcuffs and watched Finn and Camille Jones standing at tables side by side in front of the bench. Camille was dressed impeccably in a navy blue pant suit and white silk blouse. Tony Garcia sat next to her at counsel table, looking professional in a jacket and tie, but also seeming weary from lack of sleep.

Finn left his table and came to stand next to Mark in front of the dock, whispering words of encouragement. The clerk read the charge and Mark was asked how he pleaded. "Not guilty, your honor," Mark answered in a loud and steady voice. As Mark recited those critical words, he looked purposefully at Katie and Archie seated in the front row, managing to catch their gazes. Although his words did not falter, his face betrayed his anguish.

"Question of bail?" the judge asked the prosecutor.

At this point Camille Jones rose from her chair and proceeded to lay out the state's case against Mark. It was a powerful summary of the evidence, more akin to a closing argument than an arraignment. Camille knew that the reputation of her office was on the line, and that her visage would be broadcast across every major news outlet in New England throughout the day.

"Your honor, the Commonwealth requests that the defendant be held without bail."

Jones talked about the horrific nature of the crime, the loss of an esteemed member of the legal community, and the danger to the public. She then began to lay out the strength of the state's evidence against Mark, beginning with motive.

"The defendant's career was in a free fall. He was drinking too much. He knew that his wife had a five-million dollar life insurance policy through her prestigious law firm naming him as sole beneficiary. And, his lover of over one year—a teaching assistant—had just given him an ultimatum."

Camille Jones then recounted the search of the Price family home on Friday.

"The chief magistrate of this court issued a warrant last Friday giving the State Police authority to search the defendant's residence. Your honor has a copy of that warrant in front of you. During the search, a trained canine alerted to an area of upturned soil in the rear of the yard. Police recovered a kitchen knife with a four-inch handle and a six-inch blade buried in the back yard. The coroner has examined the knife and concluded that it is consistent with the type of weapon used to inflict the wounds that killed Susan Price. That knife has also been tested at the state police crime lab. It harbors the blood of the victim, Susan Price, and the fingerprints of her husband."

Jones reminded the court that a first degree murder conviction carries a mandatory sentence of life in prison without parole, and asked the judge to hold the defendant without bail "in light of the overwhelming risk of flight."

Now it was Finn's turn.

"Theodore Cummings for the Defendant, your honor. The Price family has deep roots in our community. My client is grieving the loss of his wife, whose accomplished life was cut far too short by this extreme act of violence. But in their rush to solve a horrific crime, the state has simply arrested the wrong man. Mark Price is anxious for the police to track down the real killer, who is out there and may pose a threat to his children."

"For a week prior to the crime, the Price family was receiving threatening letters from someone with evil intent. My client turned those letters over to the police, but Assistant District Attorney Jones neglected to even mention those letters or explain their significance in the summary she just gave you of the evidence. Ms. Jones also failed to mention that no bloodstained clothes, shoes or traces of Susan Price's blood were found anywhere in the Price home."

"My client was home cooking dinner for his children at the time of the attack, as their testimony and cell phone records will prove. He would not have had time to leave his house, walk to Harvard Square, commit this heinous crime, walk back, wash up, and dispose of evidence before the police arrived at his doorstep at 8:30 pm. It is simply impossible, and the government's account of the timeline does not make any sense."

"As for the knife found in the backyard of the Price property, the same person who sent the threatening letters is trying to frame my client. That area of the yard is accessible from the side of the house to anyone walking down the street. Ms. Jones says that preliminary reports indicate my client's fingerprints were on that knife. She has not yet shared with me any final report from the crime lab setting forth that expert analysis, as she is constitutionally required to do. But even if that fingerprint analysis is accurate, there is an obvious explanation that the state has simply chosen to ignore. Susan Price ordered a new set of kitchen knives on Amazon Prime ten days before her attack. I am passing to the clerk a copy of the computer record from the Price's Amazon account showing the knives that were ordered and delivered. The defense will prove that the Price family discarded the old knives in their trash during the last week of October. That is the very same week that the Prices received the first threatening letter. Someone retrieved one of those discarded knives, used it to murder Susan Price, and then buried the knife in the Price's backyard. A private detective employed by my law firm interviewed the Price's neighbors and discovered that the Clarks, who live right across the street from the Price's home, have a Nest doorbell camera that reaches the end of their driveway and the front of the Price's lot where their garbage barrels are placed. I am handing the clerk a copy of a still image from the Clark's doorbell camera on October 27th that shows a hooded man sifting through the Price's garbage."

"Your honor, in just three days my detective uncovered evidence that casts substantial doubt on the government's theory of this case, evidence that the state was simply too uninterested in or too harried to pursue. In their rush to judgment, the state has ignored alternative evidence and arrested the wrong person. I urge you to return Mark Price to his family while this investigation is sorted out."

When Finn was finished, Judge Lee seemed to hesitate on the bench. She was obviously stunned by the Amazon records and the Nest image before her. Judge Lee sat silently for several moments, scrutinizing the search warrant in her file. The judge had two forceful and accomplished advocates in front of her, both of whom had performed impressively. Yet she didn't have much room for discretion, given the severity of the charges.

> "I agree with Mr. Cummings that the search warrant affidavit is rather sparse in this case. There is not much beyond conjecture in the application to suggest that evidence would be found on Mr. Price's property. I am going to hold the defendant without bail. But instead of a pre-trial conference date, I am going to set this down for a motion to suppress in seven days. I'll hear legal arguments then on the validity of the search warrant."

> "That's fine, your honor. I expect that the grand jury will return an indictment before that date anyway," Jones replied.

> "Ms. Jones," the judge admonished, "if that is the case, I hope your office will make the grand jury aware of the highly relevant evidence Mr. Cummings has offered to the court today. The court will be in recess."

With that, the gallery rose and reporters began to call or text their producers. Mark Price was escorted out of the courtroom in handcuffs, without any opportunity to interact with his children.

Finn knew that he had at least scored a victory in front of the cameras by having the judge question the validity of the warrant. It may have been a pyrrhic victory, because once the grand jury returned an indictment, the case would start all over again in Superior Court, and the motion to suppress would be heard by another judge. Still, Finn had landed some major blows against the government in their opening skirmish, which was all that mattered right now in the court of public opinion.

As they walked out of the courtroom together, Camille Jones whispered to Finn, "We need to talk."

43

Forlorn in his sparse cell, Mark went over the events of that morning's arraignment. He was grateful to Finn for doing such an amazing job casting doubt on the government's case, and to Paul Troy for uncovering the Nest image from the Clark's front door. Still, Mark could not sort out why anyone would want to hurt him. Although he normally functioned like a rational person, Mark's thoughts and emotions during the past two days had been hopelessly tangled. He felt unmoored and increasingly unhinged.

Loneliness seemed to be Mark's most overpowering emotion right now. As an only child, he had no siblings to visit him in prison. He felt abandoned. Although it was small solace, Mark was grateful that his parents were not alive to witness the arraignment. Having prided themselves in Mark's accomplishments throughout his life—including graduating from Princeton and Harvard—he knew they would not have been able to bear the spectacle of today's downfall.

Mark was also extremely worried about Katie. She clearly felt confused about her sexual preferences. And she likely had been taken advantage of by an adult at school. Susan's unilateral decision to attempt to sweep that latter issue under the rug had backfired horribly, perhaps jeopardizing all of their safety. Mark was obsessing about ways to disentangle his own predicament from Katie's best interests and the school's need to know about Heidi Wilson. Right now, what he felt most acutely was the need to get home to protect his children.

Late in the afternoon, Mark was told that he had a visitor. His heart leapt as he was led down to the visitation room, hoping it would be Katie or Archie. As he entered the room he was slightly disappointed to see Finn Cummings waiting for him, briefcase on the table.

"I'm sorry I couldn't come down to the lock-up to talk to you right after the arraignment, Mark. I had another court appearance."

"I figured that was the case."

"I thought it went well. The media coverage has been surprisingly balanced. Camille wants to meet with me. That's a good sign. I am heading over there tomorrow morning."

"What's your theory, Finn?"

"We need to establish a connection between the person going through your trash and the person who left those letters in your mailbox. We're only halfway there. My working theory is that whoever left you the first letter stole the knife out of your trash barrel the same day. When he returned to leave the second letter the day of Susan's funeral, he planted the knife in your backyard. But the Clark's Nest camera image does not reach your mailbox. It only reaches to the side of your front yard where you put your garbage can. I am having Paul Troy go back to the Nicholson's house next door to the Clarks and try to get them to show him their doorbell camera footage. They refused when Paul first approached them, but I hope today's proceedings will convince them to cooperate."

"Olivia Nicholson was very close with Susan. I'm sure she is horrified by all of this."

"Well, we're working on it. If we can't get it from the Nicholsons, I will tell Camille to have Tony Garcia get it. But it's risky. Who knows what it might reveal?" Finn lingered on the last comment, watching Mark's expression carefully. "I would like to get there first."

The two friends stared at each other quietly, assessing each other's moods. Right now Mark felt abandoned by everyone in the world except Finn Cummings. He was Mark's life jacket in a shipwreck.

"Mark, do you need anything in here?" Finn asked quietly.

"I need to see my kids, Finn. They haven't been to visit. Anne isn't answering her phone."

"She's a tough nut, Mark. I've been begging her to bring them. I'll try again this afternoon. I get the sense that she actually thinks you could have done this. The revelation about Julia Hoffman did not help matters."

Mark cringed, realizing how the situation must look to Anne and probably others, including colleagues and former friends. He knew that he had betrayed his wife, but how could anyone possibly think that he could have killed her?

"On the subject of Julia," Finn added. "She wants to be added to your approved visitor list. She wants to come see you."

That was a shock to Mark. He assumed Julia had turned on him. Why would she want to talk?

"I'm not sure I could face her, Finn. It was a huge mistake in my life. What good could possibly come of it?"

"Well, so far she has refused to talk to Paul Troy. She may only be talking to the government. It might be good to open a line of communication to see what she would testify to at the grand jury and trial. Smoke her out."

"Yea, but she may be going right back to Tony Garcia and reporting whatever I say. This could be a set up. If I break down I might say something I regret."

"That's a risk. But if we are going to do it, we better strike while the iron is hot."

"I'll think about it, Finn. In the meantime, I need a laptop in here. Is that allowed? Is my laptop still at the house?"

"No, they seized it. I could get you a loaner from my office. Since you are essentially in solitary without access to jail computers, I might be able to convince the sheriff to allow you to have one—in aid of your defense. What do you need it for?"

"I helped Susan with her judicial application. We kept it on a common google drive. I want to see if there's anything on there that could provide a clue to motive. It just can't be a coincidence that this killing happened right during her confirmation hearings."

"I'll have Paul Troy deliver it as soon as possible. Along with some books and magazines to keep you occupied. Need anything else?"

"My kids, Finn. I need to see my kids."

44

On Tuesday morning, Finn Cummings arrived at the District Attorney's Office at 10:15 am. "Fashionably late," he thought to himself. Camille Jones had requested the meeting, which they had set for 10:00 am. She was anxious to see him for some reason. Leaving her cooling her heels for a few minutes might correct the imbalance of power in their relationship.

Camille led Finn back to her office. Finn was surprised to see Tony Garcia sitting in one of the guest chairs at Camille's small conference table. While it was not uncommon for a prosecutor to ask the chief detective on a case to sit in on meetings with defense counsel, Garcia's presence was disconcerting. Finn made a quick tactical decision not to request a private meeting with Camille. Perhaps he could learn something valuable from Tony.

Camille cut right to the chase. "What was that stunt yesterday with the garbage can photograph?" she asked, pushing a copy of the Clark's ringcam image across the table.

"That wasn't a stunt, Camille. The murder weapon was retrieved from the Price's garbage barrel."

"You don't know that, Finn. The image is grainy. We checked the full roll. You can't see what the person takes from the bin—if anything. Plus, homeless people sort through garbage barrels in Cambridge all the time."

"Do you think it's a coincidence that this person sorted through the Price's garbage can on the same day the first note was left in their mailbox?"

"Maybe. What's your theory?"

"Whoever left those notes is the killer. On the day he delivered the first note, he swiped a knife from the Price's garbage bin. On the day he delivered the second note, he buried the murder weapon in the Price's backyard, knowing everyone in the family was attending the memorial service."

"That's pretty farfetched."

"I don't have to convince the jury of anything, Camille. That's your burden. I just have to create reasonable doubt."

"Mark Price could have left the notes himself as a way to deflect attention."

"Now *that's* farfetched," Finn replied. "Have you gotten any fingerprints or DNA off the notes or envelopes?"

"No DNA. The sender did not lick the envelopes. Smart. Three sets of prints on the first letter, though. Mark, Susan, and the Dean of the Law School."

"They all read the letter."

"Finn, Mark Price had a powerful motive. And, he had a huge argument with his wife within days of the murder."

"C'mon Camille. Couples argue. I saw your police reports about the contents of Susan's text messages that day with Mark. Those will get kicked out of evidence under the spousal privilege. Husbands are allowed to have private conversations with their wives. So will the conversation on the patio that the neighbors allegedly overheard. The Prices had a legitimate expectation of privacy in that conversation as well. None of that is coming into evidence."

"Not if they were talking loudly enough for the neighbors to hear."

The two stared at each other silently for a few moments. It wasn't common for Finn to reveal his defense strategies so early in the game. But in this case he was truly convinced that the state had arrested the wrong guy. Now it was time for him to get Camille talking.

"I would think you and Tony would be doing everything in your power to chase down other leads. Have you looked at Heidi Wilson's bank accounts? She had a powerful motive."

"What are you suggesting? That she paid for a hit?"

"It looks like a hit to me. Targeted killing. Someone was following Susan from the subway. No robbery."

"Not only is Wilson's alibi solid, but there is no strange activity in her bank accounts."

"She may have been diddling a minor student. Why don't you bring her in under the computer sex image of a minor statute?"

"We don't have proof of that. You haven't let us talk to Katie."

Camille had a valid point. Now Finn needed to redirect the conversation.

"What about Carter Ellis?"

"*Judge* Carter Ellis? You can't be serious."

"Well, he had a motive. Gets him the appointment to the top Court. And you seem to have decided that motive was strong enough evidence to make an arrest of my client."

"Motive *and* a murder weapon with his prints on it," Camille snarked.

"Have you checked all the public video cameras in the square?" Finn asked.

"Nothing unusual."

"What about the neighbors' doorbell cameras? We got the Clark's. The Nicholsons won't talk to us."

"We have the Nicholson's. One of my detectives is going through it right now," Tony interjected. This was the first time he had spoken at the meeting other than to say hello. He was still somewhat smarting from the fact that Finn's private detective had beaten him to the Clark's doorbell video.

"You should focus on the dates the letters were delivered—October 27th and November 6th," Finn responded, mindful of Mark's unexplained departure from the house on the night of the murder.

"We'll focus on everything," replied Garcia, with a steely gaze fixed on Finn.

Finn knew they would be presenting this case to the grand jury in the next week, and probably indicting his client. He had to make sure they presented all evidence helpful to the defense.

> "If this case goes to trial, which I very much hope it does not, I am going to ask for an instruction allowing the jury to consider the failure of the police to pursue all possible leads."

Camille was familiar with the *Bowden* instruction and its implications for reasonable doubt in Massachusetts. She had lost cases before because the jury thought the police department had done a lousy job with the investigation. Nevertheless, she considered this to be just another example of Finn flexing his muscles in front of Garcia. Macho crap.

> "We've got our top talent on the case, Finn, and they are working around the clock."

Finn stared at Camille and thought about the search warrant. He had to make a split-second decision about whether to reveal what he knew about Tony's prior intimate relationship with Susan. It might help put Camille on the defensive and question whether she could win the case. It might also backfire and eliminate Finn's advantage of surprise. He decided to go for it.

> "There is one more thing, Camille. I think I have a strong motion to suppress the search in this case. The affidavit is weak, as Judge Lee even acknowledged. I will be cross-examining Tony about his application for the warrant."

"I would expect nothing less," Camille responded.

"And, I will bring out on cross-examination that your lead detective had a sexual relationship with the victim about nineteen years ago. I think that might influence the judge's determination of whether Lieutenant Garcia was fair and objective in crafting his search warrant application."

45

Tony Garcia's head was spinning as he left Camille Jones' office. He had just received a tongue lashing of the sort rarely experienced between prosecutors and police officers. "What were you thinking?" "Why am I just finding out about this now?" and "This could screw up our entire case!" were just three of the milder invectives she hurled at Tony as soon as Finn left the meeting. The rest of the tirade was interspersed with F-bombs, totally uncharacteristic of the normally poised prosecutor. Camille walked Tony to her door and said she would have to talk to the DA and Emily Cronin before she made any decisions about his continued involvement in the case.

The truth was, Tony did not know what he had been thinking. Shock at Susan's murder, a longing to play a role in finding her killer, and a desire for stature in the office clearly had clouded his judgment. But that was not all. Tony had gambled that nobody else knew about his affair with Susan, except perhaps her husband. And he had also miscalculated from the beginning the likelihood that Mark himself would end up being a realistic suspect. In retrospect, Tony realized how risky those two calculations had been.

Bedraggled, Tony plopped himself down beside Ray Jones in the junior detective's cubicle and asked him about the status of the neighborhood video footage.

"What did you get from the Nicholson's doorbell camera?"

"It doesn't reach the Price's driveway or their front door."

"Does is reach their mailbox?"

"Only a very limited view. But it does give us something," Ray replied.

"Let's take a look."

Ray took his boss through the video footage on October 27th and November 6th. The view of the Price's mailbox from the Nicholson's front door was distant and grainy. The mailbox only captured about a quarter of the frame. They scanned through the usual activity of pedestrians walking up and down the street, the mailman parking his truck, and cars traveling back and forth. Someone looking like Mark Price could be seen retrieving the mail in the evening, although those images were dark due to the faint light cast by the streetlights. But in midafternoon on both days, a pedestrian could be observed stopping briefly in front of the Price's mailbox. Ray zoomed in on the images. It appeared to be a male, trim, fairly tall. On both dates the suspect was wearing a baseball cap and a sweatshirt with an upraised hood that obscured his face. It could be Mark Price. Or it couldn't.

"Print those," Garcia ordered. "Now take me to the Clark's camera on October 27th at the garbage can."

Ray called up the Clark's video roll on his computer and reversed the footage to October 27th. The person sorting through the Price's garbage can was also wearing a baseball cap and an upraised hoodie. There was no clear view of the face. But the person was of the same general size and build as the image from the Nicholson's camera.

The detectives stared at each other silently for several moments, each wondering the same thing. "Did we jump too quickly on this case?"

Ray finally broke the tension. "Does that look like the same guy to you?"

> "Could be. Different camera angle so it is hard to tell. The hoodie looks the same on October 27th in both images. Medium to light gray. But on November 6th it looks black."

> "What should we do now?"

> "Print all these and get them up to Camille ASAP. She's going to have to disclose the Nicholson's footage to the defense.

As Garcia got up to leave Ray's cubicle, he had one more thought.

> "Did you subpoena the footage from the Price's doorbell camera?"

> "Yea, nothing there. The Ring camera wasn't installed until after the murder."

46

Mark finally received a visit from Archie and Katie on Wednesday. He knew Finn had worked hard to make this happen. But it couldn't have come soon enough. Mark was desperate to know how they were doing and what they were feeling.

When Mark entered the visitation room, his children were seated at a corner table waiting for him. Anne was standing by the doorway, her folded arms and her stance signaling stone cold disapproval. Clearly she did not want to have any contact with Mark herself. Anne must have felt obligated to be present to protect the kids. So Mark ignored her and went straight to Katie and Archie. Mark could see the hesitation in their faces. As they stood up, Mark gave each of them a great big hug. He let the warmth of their embraces wash over him like a shower, knowing that he would need to remember those brief connections to get him through the tough days ahead. Usually there was no physical contact allowed between prisoners and visitors, but luckily the correctional officer who had escorted Mark down today looked the other way. Maybe he was a father himself.

Mark had been rehearsing what he wanted to say to Katie and Archie for five days. He had promised himself that he would stay strong, for their sakes. But as soon as Mark sat down and opened his mouth, he began to choke up.

"I know you have lots of questions. What matters most to me right now is that you understand one thing: I could never have killed your mother. What you heard in that courtroom about fights and ultimatums was not a true picture of our life together. We loved each other. Sure, we had disagreements. All couples do. But we loved each other, and above all, we loved you two more than anything else. You know me. I would never have done something like this to my family. Finn is helping me prove that they arrested the wrong guy. But what matters most to me right now—more than getting out of here, more than catching your mother's killer—is that both of you believe in me. I couldn't go on if the two of you didn't believe in me."

Archie was the first of the two kids to speak.

"Is it true what they said—that you were having an affair? Did Mom find out?"

"I was in a brief relationship with a law student," Mark started. "I made a huge mistake, Archie. I was weak, and for that I am very sorry. Someday you and Katie may understand. Maybe you will even be able to forgive me. But there are no excuses. What I did was wrong, and I broke my promise of fidelity to your mother. Your Mom never found out, thankfully. The relationship was over before she was killed."

"Were you in love with her?" Katie asked, her eyes glistening with tears.

"No, Katie. It was just a physical attraction. I was flattered by her attention. I've always loved your Mom."

"Dad, the news is making it look like this is a slam dunk case," Archie interjected. "The murder weapon was buried in our back yard. It has your fingerprints on it."

"Archie, I didn't put it there. You have to believe that. Someone is trying to frame me."

"Why would anyone do that?" Katie pressed.

"I don't know sweetheart. That's what we're trying to figure out. Finn is going to get to the bottom of this. It has to be the same person who left those threatening letters in our mailbox."

The kids' hesitance at the beginning of their meeting had begun to soften slightly. Mark could see it in their faces and their change of posture. Seeing their father and hearing his voice had reminded them of the person he actually was, rather than the monster being portrayed in the media.

"Have you gone to school this week?" Mark asked.

"Aunt Anne was going to keep us home all week. But we got bored and decided to go today. It was awful," Archie complained. "Everyone was staring at me."

"You can stay home until we sort this out," Mark offered. "The teachers will send you homework."

"Dad, what's going to happen to us?" Katie almost whispered. "We just lost Mom. We can't lose you too."

Mark was fighting back tears now. As uncertain as he was about his own future, he hated to see his children feeling vulnerable. Like most parents, he had always put their safety as a top priority.

"We're going to get through this, I promise you. You have to stay confident."

The C.O. came over to escort Mark back to his cell. Anne was still standing by the visitor's entrance, pretending not to listen, but nonetheless keeping a close eye on her brother-in-law seated less than twenty feet away. Katie and Archie gave their father a final hug and started toward the door. Katie held back for just a second until she was sure her brother was out of earshot.

"Dad, I feel bad," Katie croaked. "I lied to you about something the other night. I thought you and Mr. Cummings should know in case it has anything to do with Mom's murder. I don't know if it matters, but I felt guilty not telling you the whole truth on our run."

"It's okay, honey. It's okay. What is it?"

"I did have sex with Heidi Wilson."

47

Getting a laptop in jail was the beginning of salvation for Mark. He knew Finn had pulled a lot of strings to make it happen—even threatening to sue the sheriff for violation of Mark's right to mount a defense. But Mark didn't care what it took—he was happy to have a lifeline to the real world, and a way to pour himself into the hard work of proving his innocence.

Mark had told Finn over the phone last night about his conversation with Katie and her sexual relationship with Heidi Wilson. Paul Troy was going to continue to track down that angle. Mark still found it hard to believe that Wilson was capable of murder, or that she could possibly have felt cornered enough to go to such extremes.

Mark was convinced that Susan's murder must have had something to do with her nomination to the high court. The timing just couldn't have been a coincidence. So Mark spent hours Thursday reviewing Susan's judicial application, which she had asked him to review and comment on just two months prior to her death. They had shared it on Google Drive, and it comprised over one hundred pages. Maybe something in her prior cases or work references would reveal a motive.

Earlier in the week, when Mark had nothing to occupy himself, time had passed extremely slowly. Minutes had seemed like days. Now that Mark had a computer and a purpose, he felt energized. The day flew by. He felt like a lawyer again for the first time in a very long while.

Mark pored over the high-profile cases Susan had handled as a prosecutor, doing research on the internet to see if any of those defendants were out on parole and where they were living. He looked at her pending matter list at the law firm, searching for a disgruntled client or opposing counsel. He scrutinized her references and did media research on them to see if anyone could have held a secret grudge.

Late in the day, Mark was staring at Susan's list of trials while she was a partner at Wright & Graham, and something struck him. Something was missing. Mark remembered the case of Anton Jenkins, a defendant who was charged with murder. Susan had taken the case pro bono at the law firm as a way to keep her skills up. The kids had been young—maybe only five and three years old. Mark remembered that the lead-up to the trial had been extremely stressful for Susan, requiring Mark to take on close to 100% of household responsibilities for weeks. After jury selection and on the third day of trial, Jenkins had decided to plead guilty to manslaughter, which gave him at least a chance of parole. But the Jenkins case was missing from Susan's judicial application submitted to the Governor.

Mark went back to the version history of the Google document. Two weeks prior to being finalized, the Jenkins case was listed on Susan's form. Susan described it as "Defendant had prior convictions for drug dealing and weapons. Accused of robbing a stash house for cocaine. During escape from robbery, shots were fired. Bystander in back yard of apartment complex was hit and killed. Defendant was charged with first-degree murder and pleaded guilty to manslaughter."

Why had Susan removed the Jenkins matter from her judicial application? It had been a notable case in the media that winter—Jenkins was portrayed as a vicious gang banger. The public defender's office had asked Susan to take the case as a way to challenge the state's felony-murder rule, which made every killing happening during the course of a violent felony a murder, even if it was accidental. What had prompted Susan to omit this case?

That evening, Mark reached Finn on the telephone. Finn was excited to hear his voice. Even jubilant.

"I was going to come see you first thing tomorrow morning. I think I have some very good news," Finn started.

"Me too," Mark said. "I may have found something."

"You go first," Finn demurred.

"Have Paul Troy look into the case of Anton Jenkins. Boston homicide case, around 2012. Susan defended the guy. But at the last moment, she left the case off of her judicial application. I can't understand why."

"Okay, I will. But I have better news. I may be able to get you out."

"What?" Mark almost screamed, loud enough that the C.O. standing at the end of the telephone stalls turned and stared.

"I got Camille Jones between a rock and a hard place. She gave me a packet of reports in discovery yesterday. Photo cam shots of a guy fishing out of your garbage and hovering around your mailbox look like they could be the same guy. Seemed to be wearing the same sweatshirt that day. Camille knows that she has to present that evidence to the grand jury if she chooses to indict. But she wants more time to investigate. She's faced with a court date in District Court on Monday for the search warrant hearing. She doesn't want to go forward before Judge Lee. She asked me to agree to a continuance."

"What did you say?"

"I told her I would agree to a two-week continuance in district court if she agreed to let you out on bail while we sort out new information."

"Would she really do that?" Mark almost whispered. He was hesitant to get his hopes up.

"She will if she wants to avoid having me crucify Tony Garcia on cross-examination. Get this. Paul Troy went to the security office at Verizon to get print outs of the numbers reached on all of your family's calls. He talked to a former friend on the force who now works for Verizon. That friend told him it was the second time someone had pulled Katie's call logs. Tony Garcia from the state police asked for Katie's records two weeks before Susan was murdered. The guy did Tony a favor and gave them to him without a subpoena."

Mark was speechless. His mind raced to sort through all of the implications of that. Susan didn't use a private investigator at the firm to get to the bottom of Katie's sext messages. She used Tony Garcia, which meant that she had lied to him. Why? It also meant that she had been in contact with Tony. For how long?

"How did you leave it with Camille?" Mark finally asked.

"She's going to talk to the DA and see if he will agree to a bail release on Monday. She wants to avoid a hearing right now at all costs."

48

Souza-Baranowski State Prison lies approximately sixty miles northwest of Boston in Lancaster, Massachusetts. As a maximum security facility it houses the state's most dangerous prisoners—lifers and near lifers. Because Anton Jenkins was serving a twenty-year sentence for manslaughter and had a prior history of violent felonies, he was sent to Lancaster.

Paul Troy drove out to see Jenkins on Friday. It was a long drive from Cape Cod; most true locals from the Cape hated traveling over the bridge if they could possibly avoid it. Troy had been doing a lot of legwork for Finn Cummings since the Price case had started. He knew Finn would reimburse him for the cost of a hotel if he had to stay over. More importantly, Troy was kind of enjoying being back in the fray of detective work. His wife had died of pancreatic cancer just fifteen months after he had retired from the Boston Police Department over two years ago. His kids lived out of state. It was just him, his dog, and his small fishing boat down on the Cape. The Price case had made Troy feel somewhat alive again.

Troy was taking a gamble that Jenkins would see him. But his instincts told him he probably would. Jenkins had been assigned to a prison with little programing for inmates. His liberty was severely curtailed—so-called "hard time." Jenkins was serving this time far from his family members, which made it difficult for them to visit. Jenkins was likely mad at the world and at the government in particular. Having someone new to bitch at would likely be the highlight of Jenkins' week.

Troy had interviewed hundreds of inmates during his career as a police officer. Many wanted to cut a deal to shorten their time by supplying tips on cold cases. Some wanted to rat out fellow inmates by giving information about things going on in the jail. Troy approached each of these convicts with a weathered sense of skepticism. Many would sell out their own mothers if it would lighten their loads.

Jenkins entered the visitation cubicle and sat down behind the plexiglass separating him from Troy. Jenkins appeared thinner and older than the photographs of him that appeared in the police file almost ten years ago. The intervening decade had not been kind to him.

"You Boston Police? I don't recognize you?" Jenkins began.

"Retired. I wasn't on your case."

"What are you doing here then?"

"I'm a private detective now. Working for the family of Susan Price. She was murdered. You remember her?" Troy asked.

"Sure, I remember her. She defended me. Her hit has been all over the television."

Troy was happy that Jenkins was talking. He asked him some general questions about his classification and parole status just to keep the conversation going.

"Been denied parole twice so far. Same bullshit about too many disciplinary infractions. Guy's gotta protect himself in here."

"What's your wrap date?"

"2029."

"Can you tell me a little bit about your manslaughter conviction?"

"What does that have to do with my attorney's murder?"

"I don't know if it does. We are looking into some of her prior cases to see if there may be any connection."

"I got no motive, man. I liked the lady."

"Why did you plead guilty?"

"They were offering me a manslaughter deal. If I went ahead with the trial I could have been hooked for murder one. She laid the options out for me. Explained the law. Even if I wasn't the shooter, I could have gone down for murder if I was an accomplice to a felony."

"Were you the shooter?" Troy asked gently.

"No, man. Shot must have come from some guys chasing us out of the apartment."

"What did your attorney want you to do?"

"She was all revved up for trial. Willing to go for it. She thought she could win on appeal even if she didn't win before the jury. I wasn't willing to chance it."

"Do you think she did a good job for you?" Troy asked.

"I told you, man. I got no problem with how she handled my case. What she did after that was fucked, though. 100%."

"What do you mean, 'what she did after that'?"

"I told her I had no problem with pleading guilty to manslaughter. I had blood on my hands anyway for a stabbing that happened on Humboldt Avenue two years before. Cops never arrested me for that. Arrested the wrong guy that looked like me—Darius Brown. Dude I sometimes ran with in the neighborhood. I told Attorney Price that Brown didn't do it. I thought she would do something to help him out. But she never did."

"Where did Brown serve his time?"

"Here."

"Still in?"

"No, he got out in September."

Troy was anxious to get back to his car and contact Finn Cummings. But first he needed Jenkins' help with one more thing.

"Anton, are you okay with us looking at your file at Susan Price's law firm?"

"I got no problems with that, man. It ain't my property."

"Well, actually it is. You were her client. You get to decide if anyone can see confidential information in her files. Her law firm can't turn it over to us without your permission."

"If I do this and it helps the cops find her killer, will you tell the prosecutor that I cooperated? Help me with my next parole hearing?"

"I promise."

Before he left Souza-Baranowski that day, Troy hastily wrote out an affidavit waiving the attorney-client privilege, which Jenkins signed.

49

Tony Garcia was in the office over the weekend getting ready for the motion to suppress hearing in District Court. At about 11:00 am he was summoned into a meeting with Captain Cronin. She wasn't usually in her office on Saturdays, so he knew this wasn't a good sign. He walked down the hallway and knocked softly on her door.

"C'mon in."

Tony entered to see Camille Jones sitting on the opposite side of Emily's desk. So, this was his moment of reckoning. He had been dreading it for days. Tony sat down in the empty seat next to Camille and waited nervously for his execution.

"Captain, I just want to...."

"Wait a minute Tony. I'll give you a moment to explain, if there is any explanation. But first the DA's office has something to say."

"Tony, this is the biggest case our office has handled in years, perhaps decades," Camille began. "All eyes are on us. You were assigned to the case because you're the best detective in the office. I was looking forward to working with you on it."

"Camille, I..."

"Hear me out, Tony. You normally have the best judgment and the best instincts of any cop in this office. But you really blew it on this one. I don't know how you could have taken the assignment without telling either me or Emily about your romantic involvement with the victim."

"It was almost twenty years ago," Tony protested. "Captain, you need to understand," he said, turning to Emily. "I never thought it would come out. On the night of the killing, I didn't think that Susan's husband would be a suspect."

"Exactly, Tony. You didn't think," Camille continued. "And now, you have put this office and this prosecution in incredible jeopardy."

"I fucked up," Tony began. "I...."

"Hold on, Tony. We understand your personal life has been stressful lately. We get that. It's no excuse, but it might help explain your bad decision here. Emily and I have been discussing how to staff the case going forward. You have conducted the witness interviews, you have handled the physical evidence, you have transported material to the crime lab. Your signature is on lots of the subpoenas. If we could get you out of the case entirely, we would. But we can't. Your fingerprints are all over it. You may have to be a witness at trial, even if we don't want you to be. So, we're going to keep you on the case. But from here on out, you don't take a piss without the direct involvement of Ray Johnson standing over your shoulder. He is going to be your partner on the case, and we want him involved in everything you do, so we can rely on his testimony if necessary. You are both going to report directly to Emily. She's also going to be involved on a day-to-day basis. Do you understand?"

"I get it. Thank you."

"No time for gratitude," Camille interjected. "We've got looming deadlines, and we don't know whether we've got the right guy in custody. We need to figure out if that shadowy presence at the mailbox is something real. I can't indict the matter without a theory of how those letters fit into the case—if at all."

"What are we going to do with the motion to suppress on Monday?" Tony asked.

"I can't run the risk that Judge Lee will suppress the knife. The DA has given me permission to move for a continuance and agree to let Price out on bail, with strict conditions. Cummings is on board. That will buy us some time, but it'll probably only be a week or two. We need to lock down all the loose ends on this case."

Tony sat in Captain Cronin's office for another hour, the three of them strategizing on what leads they needed to track down and what evidence remained to be gathered for the grand jury.

When he got back to his desk, the message light on Tony's phone was flashing. It was Finn Cummings. "Tony, Paul Troy and I want to come see you. As soon as possible."

50

Paul Troy sat in the small conference room of the Cummings law offices with a mound of paper in front of him. He and Finn had been at it all day Saturday, reviewing files, going over timelines, and hashing and rehashing theories. Finn was one of the smartest lawyers Troy had ever known. And he was tireless, as the full ashtrays and empty coffee cups scattered around the room attested.

Troy had told Cummings about his meeting with Anton Jenkins via telephone on the way home from the jail yesterday afternoon. Finn suggested an all-day strategy session Saturday. Troy used the remaining time Friday to pull the publicly available material on Darius Brown, talk to his parole officer, and get Anton Jenkins' file from the records department at Wright & Graham. He accomplished all this in three hours, before crashing for the night at a cheap hotel in Revere. It was fun to be back in the game.

Finn was intrigued by Jenkins' claim that Brown had gone down for a violent crime that in fact Jenkins had committed.

> "Why would Jenkins have told Susan that? It was an unrelated case? Why admit an uncharged crime to your own lawyer?"

> "Jenkins is a talker. And a braggart."

"What did he expect Susan to do with the information? She couldn't reveal it to Brown or the police without violating attorney-client privilege," Finn explained, half to himself.

"I think Jenkins hoped that if he told Susan, she could do something to help Brown on her own. Like represent him on appeal or something. Or plead with the DA."

"Do Susan's notes in the Jenkins file corroborate that Jenkins made the confession?" Finn asked.

Troy pushed a yellow legal pad across the table toward Finn. It contained Susan's handwritten notes from her meeting with Jenkins the day of his guilty plea.

"Explained felony murder rule to client. Defendant says he is willing to take the deal to manslaughter, even though he was not the shooter. Defendant feels guilty about a prior armed assault where he escaped charging. Darius Brown, convicted in 2011," Finn read aloud.

"Susan's notes do not specifically say that Defendant admitted to the crime, but they strongly hint at it," Troy added. "That backs up Jenkins' version of events."

"Susan was in a jam," Finn explained. "That conversation was privileged. She could not have revealed her client's confession to another crime under the attorney ethical rules unless she had her client's permission. Does the file indicate that she sought Jenkins' permission to disclose?"

"No. Her notes end there. The next annotation is, 'Change of plea, manslaughter, June 14, 2012.'"

Finn was perplexed. He pulled a copy of the attorney ethical rules down from his bookshelf. None of the exceptions to the duty of confidentiality under Rule 1.6 applied. In 2015, the Massachusetts High Court had added an option to disclose confidential communications "to the extent the lawyer reasonably believes that disclosure is necessary to prevent the wrongful execution or incarceration of another." But that exception to the duty of confidentiality did not exist when Susan had handled the Jenkins matter. Susan would have had to seek Jenkins' permission to disclose her conversation with him. Why had she not asked for it?

"Did Brown serve time with Jenkins at Souza-Baranowski?" Finn asked.

"They were in the P-Wing together for eight months before Brown was paroled," Troy replied.

"We need to get a meeting with Tony Garcia."

51

The pace of business was brisk on Monday morning in Cambridge District Court. The police had arrested thirty people over the weekend, so Judge Veronica Lee had lots of arraignments to clear off her docket between 9:30 and 11:00 am, when she had scheduled a motion to suppress hearing in the Mark Price murder case.

Although it was difficult to see under her traditional black robe, Judge Lee had chosen an impeccable blue suit and silk blouse for the day's main event. She had hated the way she looked on television last week covering Price's arraignment. Even her husband and kids teased her about it. Today, she made sure she was perfectly polished and coifed for the media, who had started to set up their cameras as soon as the doors were unlocked by the court officers.

Judge Lee anticipated that the day's events would be anticlimactic. Usually the prosecutor indicted major felony cases and transferred them to Superior Court before the second scheduled date in the lower courts. She fully expected that the Assistant District Attorney would announce in court that the defendant had been indicted and move to dismiss the district court complaint, making the motion to suppress argument in the lower court moot. Still, she wanted to look her best. Judges were people too.

The courtroom clerk called the Price case at 11:05 am. Mark

was led into the courtroom in handcuffs. Finn Cummings and Camille Jones made their way up to the front of the courtroom, pushing through a crowd of onlookers to sit at their respective tables. Judge Lee eyed the defendant with reserve and a little bit of pity. His physical appearance had changed dramatically in just seven days. "Oh how the mighty had fallen," she thought to herself. Mark appeared pale, gaunt, and disheveled. His new beard growth was coming in straggly and gray. Even his weight and his muscle tone had diminished. Jail can do that to a person. Judge Lee suddenly had a pang of guilt. Undoubtedly she noticed Mark's change in appearance because he was white and privileged. How many defendants appeared before her on a daily basis where she failed to truly see them?

Composing herself, Judge Lee gaveled the court into session and quieted the crowd.

> "Ms. Jones, are you prepared to go forward on today's motion to suppress hearing?" the judge asked, relatively certain of the answer.

> "No, I'm not, your honor. The Commonwealth is still presenting this case to the grand jury. We have run into some complications. The government would request a continuance for one week."

Judge Lee raised her eyebrows and glowered at the prosecutor. That was a curveball she had not expected.

> "That's highly unusual, Ms. Jones. The defendant is being held without bail. What sort of complications?"

Finn Cummings stood up to save Camille. Neither the prosecutor nor the defense wanted to disclose in front of the media all the investigative twists and turns in the case.

"Your honor, the defendant doesn't object to the continuance. While we were looking forward to litigating today the sufficiency of that very bare-bones search warrant application, the defendant is prepared to put the matter over for one week, provided that the defendant is released on conditions of bail."

Judge Lee turned to the prosecutor, certain that she wouldn't agree to any such a thing. Letting murder suspects out on bail was practically unheard of.

"Your honor, the Commonwealth believes that a $500,000 bond will be sufficient to secure the defendant's attendance, given his deep roots in the community. We have no objection provided the defendant is willing to wear an ankle monitor and remain in his home during evening hours."

At this point it was apparent to the judge that the parties had worked out an inside deal. Something was up, and the judge was being treated like a potted plant inside her own courtroom. That might antagonize some judges. But it often happened with defendants who were cooperating with the government. Judge Lee knew and trusted Camille Jones. The district attorney would not let a suspected murderer out on bail unless she had a really good reason for doing it. So Judge Lee acceded to the request, not wanting to screw up the government's investigation.

"This matter will be put over to the third Monday in November for a motion to suppress hearing. The defendant's bail terms are changed to a $500,000 bond and home monitoring. The matter is adjourned."

When the judge's gavel came down, the court erupted in pandemonium. Reporters were calling their editors and producers. Some were reaching over the bar to seek an interview with Camille Jones. Suddenly, a court officer approached the defense table and unlocked Mark's handcuffs. Mark couldn't believe he was free, at least temporarily. He felt elated and disoriented at the very same time. Everything was happening so quickly.

Katie and Archie approached their father and gave him big bear hugs. Katie had tears in her eyes. Neither of the kids seemed at all tentative, like when they met him just days before in the jail. Both were beaming with joy at the prospect of having their father home. Mark felt reassured; the warmth of their love flowed through his body like a current.

Finn was packing his briefcase when Tony Garcia approached the defense table.

"How about we meet in my office in twenty minutes?" Tony asked.

"We'll see you there," Finn replied.

52

Mark breezed through the probation department and was out on the street in relatively short order. He was in the car with Anne and the kids driving back to his house slightly after 12:30 pm. Finn had greased the skids by alerting one of his friends in probation that the bail was likely going to be revised; much of Mark's paperwork had already been processed by the time court adjourned.

Anne insisted on driving Susan's Volvo, as she had done earlier that morning on the way to court. Mark didn't object. It freed him to concentrate his attention on his children. Archie sat in the front passenger seat and Katie sat with Mark in the back.

The kids were bubbling over with questions as soon as their car pulled out of the courthouse parking lot. Katie was the first to jump in.

"Does this mean they know you didn't do it?"

"Well, Finn and his private detective have given the police some hard evidence that could point to other suspects. They are running down those leads."

"Like who," Archie asked.

"Too early to say," Mark explained. "They got some grainy video footage from doorbell cameras of a man lurking around our neighborhood."

"Was it Mullet?" Archie asked.

"No, the description doesn't match Mullet," Mark answered, watching the visible relief wash over Archie's face.

"Why didn't they just dismiss the case against you today?" Katie asked.

"It's not that easy, honey. The government is not going to admit they made a mistake until they track down other leads."

Katie wasn't entirely mollified.

"What's going to happen in court next week?"

"We just have to take one step at a time. Hopefully, they will find Mom's killer and indict that person. Then they can dismiss the charge against me. Finn is working with Detective Garcia right now to go over what they found."

They were just pulling into the driveway. Mark got out of the car and stood gazing up at the house. He had never felt so unbelievably grateful to be home.

Katie and Archie went into the house ahead of the others. Anne pulled Mark's sleeve gently to hold him back for a private conversation.

"Mark, you shouldn't be filling the kids' heads with false hopes," she whispered.

"It's not a false hope, Anne. I didn't kill Susan. Besides, it's my *only* hope."

"Well, the government didn't concede today that they arrested the wrong person."

Mark was stung by Anne's comment. Clearly she still entertained the possibility that he had murdered her sister. He paused a few moments in order to choose his words carefully.

"Anne, I really appreciate what you have done for my family over the past two weeks. And I know you are grieving Susan's death. But I think it may be time for you to go back to New Jersey. The kids and I need some time alone together to process all of this."

53

Finn Cummings and Paul Troy made the short drive over to Tony Garcia's office immediately after court on Monday. They felt quietly optimistic that they could convince Tony to check out Darius Brown as a possible suspect. The two of them had spent most of the weekend getting their ducks in a row so that they could present the most compelling theory possible. Convincing someone in authority that they had made a mistake was never easy—especially when that someone was so personally invested in the case.

Tony introduced them to his colleague Ray Jones, who apparently was now working the case. The four men entered the conference room and started to spread out files before them. Tony offered Paul and Finn coffee, which they gladly accepted. Stale and acrid as it was, it served its purpose in jolting them awake.

Tony started the conversation. "Your dime. What do you have for us that is so urgent?"

> "Tony, it's no secret that if we go to trial on this case, we are going with an 'other culprit' defense," Finn began. "And we will be asking the judge to instruct the jury that they can consider the police department's failure to investigate other leads in making their decision about reasonable doubt."

"I understand."

"But our possible 'other culprit' is not Heidi Wilson or Julia Hoffman. I take it you have ruled them out as potential suspects?"

"We have. They have solid alibis. And, we have looked at their bank accounts. Absolutely no evidence that either of them solicited a hit."

"As I suspected," Finn continued. "We think another possible culprit is a guy by the name of Darius Brown. Recently released from prison on an attempted murder conviction. Paul Troy can explain the connection."

Paul Troy then laid out two booking photographs on the conference table and showed the similarity in appearance between Darius Brown and Anton Jenkins.

"Anton Jenkins was one of Susan's prior clients. She represented him on a murder case. She omitted that case on her judicial application. We wondered why, so I interviewed Jenkins in prison. He told me that Brown was convicted for an attempted murder that Jenkins actually committed. Slash and grab on Humboldt Avenue in Dorchester. Jenkins told Susan about having committed that prior crime, but Susan did nothing to help Brown."

Tony and Ray were looking confused. So Finn jumped in.

"When Brown was transferred to Souza-Baranowski, he was placed in the same unit as Jenkins. At some point Jenkins confided to Brown that he had done the slash and grab, and that he had told Susan about it. Brown was angry about doing time for a crime he didn't commit, and he blamed Susan."

"Sounds far-fetched," Tony interjected. "Exactly what's your theory here."

"Susan left the Jenkins matter off of her judicial application because she always felt guilty about the case. Ethically she was in a bind—Jenkins' disclosure to her was confidential, and she could not reveal it to anyone without his permission. Which of course Jenkins was unlikely to give because it would expose him to an indictment for another violent felony. Darius Brown did not understand those legal niceties—he blamed Susan and Jenkins for making him do time for an attempted murder he didn't commit. When he got out on parole, he read about Susan's nomination in the newspaper and was outraged. He hatched an idea for a revenge killing."

Tony was looking at the photograph of Darius Brown, and comparing it to the doorbell camera images in front of Mark's mailbox and garbage can. Could be the same guy. Same general build and height. It was difficult to tell, though; the images were so distant and grainy. The stranger did not look Caucasian in the camera images. Darius Brown and Anton Jenkins were both light-skinned African Americans.

Finn took Tony's silence as a license to continue:

"Brown got out of prison in September and plotted revenge against Susan. He pulled an old kitchen knife out of the Price garbage barrel the same day as he left that first threatening letter. Ten days later, the day of Susan's memorial service, he left the second letter and planted the knife in Susan's back yard, implicating Mark. He knew that nobody would be home that day.

Look at the images on both October 27th and November 6th. The stranger seems to be wearing light gloves.

> Cotton or latex. Why would Mark Price be wearing gloves if he was retrieving a knife from his own garbage can that he knew already contained his own fingerprints? Or, why would he wear gloves if he was planting a threatening letter in his own mailbox to cast a motive elsewhere, if he knew that he was going to touch and read the letter the very same day?"

Tony appeared deep in thought, shuffling the images of Brown, Jenkins and the neighbors' doorbell cameras. He didn't want to undermine his own case by suggesting Finn's theory was plausible, certainly not without discussing it with Camille Jones.

> "That theory might suggest Darius Brown had a motive to kill Susan. But why would he falsely implicate Mark?" Tony asked.

> "He did prison time for a crime he didn't commit. Brown wanted Susan's husband to suffer the same fate," Finn responded. "Tit for tat. We checked Brown's records at Souza-Baranowski. He was the leader of the prison Bible Group. That explains the second bible verse."

Just then, Ray Jones interjected.

> "Lieutenant, look at these photos. I've been wondering whether they meant anything. This is from the crime scene. A tree in the cemetery about twelve feet away from the victim's body. About five feet up from the trunk of the tree, somebody carved the initials 'DB.'"

Ray Jones passed around two photographs with a magnifying glass. The photos showed the tree surrounded by yellow tape and evidence placards. The initials were barely noticeable, less than two inches high and two inches wide.

> "I didn't know if these meant anything," Jones continued. "They could have been there for years. Just some kids goofing around in the cemetery."

Now it was Paul Troy's turn to feel chagrined. He hadn't noticed those images in the reams of discovery provided by the prosecution. There had been way too much evidence to scrutinize.

> "People who commit revenge killings often leave markers," Finn interjected, growing excited now. "Psychologically, they need to create some historical record of the fact that they have gotten even with their enemy. That is why Brown carved his initials in that tree. That is why he left the letter with the bible verse about atonement in the Price's mailbox."

After several long moments of silence, Tony finally spoke:

> "I'm not saying it's impossible. Improbable maybe, but not impossible. What exactly are you guys asking from us?"

"There are two sources of records we can't get," Paul Troy responded. "The video cameras on the Red Line from Brown's house in Dorchester to Harvard Square. See if Brown traveled to Cambridge on October 27th, November 1st, or November 6th. Also, Brown was on parole. He was wearing an ankle bracelet. The GPS would show his movements. But his parole officer will not give up the GPS information without a request from you."

"We'll look into it," Tony assured them, rising to signal that the meeting was over. "That's all I can promise."

As they were leaving, Finn took a gamble. He wanted to have a private word with Tony. Finn thought he could connect with him on a personal level due to their history of working together. So he touched Tony Garcia's elbow and met his gaze.

"Tony, can I have a quick word with you in private?" Finn asked.

Tony was momentarily speechless, mindful of the Captain's conditions of his continued involvement on the case. He, too, decided to take a chance, catching Ray Jones' eyes and motioning him toward the doorway.

"It's okay, Ray. I'm sure this will only take a minute."

As their colleagues left the conference room, Finn and Tony stood just inside its closed doorway. Finn was quick to capitalize on the opportunity to get Tony alone.

"Tony, I just want you to know that I appreciate how hard this is for you. Both because you were close to Susan, and because I threatened to make that relationship an issue on the witness stand. I hope you understand I was just doing my job. I have a client to protect."

"I get it, Finn. This isn't my first rodeo."

"I know it isn't, Tony. I just wanted to acknowledge how hard it must be for you."

"Thanks."

"And Tony, there's no reason this can't still be a big career victory for you. If you catch Susan's real killer, you come out of this smelling like a rose. Win-win. I hope you get that."

Tony stared at Finn pensively but did not reply.

54

Mark spent his first few days at home catching up on emails from some friends and supporters, and taking long, chilly runs. It felt good to feel the fresh air against his skin after ten days in confinement. The neighbors were still frosty to him and avoided his glance when he was coming and going from the house. Mark understood. The cloud of suspicion still hung heavily over Mark's head. It would take time.

The family had settled into a fragile 'new normal' since Mark was released from prison. He was trying to play the role of two parents. While Mark understood how acutely they were all grieving the loss of Susan, he figured the best way forward was to focus on routines—getting the kids to school, helping them with homework, talking about their activities. It helped get all their minds off the white elephant in the corner of the room.

Mark was worried about Archie the most. Periodically, Katie would break down in tears while cuddling with Mark on the couch. Archie hadn't really opened up yet about how he was feeling. Not normally a 'talker,' the trauma of Susan's killing had driven Archie deeper inside himself. Mark wished Archie could find a way to let it out, either with tears or with rage.

On Wednesday evening, Mark was helping Archie with his

algebra homework at the kitchen table while Katie stacked dinner dishes in the washer. They were interrupted by the doorbell. "Probably flowers or food being delivered," Mark thought as he made his way to the mudroom door. He was surprised to see Finn standing on the back stoop carrying a brown paper bag and a large, helium-filled balloon. Finn was grinning from ear to ear.

"Finn, what's up?"

"I've got some great news. Are the kids around?"

Mark ushered him into the family room, where Katie and Archie both stopped what they were doing to give him big hugs. They hadn't seen Finn since court on Monday.

"What's with the stupid balloon?" Mark asked.

"Dad, that is so rude!" Katie joked.

"It's okay, Katie," Finn laughed. "You all need to sit down to hear this."

As they assembled around the sectional sofa, Mark opened the brown paper bag that Finn had thrust in his arms. It was a bottle of Woodford's bourbon and a package of his favorite Cuban cigars.

"Camille Jones called me about an hour ago," Finn started. "They made an arrest in your Mom's case. A man named Darius Brown. His GPS tracker on his ankle bracelet put him in Harvard Square on the day those letters were delivered to your mailbox. So did the video footage from the subway. They searched Brown's apartment in Dorchester this morning. They found two hoodie sweatshirts. Both had been laundered, but one looks like it contains occult blood. The lab is analyzing it now. They also found sneakers in his closet with blood on them, also being analyzed at the lab. His GPS bracelet had been cut off his ankle. The tracker indicates it was disconnected on the day of your Mom's murder."

Finn could hardly catch his breath. He was talking so quickly that it was hard for the kids to absorb it all.

"Darius Brown was taken into custody around noon today. After a couple hours of questioning, he confessed to the murder. He admitted to Tony Garcia that he killed your Mom."

Katie erupted with a shriek, jumping up to wrap Finn in a warm embrace. Archie's mouth hung open in confusion.

"Who is Darius Brown?" Archie asked. "And why would he want to hurt Mom?"

Finn chose his words carefully in describing Darius Brown's history and his relationship with Anton Jenkins. He knew that the narrative would be difficult for a non-lawyer to digest, not to mention teenagers. So he went over the background slowly and methodically, explaining Brown's motive.

"So, Mom let an innocent man go to prison for a crime he didn't commit?" Katie asked.

"She didn't have a choice," Finn explained gently. "She was ethically obligated to keep her client's secret. That's her job. She could have been disbarred if she revealed it."

"That seems so messed up," Archie almost whispered.

"Your Mom was a great lawyer," Finn assured him. "She took her oath seriously. She can't be faulted for that."

"Why didn't she tell Dad about that ethical problem when it happened?" Katie asked.

"That is something I've been turning over and over in my head," Mark interjected. "You kids were young. I was going up for tenure. Our lives were busy. Maybe Mom didn't want to bother me. Or maybe she didn't want to hear my answer."

"What would your answer have been?," Katie asked.

"I honestly don't know, Katie. For your Mom, the law was the most important thing. For me, I guess people are the most important thing."

Mark gathered Katie in his arms and consoled her. The enormity of Susan's death suddenly washed over them all, momentarily overshadowing any reason to celebrate Mark's exoneration.

Finn was the first to break the silence.

"Brown is going to be arraigned on the murder charge tomorrow in Cambridge District Court. The prosecutor is going to dismiss the charge against your father. You should all be there for the television cameras. Your Dad's reputation has been mutilated over the past couple of weeks. It will be important for the media to see the family getting back on its feet."

"Uncle Finn, thank you," Katie interjected through soft tears. "Archie and I could have lost both of them. You got our Dad back."

Finn's own eyes began to mist up. He tried to lighten the mood by reminiscing about Susan and their times together back in the District Attorney's office when they were younger. Finn wanted the kids to know what a skillful lawyer and a vibrant person their mother was. He wanted them to have good memories.

"I had a huge crush on your mother back then, you know. Everybody did. Your dad just got to her first."

Around 9:30 pm, Mark broke up the gathering by telling the kids they should go up to their rooms and finish their homework.

"I've been rude to Finn. I need to offer him a cigar and a glass of this bourbon."

After Katie and Archie had gone upstairs, Mark poured two whiskeys, and the men grabbed their jackets to go out onto the patio. Molding brown leaves were piled high in bunches around the deck furniture, reminding Mark of all the chores that had been neglected for the past several weeks. Autumn was slowly turning into winter, and Thanksgiving was just days away. Mark hadn't given any thought whatsoever to their first holidays without Susan.

As they lit cigars and settled into their chairs, Mark felt enormously grateful for his old friend.

"Finn, Katie is right. I don't know how to thank you."

"You haven't gotten my bill yet."

"I'm not kidding. I owe you my life."

"You would have done the same for me. Besides, you're the one who made the Jenkins connection."

The whiskey was warming Mark up and making him pensive. He scanned the backyard and remembered how Darius Brown had snuck back there to plant the murder weapon by the hedges. He must have been carrying such an enormous grudge against Susan.

"Whatever the District Attorney says at his press conference tomorrow, I hope he doesn't vilify Susan. She doesn't deserve that," Mark said.

"I don't think he will. I talked to Camille. They understand that it would just make the entire system look bad."

"You appreciate the irony here, right Finn?"

"What irony?"

"The law of attorney-client privilege destroyed Susan. But it also saved me. If you hadn't had the foresight to tell me to take that ring camera off my door and deliver it to you, the cops might have discovered that I left the house that night. That would have made their case against me so much stronger."

"It was a gamble."

"It was much more than a gamble, Finn," Mark said. "You could have been accused of obstruction of justice by taking possession of that Nest camera."

"I was willing to take that risk for you," Finn said. "By the way, where *did* you go that night?"

"I went outside to smoke a joint. One that I found in Archie's backpack. I was under a lot of stress."

"You should never lie to your own lawyer," Finn laughed.

"I know. I was embarrassed."

Finn took another sip of his whiskey. He was feeling satisfied but also a little bit nostalgic. He and his old friend did not do this enough—just sit and talk. Families and careers had intruded on their friendship over the past twenty years. Now that Susan was gone, Finn would have to check in on Mark more regularly.

"What are you going to do now?" Finn asked.

"What do you mean?"

"With your life...."

"I've been thinking about that. I have to see if I can make amends at work. Who knows how seriously those bridges have been burned? I also need to talk to Julia. But first and foremost, I need to focus on the kids. They're my top priority. I'm going to get both of them into counseling."

"Katie seems to be doing okay," Finn responded.

"Katie is confused about her sexuality. She doesn't feel comfortable talking to me about it. Archie is totally bottling up his emotions. I'm going to suggest that he transfer back to Cambridge Rindge and Latin in January so he can be with his friends."

Finn scrutinized his best friend carefully as they let the silence wash over them for a few more moments.

"Mark, you should be prepared to say a few words to the media tomorrow. They will want a comment from you."

"Maybe, Finn. I'll sleep on it. But you should speak first. You deserve the limelight."

"Limelight isn't my thing. You know that."

55

The Prices drove together to the Cambridge District Court early Thursday morning. At least by outward appearances, the scene was not significantly different than two weeks earlier at Mark's arraignment. Television vans lined the streets in front of the courthouse. Reporters, who were bundled up against the November wind, scurried around on their cell phones making calls to their producers. Extra court officers had been brought in to manage security in the lobby.

Although outwardly the scene appeared the same, inwardly Mark felt very different. Two weeks ago he cowered in the dock feeling like a caged animal. This morning, he was watching the proceedings from the outside looking in. Mark now felt like he was a master of his own destiny rather than the object of another person's will. That rekindled sense of personal agency seemed poignant to Mark. A new chapter was beginning in his life, and he alone was empowered to take control of its direction.

To her credit, Camille Jones had choreographed every detail of that morning's proceedings to accommodate Mark and his family. She had filed a written dismissal of Mark's case with the clerk before the proceedings began. She had worked with the clerk's office and the probation department to have Mark's ankle bracelet removed before court was called into session. She had arranged with the court officers to allow Mark to sit with his children in the front row of the courtroom.

Judge Veronica Lee took the bench precisely at 9:30 am. The judge's clerk had already briefed her on the Commonwealth's motion to dismiss the murder charge against Mark Price, and the arrest of a new suspect. The clerk called the case of Darius Brown, and the defendant was led into the dock in shackles. For the first time, Mark and his kids got to look Brown straight in the eyes. Mark's stomach gripped and he felt a wave of nausea rising in his body as he stared down Susan's killer. What had once felt conjectural now felt very real. Mark was torn between hatred and sadness as he heard the judge appoint Brown a public defender.

> "Assistant District Attorney Camille Jones for the Commonwealth, Your Honor," the prosecutor began. "A new suspect has been arrested in this case, and the government is moving to dismiss the charges against Mark Price. Darius Brown, the defendant present in the dock, is ready for arraignment on one charge of murder in the first degree."

> "The Commonwealth will prove that Mr. Brown stabbed Susan Price to death on November 1st, in the Church Street neighborhood of Cambridge, out of revenge for her representation of one of his gang associates, Anton Jenkins. Surveillance footage from neighborhood cameras, plus GPS data from Mr. Brown's parole bracelet, put Mr. Brown in the Price's neighborhood on the dates two threatening letters were left in the Price's mailbox. Video footage from the MBTA Harvard Square subway station puts Mr. Brown in Cambridge on the night of Ms. Price's murder, where he was seen following her out of the station. The State Police executed a search warrant at Mr. Brown's home

yesterday and recovered evidence specifically linking him to the killing, including sneakers containing the blood of Susan Price. Upon his arrest and being provided with *Miranda* warnings by Dt. Lt. Tony Garcia of the Massachusetts State Police, Mr. Brown confessed to the crime and provided details that could be known only by the perpetrator. The motive for the heinous offense is that Mr. Brown, recently paroled for a sentence on an attempted murder case, believed he had been wronged by Ms. Price and convicted for a crime committed by another."

Mark could not take his eyes off Brown while Camille was speaking. During his many years as a prosecutor, Mark had observed hundreds of defendants in the dock facing serious accusations against them. Their demeanor typically fell into two camps—dazed and confused about what was going on, or indifferent, like they had 'been here, done this.' But Darius Brown was different. He was defiant—almost arrogant—staring down the prosecutor and the judge with his head held high. Clearly Brown had no regrets about what he had done. He felt that Susan had deserved it. That composure sent a chill down Mark's spine.

Mark was grateful that Camille Jones did not go into detail about Susan's ethical dilemma and her withholding of exculpatory evidence against Brown. Undoubtedly those facts would come out at trial—if there ever was a trial—but Mark did not want that issue to be the lead story in tomorrow's newspapers.

On the steps of the courthouse after the arraignment, the staff of the District Attorney's office set up a podium for an impromptu press conference. Finn Cummings and Mark Price had been escorted to the steps and told where to stand, flanking the prosecutors and the police. District Attorney Kevin O'Sullivan, looking impeccable with a pressed blue suit and neatly trimmed gray hair, was the first to speak.

"Our mission as prosecutors is to get it right—to solve crimes and hold the perpetrators accountable. In pursuing that mission, we need to be nimble and follow evidence wherever it may lead. We also need to be humble and transparent in our work so that the public has faith in our efforts. In this case we initially got it wrong, but I believe we have ultimately gotten it right. It turns out that Mark Price was framed by a recently released prisoner who had a grudge against his wife for her work as a criminal defense attorney. Today, we have rectified that error and charged the man we are convinced beyond a reasonable doubt actually committed the brutal murder of Susan Price— Darius Brown. I applaud my lead prosecutor, Camille Jones, Detective Lieutenant Tony Garcia from the State Police, and their entire team for following every lead in this case in order to bring the perpetrator to justice."

"To Mark Price and his family, I apologize for the ordeal of the past two weeks. I am relieved that the court has granted our motion and restored Mr. Price's freedom."

"We are not going to take any questions today, as further details of the crime will be revealed in court as the case proceeds."

Finn Cummings appeared slightly less comfortable compared to the seasoned politician standing beside him. Like many defense attorneys, Finn could wax eloquent in a courtroom where necessary, but he often felt tongue-tied in front of a camera. Today, however, Finn felt buoyed by his unique emotional attachment to the Price family. He stepped up to the podium with a full heart.

> "I am relieved and gratified that my old friend, Professor Mark Price, has been cleared of suspicion in this horrific crime. Knowing him as I do, I personally never had any doubt about his innocence."
>
> "Over the past month, members of the Price family have suffered double tragedies—the terrible loss of their beloved wife and mother, and then a wrongful, very public accusation against Professor Price. My client is now anxious to get back to life with his children, who have suffered enormously over the past three weeks. He is also anxious to get back to his teaching and research responsibilities. Today, most of all, he is overjoyed that he has been exonerated. I applaud the DA's office for being willing to admit their initial mistake and to follow important new leads as they arose in the case."

When Finn finished, he shook hands with Mark and pulled him in for a heartfelt embrace. Mark then approached the podium with tears already forming in his eyes.

> "As a result of this atrocious crime, my family has lost the love of a beautiful, generous and caring woman. The Commonwealth of Massachusetts has lost an exceptionally talented lawyer, public servant, and leader in the profession."
>
> "Our loss is indescribable. But we are not the only victims here. Darius Brown was the victim of wrongful imprisonment for a crime that he did not commit about a decade ago. He spent close to ten years in prison as a result of a misidentification by a victim in a robbery encounter—a cross-racial identification by a white victim who had been attacked after dusk on a city street by a light-skinned African

American unknown to him. Scientific studies have shown that cross-racial identifications such as these have extremely high error rates."

"I know it will come as a shock for some of you to hear me describe Darius Brown as a 'victim,' given the precious life he took away from me and my family. But before he was a cold-blooded murderer, he was indeed a victim of an unjust accusation, just as I was a victim of an unjust accusation two weeks ago."

"We need to understand that the criminal justice system is not infallible; people are wrongfully accused and convicted all the time—whether because of misidentifications, prosecutorial misconduct, coerced confessions, or shoddy representation. That is not news. These ills have plagued the administration of our criminal laws for centuries. What is news is that I have now been on the other side of those deficiencies, and I have experienced them first hand. That experience, while extremely painful, is going to shape the way I think about criminal law going forward. I pledge to make it a part of my professional life to take on cases of defendants who were wrongfully accused and incarcerated. That will be my wife Susan's legacy. That is what I owe to her and to all the Darius Browns out there."

"Thank you all for coming today, and for respecting my family's privacy in the days and weeks to come."

Mark was trembling as he stepped away from the podium. He dodged the microphones being shoved in his face and made his way down the courthouse steps toward Katie and Archie. He wanted to get them out of there. He wanted to take them home so they could all unpack today's events together, in private. But as Mark left, he felt a tug on his elbow and turned to see Tony Garcia standing right behind him.

"Mark, can we talk?" Tony asked.

"Sure, Tony. But let's make it quick," Mark said, scanning the crowd for the kids.

Tony led Mark quickly down a side street next to the courthouse and through a door reserved for the police and sheriff's offices. Flashing his badge, Tony nodded to the court officer inside the small hallway and walked down the corridor to a breakroom set aside for court personnel. Luckily they found the room empty, and Tony shut the door behind them.

"Mark, thanks for meeting with me," Tony began.

"Tony, if you're trying to apologize, there's no need" Mark interjected. "I don't blame you for jumping the gun on this. You had a murder weapon and evidence of motive. Plus a lot of public pressure to solve the case. I might have done the same thing."

"Thanks, Mark. I let my emotions get the better of me by accepting this assignment in the first place. And, by helping Susan with that phone number. I regret both of those decisions. But that's not why I asked to meet with you."

"Can I ask you something?" Mark interrupted. He was nervous, and eager to seize a long-awaited opportunity to talk to Tony candidly. "There's one piece of the puzzle that has been gnawing at me. It's weird how you and Susan reconnected after all these years. Were the two of you having an affair?"

"No, Mark. We belonged to the same gym. We met for coffee a couple times after our workouts. It never went any further than that. I promise you. I adored Susan. You know that. But I think she was loyal to you."

"Thanks Tony. For some reason I needed to hear that. I certainly don't deserve to be jealous, given my own infidelity. But I just wanted to know."

"Mark, I asked to see you today because Darius Brown's lawyer told Camille and me just now that she wants to talk to us about information her client can provide the government. About the murder."

"I thought he already confessed."

"He did. But the public defender says Brown has more information. He wants to cut a deal."

"A deal for what? What could he offer you?"

"She didn't say. She was vague. We'll see tomorrow when we meet with her."

"What do you think it could be?"

"I'm not sure, but I have an idea. I pulled Brown's parole file in preparation for today's arraignment." Tony pulled a folder out of his briefcase as he spoke. "I was reviewing it this morning. Brown was represented at his parole hearing in September. Does your law school have a clinic that works in the parole system?"

"Yes," Mark almost whispered, still not comprehending.

Tony put the file on the desk and pulled out one of the pleadings from the folder, opening it to the last page where Brown's attorney had signed on his behalf. He pointed to the signature line on the document.

"Julia Hoffman

Student Attorney"

Mark stared at the page, frozen in disbelief. The room was spinning. Feeling like he was about to lose consciousness, Marked gripped the edge of the table and struggled to parse the implications of those four simple words.

Acknowledgments

For MB, Seamus and Jack, who make all things possible and worthwhile.

I am grateful to my friend and colleague Professor Judith McMorrow for consulting on several thorny legal ethics issues embedded in the story.

Author's Note

When the Past is All Deception was factually inspired by the brutal murder of New England Law Professor Mary Jo Frug near Harvard Square in 1991. Frug's gruesome slaying has remained unsolved for over three decades. Given the savage stab wounds and the fact that no personal belongings were taken from Prof. Frug, the police operated on the premise that the perpetrator was someone known to the victim. Prof. Frug's husband, Prof. Gerald Frug of Harvard Law School, died in 2023. He was never named as a suspect.

I served as a prosecutor in Massachusetts when this grisly crime was committed, and I have been haunted by the slaying ever since. When I decided to turn my attention from legal scholarship to fiction, I resolved to revisit this "cold case" and use it as a launching pad for my first novel. I have re-imagined the characters, and I have situated their conflicts amid the contemporary culture wars rampant on college campuses today. In doing so, I hope I have drawn faithfully on my experiences as a prosecutor, a law professor and a Bostonian.

The characters in this novel are fictional, and any resemblance to persons living or dead is unintended.

About Atmosphere Press

Founded in 2015, Atmosphere Press was built on the principles of Honesty, Transparency, Professionalism, Kindness, and Making Your Book Awesome. As an ethical and author-friendly hybrid press, we stay true to that founding mission today.

If you're a reader, enter our giveaway for a free book here:

SCAN TO ENTER
BOOK GIVEAWAY

If you're a writer, submit your manuscript for consideration here:

SCAN TO SUBMIT
MANUSCRIPT

And always feel free to visit Atmosphere Press and our authors online at atmospherepress.com. See you there soon!

About the Author

R. MICHAEL CASSIDY is a Professor and Dean's Distinguished Scholar at Boston College Law School. Before entering the legal academy, Professor Cassidy served as the Chief of the Criminal Bureau in the Massachusetts Attorney General's Office, where he prosecuted hundreds of complex felonies at both the trial and appellate levels. He is a graduate of Harvard Law School.

Professor Cassidy is the author of dozens of scholarly articles and three nonfiction books in the fields of Evidence and Legal Ethics. This first novel—a legal thriller set on a college campus—draws heavily on his knowledge of both academic life and criminal procedure.

Printed in the USA
CPSIA information can be obtained
at www.ICGtesting.com
LVHW042003271024
794899LV00006B/1064